For my mother
Betty Louise Hulett Crouch

Praise for
Granted

"In her wonderfully imagined stories, Angela Correll opens a window into the way life sometimes is, and maybe even ought to be. Threaded through the community of May Hollow with its farmhouses and families, cafes and banks, what's prized and what isn't, she sets forth a counter-narrative to the 'industrial economy' that her fellow Kentuckian Wendell Berry critiques— all the way down into the pies and garden of dear Beulah, who lives her life for the sake of others, teaching all of us about the meaning of a very good life."

> —**STEVEN GARBER, Professor of Marketplace Theology, Regent College, Vancouver, BC, and author of *Visions of Vocation: Common Grace for the Common Good.***

"I've had the immense pleasure of adapting both *Grounded* and *Guarded* into stage plays. As a storyteller, I love Angela's bone-deep sense of place, her appreciation of faith and family, and how she masterfully chronicles one Kentucky family's journey in a way that richly reflects larger historical trends and context. There is so much soul and heart in these books!"

> —**ROBBY HENSON, filmmaker and stage director**

"The May Hollow trilogy is regional writing at its best! Correll perceptively and affectionately portrays small town relationships, farm life, and family dynamics against the backdrop of rural Kentucky. You'll laugh and cry with Annie as she rediscovers her roots, reconnects with neighbors, and— most importantly—reconsiders the boy next door in this heartwarming series."

> —**NANCY SLEETH, author of *Almost Amish***

". . . a sophisticated and charming series that makes you fall in love with small town America."

"The May Hollow trilogy is like a family reunion that gets better each time you attend. You'll always want to go back to have tea and pie with Beulah, Annie and the rest of the family."

"I always feel like I'm reconnecting with old friends and family when I step into the world Angela Correll creates for her characters on May Hollow Road. I was both happy and sad to come to the final chapter of Annie's and Beulah's multi-layered journey—happy that all the many colorful threads had been woven so skillfully into a final, beautiful tapestry; sad to say good-bye to a couple of strong Kentucky women I've come to know and love."

Granted
by Angela Correll

Published by

köehlerbooks ™

210 60th Street
Virginia Beach, VA 23451
212-574-7939
www.koehlerbooks.com

Granted

[signature: Angela Correll]

ANGELA
CORRELL

VIRGINIA BEACH
CAPE CHARLES

THE FARMS
~ on ~
MAY HOLLOW ROAD

Jake's Cottage

The Wilder Farm

Wall crossi

← To Somerville

Betty & Joe Gibson's

N

Cemetery Hill

Swimming hole

The Old Stone House

Gibson's Creek Road

Beulah's House

May Hollow Rd.

Chapter One

"ERNESTINA CHADWELL IS dead!"

The news shot through the prayer chain like a greased bullet. Beulah Campbell hung up the harvest gold wall phone and dropped into a chair. The long-time Somerville Baptist kitchen director was gone, found slumped over the Sunday paper with a pair of scissors in one hand and a two-dollar-off coupon for a Butterball turkey in the other. Blessedly quick, the ninety-year-old woman had not suffered, and Beulah was grateful.

They had served together for more years than she cared to count. It was hard to imagine a church meal without Ernestina, who flitted to and fro, adjusted tablecloths, and clucked over the order of casseroles. Erni had managed every social function for forty years, including cake and punch receptions, potlucks, and the New Year's Eve watch night dinners. She dictated the location for every plate, spatula, and trivet, and no one questioned her authority since she had survived the comings and goings of seven pastors.

It was a bad time for Ernestina to die. The annual community Thanksgiving potluck, the biggest event on the Somerville Baptist social and missionary calendar, was one week away. The church doors were flung wide for all the community to enjoy free turkey with all the fixings. They straggled in from all parts of the county, down from hills and up from hollers, and got their bellies full of home-cooked food made from scratch.

The very thought of potlucks made Beulah's stomach churn with hunger. She remembered the cinnamon rolls made by her best friend and neighbor, Evelyn Wilder, and she opened the blue Tupperware container. Beulah tore off the gooey bread, dipped it in her coffee, and popped it in her mouth. As she savored the sweet and spicy flavor, Beulah thought back on all the years she had served as Ernestina's selected apprentice, especially with the Thanksgiving potluck. Beulah could do it blindfolded, but she had always held back, in order to respect Ernestina's position as leader. Now, it was her turn to assume the full mantle of responsibility.

"I'll do my best for you, Erni," Beulah said, looking at the ceiling of her kitchen. She noticed three new cobwebs and sighed. Cleaning was impossible this time of year. Dead flies, ladybugs, and spiders piled up overnight. She thought spiders were supposed to eat flies and ladybugs, but in her house, they all lived in utopian harmony.

There was no time now for dealing with insects. The church potluck needed her. *For such a time as this*, she thought, recalling her favorite verse from the book of Esther.

The phone rang, but Beulah didn't rush to answer since she knew who was on the line. She refilled her coffee, then answered, as she settled in for her morning conversation with Betty Gibson, her across-the-road neighbor and fellow church member. There was much fodder for today's chat.

"Beulah, I reckon you've already heard. I can hardly believe it. I volunteered to coordinate the funeral meal for Ernestina, so we need to do it up right. Can you bring green beans with chunks of ham hock, two coconut cream pies, and a broccoli casserole, the one with Cheese Whiz? I need you to serve, too."

"I've gone off the Cheese Whiz, but I have a new recipe," Beulah said, and noted the ingredients she'd need to pick up at the grocery store.

"What in the world will happen to the potlucks? And Thanksgiving right up on us."

"It's a big job, there's no doubt about that," Beulah said.

"Well, I heard at homemaker's club the Presbyterians want to take it over. They'll jump right on this if we don't do somethin' quick. You know they've been salivating over the potluck ever since we got that big write-up last year in the Lexington paper. Who's going to step up and take her place?"

Surely Betty knew Beulah was next in line. After all the years as Ernestina's assistant, she was the obvious choice. Yet, it didn't seem proper to self-appoint herself before Ernestina's body was cold in the ground.

"I reckon Pastor Gillum will decide fairly quickly. I'm sure he'd like to get her buried first."

"If we don't pull it together, we'll lose the community potluck. I don't believe Pastor Gillum needs to wait too long."

Beulah felt a twinge of anxiety, but by the time they'd talked of other things and hung up the phone, she wondered at how Betty got herself so whipped up. It couldn't be good for a body to borrow all that trouble. Evelyn was a Presbyterian, and if there was talk of them taking over the potluck, Beulah would have heard it from her. Too much silly gossip—the very reason she had dropped out of homemaker's club twenty years ago.

Beulah topped off her coffee and focused on her to-do list. There were changes to make, now that she was in charge. It was very possible Pastor Gillum might appoint her overall kitchen director, but for now, it was best to focus on the Thanksgiving potluck, and not get her cart before the horse.

For one, she wanted locally grown turkeys. Jake, her granddaughter's fiancé and Evelyn's son, recently told her about the Bourbon Reds he found pasture-raised the way God intended, not crammed into a tight cage and pumped with antibiotics. They did cost more than Butterballs, but since it was a community potluck, maybe they could get help from some of the local businesses.

Second, Ernestina would hear of nothing but pumpkin pies, and Beulah knew just as many folks preferred pecan pies. This year, there would be a choice.

Third, there would be real sweet tea. Ernestina had taken to the powdered tea mix because of its ease and economy, but it was a travesty to call a mess of powdered chemicals "sweet tea," and Beulah promised herself it would be honest-to-goodness sweet tea this year, even if she had to make it all herself.

Tired papier-mâché pilgrims and cornucopias adorned the tables year after year, looking worse and worse as each holiday passed. Beulah relished the idea of a decoration overhaul, but there was a strict budgeted amount, and food quality was most important.

With no time to waste, Beulah attacked the to-do list with gusto. Her appointment was simply a matter of ceremony and that could wait until after the funeral.

***

Ernestina's visitation and funeral were held on the same day, as had become the fashion for some folks who didn't anticipate a door-busting crowd. Beulah gave her condolences to Ernestina's children, as well as the host of grandchildren and great-grandchildren. Pastor Gillum preached a fine funeral, full of Ernestina's praises for her service to others as well as her love for her church and family. There was a soothing rendition of "It is Well With My Soul" and then a foot-stomping version of "Victory in Jesus" before the service concluded and they made a somber convoy out to the graveyard, where they were met with a blustery wind. Beulah slipped out before the final amen and made her way back to the fellowship hall where she took her place in the serving line for the after-funeral meal.

The food was a bit of a disappointment. Betty had opted for buckets of fried chicken and store-bought containers of potato salad and coleslaw that mixed in with a few homemade items. Beulah was sure the cheesecake came from Walmart, despite the glass plate. It was a blessing Ernestina wasn't here to see her own funeral meal.

After everyone had gone through the line, Beulah filled her own plate and set it aside for later. First, she needed to talk with Pastor Gillum. The timing was appropriate now. Ernestina was in the ground, the potluck was a week away, and she had to rescue Thanksgiving.

The portly pastor hovered over the dessert table and eyed a third helping of chocolate cake. He had never been a small man, but since his wife died a few years back, he had simply drowned his sorrows in desserts.

"Beulah, I'm looking for your chess pie," he said.

"It was here, but we're down to crumbs now," she said, and pointed to an empty pie plate.

"Ah, yes, a good sign. Maybe I'll settle for this chocolate cake."

He sliced a piece large enough to feed three people. Beulah looked on with approval; the happier he was, the more agreeable the conversation.

"Could I speak with you a moment?" she asked, and sliced a piece of Italian cream cake for herself so the visit would seem more social.

"Why sure, come on over here and we'll sit at the end of this table. I wanted to talk to you, so this will work out just fine. I wouldn't mind a cup of coffee with this cake. Can I get you one?"

"Yes, black, please." *This is working out quite nice*, she thought. Pastor Gillum was already ahead of her. He anticipated the kitchen dilemma and was ready for action.

When he returned with the coffees, she waited for him to speak first.

"Now, I imagine you want to apologize," he said. "But there is no need for that. 'For everything there is a season,' and we're always wise to recognize when that season is over."

"What's that?"

"You've been through a lot this year, what with your granddaughter moving back home, a knee surgery, and finding your nephew in Italy. It's not unusual to go through such a time and decide to make life changes. Sometimes these things cause us to consider what life is all about and how we spend our time. It's perfectly understandable, and there is absolutely no apology necessary." Crumbs from the chocolate cake dropped into his coffee as he took a drink.

"Pastor Gillum, I—"

"When Betty informed me you didn't want to do the Thanksgiving potluck anymore, I admit I was disappointed. I guess we'd assumed you'd take over for Ernestina. Betty explained your feelings, what with all you've had going on this year."

Beulah's mouth dropped as she tried to make sense of his words.

Pastor Gillum wiped the cake crumbs off his mouth and pushed back his chair. "That Betty, she's a good one. She jumped right in for Ernestina so there won't be any disruption. You can sit back and relax, thanks to your friend. My heavens, that cake was delicious."

Beulah looked down at her uneaten slice of Italian cream cake and felt sick.

***

Beulah tossed her pocketbook into the passenger seat and slammed the key into the ignition of the old Marquis.

Betrayal. That is what it is, plain and simple. After all these years of friendship and being good neighbors to boot. All her understanding and love for Betty, despite her gossiping and churlishness, and this is how she got paid back. Beulah thought back to the conversation she'd had with Betty when Ernestina died. Not one word had she uttered about giving up the potluck. She'd simply said that it was a big job, and it should be discussed after the funeral.

Betty twisted her words to Pastor Gillum and manipulated the outcome to suit herself. Over and over, Beulah had put up with Betty's petulance and petty comments. It was time to wash her hands of that woman. She gripped the steering wheel and slowed as she approached the Gibson bungalow, which sat smugly across from her own farm drive. Betty's car was parked out front; she had slipped out of the funeral meal early, which left the rest of them to clean up. Beulah tapped the brake and considered a right turn in order to unload everything she thought about Betty Gibson at the moment.

In your anger, do not sin. She swerved left into her own driveway instead of the Gibson's, aggravated at how those scriptures seem to come unbidden and unwelcome at times. The leafless walnut trees flew by in a blur as she bumped up and down into gravel potholes and skidded to a stop next to her house.

Chapter Two

ANNIE SAT ACROSS from Jake in their favorite Italian restaurant. Candlelight danced amidst soft shadows on the white linen tablecloth. While he studied the menu, she studied him. The dark hair that curled at any sign of humidity, the small scar above his left eye from a baseball accident, and the crystalline blue eyes that made her melt. He was so darn handsome she wanted to pinch herself to make sure it was real. She looked down at her antique engagement ring, as she had so many times these last few weeks, and saw it was still there. Why did she keep thinking it might disappear? That all this loveliness might float away like a dandelion in spring?

Jake looked up. "Have you decided?"

"My usual, pasta primavera. Wanna split the calamari?"

"Yeah, sounds good," he said, and closed the menu. Orders placed, Jake leaned forward. "So, how'd it go?"

"It's a world away from being a flight attendant," Annie said as she reflected on her first day as activities director at Richwood Manor and her boss. "Colleen cares about the residents and wants to see them continue to have full and productive lives. We discussed scheduling activities for December, which is the big push now since we're so close."

Annie hesitated. "Colleen seems different to me than when I first interviewed with her. She was very business-like even then, but now I almost sense a prickliness. Do you think she has doubts about me doing the job? I don't have a background in this, so I'll have to learn as I go."

"I don't know," Jake said. "Either way, you're hired and you have time to prove yourself."

"If Vesta Givens weren't in my corner, I would be even more worried."

The ninety-something-year-old former school librarian provided valuable information to Annie in the past and had recommended her for the job.

"Everyone looks to her for her approval. We're planning breakfast together two or three times a week, so I'll have a pulse on the residents and what they need. It's so different from being a flight attendant. I hope I can do a good job."

Jake reached over and took her hand in his. "You'll do a great job, no worries about that."

The waiter brought the fried calamari and opened a bottle of sparkling water with a great flourish.

Annie delayed the bad news she dreaded telling Jake.

"I met all the residents today and one gentleman is the cutest. He's handsome and still has a lot of charisma. He kissed my hand, told me I was a 'lovely vision,' and then winked at me."

"Should I be jealous?"

"He could be my grandfather. Jealous? I don't think so."

"What's his name?"

"I can't remember his first name, I met so many people today, but his last name is Caldwell."

"Lonnie Caldwell. He owns a lot of land in the county," Jake said.

"How do you know all that after being gone for ten years— really fourteen, when you count college?" Annie asked. "I feel like I'm in a new place learning everything and everybody all over again."

"I didn't disconnect quite like you did. I still came home pretty often and helped Dad, and I kept in touch with the guys at the bank since that was my business. It helps, now that I'm back." Jake put his fork down and leaned back.

Annie realized it was true. When she flew the coop, she'd ended up in New York for ten years after college as an international flight attendant. Her trips home had been brief and centered on her grandparents.

"There's also a resident who is related to my father," she said. "I think she's his aunt. I'm not sure if it's by marriage or relation."

"Did you recognize her?"

"She knew me, but I can't remember ever seeing her. It's weird, these relatives I don't know well. That side of the family is so lost to me. None of them ever tried hard to get to know me, and I sure haven't tried at all."

"Maybe this is your chance," Jake said.

"I'll visit with her sometime this week." The waiter brought their entrees.

Annie took a breath and plunged in with the news.

"As part of my first day, I had to read the Richwood Manor employee manual and sign the back of it. So, I found out I can't take a vacation, even unpaid, for six months. That puts us squarely into May for the wedding. I know it's longer than we hoped."

Jake twirled fettuccini around on his fork and looked up at her with raised eyebrows.

"What?" she asked.

"Policies exist so grace can abound," he said.

"If I had told them I needed the time off when I accepted the position, it might fly. But I wasn't engaged then. Even if Colleen says okay, it has to be approved by corporate since it's outside the policies. At least that's what the manual said."

"I can see why you made a great flight attendant," he said, and smiled at her.

"What?"

"You're a rule follower. That kind of job needs rule followers."

"What's wrong with that?" she said, and picked up her wine glass. She stared at him over the rim.

"Nothing is wrong, it's just a fact. It's a good thing when you're in the right job. Policies are created for general guidance, but for every rule there's an exception. It never hurts to ask."

"I guess I could, but shouldn't I wait a few weeks until I actually accomplish a few things?"

"Why don't we ask Scott to marry us this weekend and think about a honeymoon some other time?"

"You're teasing."

"I'm not. It would take ten minutes," he said. "Then we're official."

"We're taking sacred vows. I want it to be more than ten minutes we squeeze into the weekend. Nothing fancy, but I want it to be marked and witnessed by those who love us. You know how much I want my dad to be there. He told you he'd try to come."

Jake had made a connection with her father, despite an ocean that separated them from his life in Spain. Annie understood the bond on several levels. They were both confident and charismatic, but where her father had arrogance that sometimes bordered on narcissism, Jake was humble and sought advice from people he respected. Where her father pursued hedonistic tendencies, Jake was loyal and self-disciplined.

"So, what do you think about May? It's a beautiful time of year, it gives Dad and our new Italian family plenty of time to make their arrangements."

"Once calving starts in early March, it'll be non-stop for me. We go right into hay season after that. If you're okay with waiting on the honeymoon, I guess it's fine."

Farming didn't lend itself to much travel, and the realization sobered her.

Jake stared at her and put his fork down.

"Annie, you're used to traveling the world. Are you sure you understand what you're signing up for here? I'm not saying we won't be able to travel at all, but it won't be what you've been used to doing."

"I understand."

"Once I get everything up and going, if I have good help, it might be possible to do a trip or two a year, but nothing like jetting off to Rome on a regular basis."

"I understand, I do," she said. "I got all that out of my system. I'd like to honeymoon in Italy, though. It's such a special place."

He reached across the table and took her hand. "I'd like that too."

"Maybe I'll wait until after Thanksgiving and then ask Colleen. We'll see what happens."

The waiter cleared away their plates and Annie leaned back in her seat.

"How about you? Do you wish you hadn't taken on the bank consulting this winter?"

"It's nice to have the camaraderie of an office, especially since farming can be so solitary. Truthfully, I miss being in nature every day, in touch with the season and cycle of life. There's no other job in the world I feel that way about."

***

On the way to the car, Annie felt her phone vibrate.

"It's my father," she said.

"Take it," Jake urged, and opened the car door for her.

"Dad," she said. "How are you?"

"Fine. Look, we just landed in New York, headed to Texas, then I thought we'd come by for a visit. I want to see Jake and have a man-to-man before this wedding."

"You're in the US?"

"Have some business in Dallas. Thought we'd swing by after that."

Annie looked at Jake and smiled. "Fantastic, Jake wants to see you, too. When do you arrive in Kentucky?"

"Not sure yet. I'll call later once we get sorted out."

"Come for Thanksgiving," she said. "Could you make it here by Thursday?"

"Not sure about that; we'll see."

"Please try. It would mean so much to me."

"Take care, Annie."

"I love you, Dad."

The phone clicked.

"Jake, he's coming. He wants to see you and have a man-to-man. He might even be here for Thanksgiving." She looked at her phone in wonder, as if carrying this good news had transformed it into an extraordinary device.

"Do you know I've never spent a holiday with my father, ever? There was always an excuse. I don't think he's been to Somerville since before Mom died. The few times I saw him after that, we met in Lexington for a few awkward hours. You coming into the picture has really turned things around," she said.

"I don't think I can take the credit for all that," Jake said. "It could be where he is in his life. Is anyone coming with him?"

"He said 'we' but I was too excited to ask. The times I've visited him in Spain, he always had an entourage around. Looking back, I'd guess the times we met in Lexington there were probably other people back at the hotel. I don't think he likes being alone."

"I'm looking forward to getting to know him better. When we were kids, I thought he was the coolest man I'd ever met. That big barrel chest, thick head of dark hair, and moustache. He'd fill the room with his presence and smoke these fat cigars. I was always fascinated by him."

"I think he would have done much better with a son. I don't think he ever knew what to do with a little girl."

"I, for one, am very grateful that he had a daughter. Where is he now?"

"New York, then on to Texas. Some business in Dallas, I assume with an oil company."

"I want to hear about his work. I don't know much about mud engineering in the oil business."

"He'll tell you, all right. Dad never had a problem talking. As for listening—well, that's another story."

Chapter Three

BEULAH PACED BACK and forth in the kitchen so long she lost track of the time. It was growing dark, with the early evening creeping into the daytime and long shadows clinging to the kitchen. She stopped pacing long enough to slump into a chair and tried to think what to do next.

Annie was out tonight and Beulah did not want to be alone. Evelyn had left the funeral before the meal, but surely she was home by now. Yes, she would drive over and see her best friend.

Beulah eyed the Gibson bungalow again with narrowed lids, turned right onto May Hollow Road, and another quick right into the Wilder driveway.

As Beulah approached the brick Italianate house, she saw a Lexus parked next to the back door. It was Tom Childress, the county attorney and Evelyn's new beau. *Well, shoot.* She'd forgotten about Evelyn's courting and resented it for interfering with her friendship.

Beulah drove on up to the house in order to turn around. Evelyn came out and waved a dish towel. Beulah rolled down the window and the chilly air smacked her in the face.

"I didn't realize you had company," she said.

"Come on in," Evelyn said. "It's just Tom."

"No, no," Beulah said, flustered.

"It's okay, really. Tom is going over some deposition notes in the living room while I fix dinner. Come on in, you can eat with us."

Beulah hesitated.

"Please come in," Evelyn said and went into the house, leaving Beulah with no choice.

Evelyn's kitchen was well lit and smelled delicious, lifting Beulah's mood.

Tom came into the room looking like he walked out of a gentleman's sport catalog. He took off his glasses and smiled

"Beulah, it's so good to see you," giving her a sideways hug.

"You look well," she said, and returned the smile as her anger softened. "I am sorry to intrude on your dinner."

"Not at all," he said. "Actually, you'll keep Evelyn company. I'm working on a case and when she invited me to work here in front of her fireplace rather than staying late at the office, I couldn't resist. Lindy's got her Bunco crowd in for the evening, so there was no working quietly at home."

"That game seems to be quite popular around here these days with the young ladies," Evelyn said. "Beulah, sit down there and let me get you some iced tea. Tom, do you need anything while you're working?"

"Not a thing. I'll get back to my work."

"Dinner will be ready in thirty minutes or so."

Evelyn poured two glasses of tea and sat at the table.

"What's wrong?" she said, her eyes wide with alarm.

"How did you know?" Beulah asked, but she chuckled a little at how well Evelyn could read her.

"Why, your face, Beulah. You're flushed red and steam is fairly coming out your ears."

Beulah poured it all out for Evelyn.

"I replayed the phone conversation with Betty in my head over and over, but I couldn't remember one thing I said that to give her any idea about not wanting to do the church potluck. I nearly went right to Betty's house after I left the church, but I don't want to say anything I'll regret later. Betty's stuck her nose in my business too many times, but this time she went too far."

"Land sakes, what was she thinking? That's out 'en out conniving."

"And for what? You know how she operates—she wants to be in charge but never wants to do the work. Who's going to pull this thing together? Somerville Baptist will fall flat on its face this year and the Presbyterians will end up taking over the community potluck."

Beulah spurted out the words and then realized Evelyn was a Presbyterian.

They looked at each other for a moment, eyes wide. Then the corner of Evelyn's mouth twitched into a grin and she smiled.

"I'm sorry," Beulah apologized. "It's really not about the Presbyterians. I have wanted to take over this potluck for years, especially with Ernestina getting more and more set in her ways as she got older. I don't know why. It sounds silly. But even if I didn't want to do it, why did Betty cut me out before I even had a chance to talk to Pastor Gillum? And she knew I was going to wait until after the funeral. It was mean of her and I feel betrayed. That's the bottom line."

"Yes," Evelyn said, her voice soothed. "That is the bottom line. A good friend turned-coat on you and we don't understand why. You need to talk to her, after you calm down."

"I'll go over in the morning," Beulah said.

"Sounds like a good plan. Now let's have dinner."

***

When Beulah finally roused herself after a restless night, Annie had already left for her new job. She poured coffee from the electric percolator, glad it was hot and ready, and sat at the kitchen table for her morning devotion time and prayers. She opened up the booklet to read, but like a broken record, the phone conversation with Betty replayed over and over in her mind, like it had last night.

How in the world could Betty have twisted her words around to tell Pastor Gillum she didn't want to coordinate the potluck? It floored her, and she needed an answer. Maybe there was some strange explanation. Either way, she could not spend another minute in turmoil. Beulah murmured a quick prayer, scanned the daily devotional, gathered her pocketbook, and put on her coat.

Beulah parked the Marquis and marched up the concrete steps to the bungalow. Out of the corner of her eye, she saw a curtain shift at the window. She rapped on the door. No answer. She could imagine Betty standing inside wringing her hands. Beulah knocked again. If she had to stand out here and knock all day, she would, for goodness sakes. Betty's car was in the driveway and there was no way her neighbor was going to wiggle out of this one.

Finally, the door cracked open. "Beulah, I thought it was a Jehovah's Witness. Come on in," she said, opening wide the door to the warm room inside.

"Betty, I thought there was something you might like to explain to me." Beulah stood barely over the threshold, her body stiff.

"Sit down, Beulah. I'll get you some coffee."

"No, I don't want coffee, thank you kindly. Simply an explanation, please."

"Well, I'm not sure I understand your question." Betty's eyes shifted to the bookshelf behind Beulah. "Look here at this," Betty shoved a picture of her granddaughter posed, hand on hip, in front of the Eiffel Tower. "Did you ever see such a pretty girl? Why, she could go to Hollywood with those looks and that personality."

Beulah knew Betty was diverting, but there was nothing to do but take the picture and look at it before she handed it back to Betty.

"She'll make something of herself, that one," Betty said. She placed the picture on the shelf and reached for another.

"I didn't come here to talk about Missy. I came to talk about the Thanksgiving potluck and why you told Pastor Gillum I didn't want to do the potluck anymore when you know that is not what I said."

"Why Beulah, you all but said it! You didn't sound the least bit interested in doing a thing about it, and with the Presbyterians chomping at the bit to get hold of it, there was no time to waste. I told him how I saw it and then I took the bull by the horns."

"I was respecting the fact that Ernestina's body was hardly cold." Beulah planted her feet firmly in the shag carpet. "There was plenty of time to pull it together after the funeral. For goodness sakes, I've done this thing for more years than I care to remember."

Betty's eyes darted and finally rested on Beulah's coat collar.

"Beulah, you're so slow in thinking about everything," Betty said, her tight blond curls bobbing as she spoke. "And you're too in control all the time. You and Ernestina have reigned like queens over the meals at Somerville Baptist for too many years. It's time you let someone else do it. You're not the only one who can do anything in the kitchen, you know."

The words bit Beulah, reminding her of a time when she stuck her hand into the leafy branch of a fruit tree and was stung by three bees.

"Besides that, it wouldn't hurt you to back away from food in general." Betty sniffed and looked at Beulah's waistline.

Heat roiled off her tongue. "As patient as I've been with you all these years, helping you, listening to you, defending you, and this is the thanks I get in return? This takes the cake."

"What do you mean, defending me?" Betty's face flushed red.

Beulah leaned in and shook her index finger in Betty's face. "You can tell Joe not to pick me up for the Country Diner tomorrow night. Nor will I be helping in any way with the potluck."

"Good," Betty folded her arms and straightened herself up two inches.

"Good," Beulah said. She whipped around, feeling a twinge in her new knee, and was nearly knocked over by the cold wall of air when she opened the door. As soon as she was on the porch, Betty slammed the door. Her heart pounded and the bristling November wind carried rain that stung her face and made her blink.

***

"Grandma." A voice from faraway sounded, and then there was a nudge on her shoulder.

Beulah searched to get her bearings. She had turned on the gas logs and must have drifted off after sleeping so poorly the night before.

"What time is it?"

"It's after six o'clock. You fell asleep."

"Good heavens, is it that late? I need to get supper ready."

"I can do it. Jake has a meeting tonight on the processing plant, so I'm home anyway." Annie bounded up the stairs. "Let me change clothes and I'll get something together," she called down. "I've got some great news to tell you."

The glow from the kitchen light beckoned her with the promise of something sweet. She scanned the contents of the refrigerator and her mood lifted when she saw eggs, milk, and butter. A custard pie was exactly what she needed.

"I can make spaghetti. Or I guess we can eat pie for supper," Annie said, and frowned at the ingredients spread out on the kitchen counter.

"Spaghetti sounds good." Beulah sighed. "You fix that and I'll make the pie."

"Are you feeling bad?" Annie asked as she opened the cupboard.

"Not the best. I had the big-eye last night and couldn't sleep."

"Evelyn called me," she said.

"There are no secrets on May Hollow Road," Beulah mumbled.

"She didn't say a word, only to check on you when I got home. What's going on?"

Beulah shaved frozen butter and worked it into the dough while she thought about what to say next. Betty had caused no little trouble for Annie not long ago and telling this story might pour gasoline on a fire. Still, she needed another perspective.

"Have I gained weight?" Beulah spurted the words out and turned to face her granddaughter.

Annie stood over the saucepan and bit her lower lip.

"Is it that bad?" Beulah said.

"No, of course not. You had knee surgery and couldn't do the things you normally do. It's natural to pick up a few pounds when you can't exercise as much."

"I got rid of my scale years ago. Useless thing, in my opinion. I can tell when my dresses are getting tight, and they are a little tight right now, I'll admit."

"Maybe you should go to the doctor and get your bloodwork checked. That's the one thing I'd be most concerned about."

Beulah pressed the crust into the pie dish, working at the task with her whole body.

"Betty Gibson took the Thanksgiving potluck from me. Stole

it right out from under me. I'm fit to be tied over it."

"How do you steal a potluck?" Annie asked, waiting on the pot of water to boil.

"I know it sounds silly, but that's what happened." Beulah spilled out the whole story to Annie.

"Betty is an immature gossip," Annie said. She dropped the spaghetti into the water and added a splash of olive oil.

Beulah exhaled another deep sigh and turned from the pie to face Annie, her hand on her hip.

"She's a has-been teenage beauty queen constantly trying to steal the show. I know her and have loved her despite that all these years. But she's never before done anything quite so scheming and ornery. I've felt sorry for Joe at times, but he's easygoing and laid-back; he knows how to handle her. Usually she pops off with something and then regrets it later. I went to her house today hoping for an apology and to clear things up. Instead, she accused me of being controlling and fat. Not exactly in those words, but that's what she meant."

Annie stared back at her with wide eyes, then shook her head. "I don't care for the woman, but it's hard to believe she'd do this to you." Annie drained the spaghetti and clanged the pan down on the counter. "You're one of her oldest friends. What are you going to do?"

"I don't know that I'm going to do anything. I do know I won't be going to the Country Diner tomorrow night and I won't be helping with the potluck a week from Sunday." Beulah plopped down in one of the wooden chairs.

"How can I help?"

"There's nothing to be done right now, other than hope she comes to her senses and apologizes. This time she has crossed the line."

"I have some good news if you'd like to hear it," Annie said.

"Oh, yes, what's wrong with me? Please, do tell."

Annie brought two plates of spaghetti to the table and sat down. "Dad called and he's coming for a visit. Possibly over Thanksgiving."

"Eddie's coming here?"

"To Somerville, to see me and get to know Jake better. He's in Texas now for some business."

"Well, now, that is wonderful. It will be good to see him."

It was a lie and her granddaughter knew it, but what else could she say?

"Where will he stay?"

"I don't know any details. You know Dad, hits the highlights but vague on details. He's supposed to call after he gets to Texas."

Here we go again, Beulah thought.

Chapter Four

AS ANNIE DROVE down May Hollow Road, she sensed the chasm that had opened between her grandmother's farm and the Gibson farm across the road. On one side, her grandmother's old Victorian sat far back down the long and winding driveway. Across the road, the Gibson bungalow sat practically on the road. It seemed as if even the mailboxes were at odds; the Gibson mailbox leaned to the right, away from Beulah's big oversized mailbox.

Annie knew it was probably too much to ask of Beulah to be excited about her father's visit, but she had hoped her grandmother would show a little more enthusiasm. Her father had a bad track record, but her engagement possibly meant a new start. With grandchildren in the future, perhaps he was thinking ahead and wanted to be a part of the family.

Annie turned down Gibson's Creek Road, the narrow lane surrounded by a line of thick trees on both sides, and thumped across the wooden bridge that spanned Gibson's Creek.

She admired the federal-style stone house, with its repaired roof and newly installed windows, in the dusky light. Outside, there was no longer any sign of the traumatic fire that had destroyed part of its roof and shattered the glass.

A glimmer of light emanated from the beautiful Palladian

window and reminded her of the long summer nights when the light inside the house served as a beacon home when she and Jake had played long after dark as children.

A baseball diamond in the side yard occupied them for countless summer afternoons where they took turns as batter and pitcher. They stopped for a supper break, and then continued until the frogs croaked dirges and crickets chirped melodies. Jake went home to the farm next door and Annie went inside to her mother's comforting presence. That had all been before the diagnosis, before their lives were forever altered.

Instead of only memories, this place would soon be filled with life—their new life together. If only they could settle the niggling details of the wedding.

"We have electricity," Annie said. Jerry Baker held a clipboard and studied an invoice.

"Turned on today," he said. The contractor looked immaculate in his pressed pants and starched shirt, a detail that always amazed Annie for a man who was fairly hands-on with the building business.

"The stair rail is up," she said, and ran her hand along the wood's smooth surface.

Annie remembered the day a few weeks ago when she'd sailed down the stairs on top of a mattress, taking out the railing as she went. That day also ended in finding the letters from her great uncle Ephraim during World War II, which included a letter written in Italian that led Annie to Italy, and the discovery of Benito, Ephraim's long lost son and Beulah's nephew.

"The boys left a few minutes ago. They wanted you to see it tonight," he said, beaming with pride.

"It's beautiful. So, what's next?"

"We're working on the woodwork. Are you planning to stain or paint it? It was originally painted, but we can take the paint off if you want and have it ready to stain."

"Paint, since that was original, but Jake and I will do the painting."

Annie watched as Jerry wrote notes.

"Now, let's look at the kitchen. Do you want to put tile or wood on the floor?"

Annie followed behind him to the one-story addition built

on to the back of the house that provided a bath and kitchen. The floor was covered with buckled linoleum.

"Wood, nothing fancy. A distressed look that fits the house. If you have any salvaged wood, even better."

He nodded.

"When will it be finished?"

Jerry tapped his pen on the clipboard and stared up at the ceiling.

"Let's see, it's near the end of November now. Holidays are coming up, so I reckon late-February for us, but you'll need time to paint and do the things you want to finish out. March at the earliest."

"That's sooner than I thought."

"Jake's help on the demo moved us along."

"He's been burning the candle at both ends, with bank consulting and farming. I think he's glad the demo work is over," she said.

"We're bringing in the heating and air guys next. You'll see them around."

"Thanks, Jerry. Call me if you need me."

***

"Grandma?"

The back-porch room was lit, but the kitchen was dark. Annie took off her coat and hung it on a hook by the door.

"In here."

Annie could not remember coming into the house at suppertime when her grandmother was not puttering about the kitchen. Now it was dark as a tomb.

Annie went through the sewing room and into the living room, still a vision of the 1970s with its faded polyester couch and oversized lamp shades. Her grandmother was lying back in the recliner, her worn-out Bible flopped open on her lap.

"Everything okay?" Annie asked, and sat down next to her on the couch.

Beulah grabbed the La-Z-Boy lever, the recliner popped, and she pitched forward with a jolt. Annie jumped, ready to catch her grandmother before she catapulted into the fireplace, but Beulah planted her feet and caught herself.

"I swanny, I've got to get this thing fixed."

"If you weren't spending the insurance money on the old stone house, you could have gotten lots of things fixed or replaced."

"And we wouldn't have known about Ephraim's son in Italy, and that's worth it all. Besides, you and Jake are putting your fair share into it as well. It'll be awful good to have you all that close as neighbors."

"Speaking of neighbors, how's it going with Betty?"

"I've gotten phone calls from several women at church. I reckon she's out there telling her side of the story."

"Which is what?"

"I gave up the potluck and now I'm jealous she has it and that's why I won't help with it."

"Maybe you should get out there and tell your side of the story?"

A few weeks ago, Annie was on the other end of Betty Gibson's sharp tongue. She had overheard Betty talking about her father's side of the family to her grandmother. They'd been hurtful words that dredged up insecurities and doubts about her relationship with Jake, nearly wrecking their fragile love for a while.

"People believe what they want to believe."

"You should defend yourself," Annie said. "Everybody knows what a gossip she is, anyway."

Her grandmother's face looked pale and drawn. The rift had aged her, almost overnight.

"I've told them that's not the case, but I'll not stoop to her level. For the life of me, I don't know what has gotten into that woman." Her grandmother shook her head. "She's always been a little difficult at times, but I never thought she'd turn on me like this. I'm trying to figure out how to do what this book says," she said, pointing to the open pages. "Love your neighbor and your enemy. Right now, they are one and the same."

"Go to her and address the gossip."

"I'm too angry right now," Beulah said. "I'm working on loving her before I go, but the Lord's going to have to give it to me, because I sure can't conjure it up at the moment."

***

Annie hiked over to Jake's cottage and stepped over the stone fence at the crossover place that divided her grandmother's farm from the Wilder's. Annie picked her path carefully to avoid the cow-pies. Days were shorter and there was little light once she got home from work, but she was determined to preserve her farm walks, especially after being bathed in florescent light all day.

The Wilder's brick Italianate sat back off the road like her grandmother's farmhouse. It was grand, and Evelyn had turned it into a showcase where she extended hospitality to her church family, her garden club, the DAR, and her book club. When Jake moved back permanently from Cincinnati a few weeks earlier, he wisely chose the empty servant's cottage behind the house so his elegant mother could continue her routine without worrying about his manure-covered boots.

She paused at the window outside and caught sight of Jake bent over documents on the coffee table. He scratched his chin, the stubble thick on his face, and she marveled once again that he would soon be her husband. A slight creak with the door, then she crept across the floor and prepared to put her arms around him. He turned and pulled her down on the couch.

"You can't sneak up on me, Annie May," he said, laughing.

"I know, and it makes me so mad."

"You'll appreciate that trait when I'm your nighttime protector."

"I hadn't thought of that," she said, sitting up. "That will come in handy. What're you working on?"

"A spreadsheet so I can track financial investment in the livestock."

"Once a banker, always a banker. Want me to make supper?"

"Beulah's vegetable soup is on the stove warming, and I made appetizers," Jake said. "I'll get them."

"This I can't wait to see," Annie said, and watched him place a dish on the coffee table. "What do we have here?"

"Cracker with cheddar and a jalapeño, or cracker with cheddar and a pickle," Jake said proudly.

"Aren't you the chef? You get an *A* for effort."

"I was hoping for more than that," he said, and pushed her hair back behind her ear. "How's the house looking?"

"It's moving along. How do you feel about skipping Christmas gifts this year? We can use so much for the house. Is that terribly unromantic?"

"Are you kidding? What could be better than setting up a life with one another?" He pulled her close.

"It's our first Christmas together, and I want it to be special."

"It's not technically our first Christmas together. Other than the last ten years, we've spent nearly every Christmas together in some form, literally since the cradle."

"True, but being neighbors and friends was one thing. This is different."

"I know one way we can make it special," he said. "Let's get married before Christmas."

"We talked about this. I have to check on my vacation."

"You do get Christmas day off."

"You're such a *man*."

"I hope so," he said. "Better, what if we got married when your dad comes to town? We can take a weekend away until we can do a longer trip later."

"That could be in the next week or so, Jake. We need time to plan, and I want us to enjoy being with him when he comes, not consumed with the wedding. On top of all that, you're so busy right now. How do you even have a weekend? The processing plant, banking, farming, working on the house."

"The processing plant takes hardly any of my time. It's a small investment compared to the guys who will run it. Either way, we have to have it in order to handle the animals humanely from beginning to end. A few meetings now will save us a lot of time and money down the road."

"All right, then farming and banking," she said.

"I can handle it," he said. "It may mean a little less time together in the short run, but it will get better once I drop the consulting. That's another reason for us to go ahead and get married. We can spend more time together."

Annie turned back to the fire and stared for a few minutes at the dancing flames.

"I want that, but there are so many other things pulling at us right now. Let me talk to Colleen so I can at least know my options for time off."

Chapter Five

BEULAH SIPPED HER morning coffee in the living room with the gas logs blazing. Work needed doing, but her energy was gone, zapped like a dead battery. The turmoil with Betty had settled like some cold ache deep into her bones that she couldn't seem to shake off.

The whole mess felt like a death to her, and somehow it had made the loss of Fred feel especially sharp, even though it had been two-and-a-half years since she lost him. If he were sitting next to her now, what would he say about all this? It was so good to have someone to balance your opinion, someone who loved you with their whole heart and, even more, knew you in all your good and bad points.

She had wanted the potluck too much. In the quiet of the morning, she had to wonder if her motive was to be in control, as Betty had accused, in order to be esteemed in the community. If that were true, then the whole thing could be traced to pride, her old, besetting sin.

The thought depressed her. Pride preceded a fall, and she had surely fallen. Everyone in the community now thought Beulah was a jealous and petty person, thanks to Betty's big mouth.

A knock sounded at the back door and startled her out of revelry.

"Beulah?"

"In here," she said. "Come in."

Joe Gibson, tall and wiry, held his cap in his hands and tentatively stepped into the den.

"Can I talk to you a minute?" he asked, his green eyes searching her face.

"Why, sure. Can I get you some coffee?"

"No," he said as he sat on the edge of the couch. "I've had aplenty already."

Beulah joined him on the couch and folded her hands in her lap. Joe looked at the floor as if gathering his thoughts, and then met her gaze.

"Your mama and my mama were best friends," he said. "I reckon I've knowed you all my life."

"I remember when you were born," she said. "Your mama was the first pregnant lady I'd ever seen. Then all of a sudden, she wasn't pregnant and there you were. It was like a miracle," she said.

"You was always good to me, puttin' up with a wild young un, and you even saved me from drownin' in the creek that one time," Joe chuckled.

Beulah smiled at the memory.

"Bound and determined to catch that one tadpole but it was too far out. There you went before I barely had time to think. I saw your little towhead bobbing in the water and went after you. Anybody would have done the same, but you were always like the little brother I didn't get to have."

"The way I see it, we're family," he said.

"I've always seen it that way, too," she nodded.

"I can't abide the thought of losing that," he said, and wrung his cap as if he were squeezing water out of it. Beulah watched his hands, scarred and weathered by the sun. It was a mannerism from his childhood and it made her see him, even for a moment, as the little boy she had known so very long ago. She could see Eunice Gibson now, standing over him with one hand on her hip, the other finger pointing at Joe, as she chided him for stealing a pie. The little shaver scuffed his feet and wrung his hat while his mama fussed, then winked at Beulah and ran off with a grin when the scolding ended.

"I don't want that, either," she said quietly.

"Betty's my wife and I made a vow to her a long time ago. I love her, but she can be difficult at times. I don't reckon I've ever said that to another person, Beulah, and I wouldn't say it to anybody but you." His eyes dropped. "But lately, she's not been normal. Betty's awful irritable and snappish. She's done gone through the change a long while back. I don't know what it could be, but she's not right. I've tried to get her to go to the doctor but she won't hear of it."

"Aging takes a toll on all of us one way or another," Beulah said, and then sighed. "It's a hard thing, adjusting both to our looks and bodies giving out."

"Mebbe so," Joe said. "I'm not a woman, so I can't say as to what it might be. I guess what I come here to say is that you're like my sister. I need you to overlook Betty the best you can. She needs you in her life, and I surely do, too. Can you come on and go with us to the Country Diner tonight?"

Beulah wondered how to respond. Joe was like a little brother to her and she never wanted to hurt him. He was caught in the middle of this mayhem.

"Joe, do you remember back when I lived with Momma and Daddy in the old stone house, back before we had a good bridge and before we owned the land that this house sits on now?"

"Why sure I do. It was that-a-way until you married, then your daddy bought this piece of land and you and Fred moved here."

"Remember how the creek rose when the rains came and we couldn't cross it?"

"Nary a road another way, you was just stuck back then," he agreed.

"Sometimes it took days before it went back to normal, before we could cross to the other side."

"I sure hope this creek goes down fast. Mebbe by next Saturday night, anyway," he stood and put on his cap.

"You're a good man, Joe Gibson," Beulah said. She saw him to the door and watched as he climbed into his truck. She hoped to goodness Betty Gibson appreciated her husband.

The conversation made her hungry, almost desperately, as if there was a hole inside that needed a warm and gooey cinnamon roll to plug it. Evelyn made them fresh only the day before. A few seconds in the microwave and warm, doughy sweetness filled her mouth. She closed her eyes in satisfaction.

Rain pelted the tin roof on the closed-in back porch. Beulah finished her pastry and put the dishes in the sink. On the back porch, she settled into one of Fred's old tweed-covered chairs she couldn't give away after his death for the memories. It was a front row seat for the weather, with the long row of windows lining the back-porch wall.

Good rain, good rain. Fred always said that when the rains came, no matter what he had planned for the day. The November rains were late this year, but it had been a blessing as they had rushed to get the old stone house closed up after the fire last summer.

Rain had a way of letting a body down a bit, allowing for relaxation and staying in the house, much the way the cold months of January and February worked when no one wanted to be out much with the cold and ice.

It also had a way of ushering in the blues. Beulah loved peace with her neighbors, but some things could not be easily forgiven.

Chapter Six

WITH A FEW minutes to spare, Annie poked her head into Virginia Taylor's room.

"Mrs. Taylor?" The woman was sitting in a chair facing the window. Had she nodded off, or was she simply enjoying the lovely scenery next to the facility? It was one of the things Annie liked about Richwood—there was a beautiful pastoral view from every window lined with white plank fence and spotted with young trees. The grass faded into a brownish green this time of year, but it was still better than looking at a parking lot.

The woman's gray head turned and Annie took that as an invitation to enter the room.

"Mrs. Taylor? I hope I'm not interrupting."

"Sit down. I hoped you'd come for a visit," she said.

Virginia Taylor wore her hair in one long braid. High cheekbones and wide set eyes made Annie think she had been a beauty in her younger days.

"You mentioned we're related, and I'd love to know how. You know I don't know much about my father's side of the family. He was an only child, and my grandparents were dead by the time I came along."

"I'll be glad to tell ye." Virginia's watery brown eyes focused on Annie.

"That'd be great," Annie said. "I'm between activities right now."

"Oh no, we can't talk now," she said, her eyes darting to a calendar hanging next to her bed.

"Oh," Annie said. "I didn't realize you were busy. I'm sorry."

"I'm not busy," she said. "It's too soon."

"What's too soon?"

"The moon is full. Come back when the moon is new. Here," she pointed to a date on the calendar. "We can talk up a storm then."

Virginia looked back at the pasture.

"All right, I'll be back then," Annie said, unsure if Virginia was really serious or if perhaps it was her form of a joke. Annie edged away, in case the older woman might beckon her back, but she held a steady gaze out the window.

Annie pondered the strange encounter and nearly bumped into one of the nursing assistants who pushed an empty wheelchair down the hall.

"You've got flowers at the front desk."

"Me?"

"Just came in," the young woman said over her shoulder. "I'm jealous."

A dozen yellow roses. Jake should not have spent money, but she flushed with warmth. There was no card.

Annie passed Lonnie Caldwell on the way back to her office and smiled at him. He winked, jiggy stepped, and grinned before he sauntered down the hall. Goodness, he was a flirt.

Once she settled the flowers on her desk, she sent Jake a quick text of thanks.

"For what?" Jake replied.

"The roses! I love them."

Jake's number rang through.

"You got flowers?" he said.

"Quit pretending you didn't send them."

"I didn't, really."

"Seriously? Well, who?"

"I don't know, but I wish I had—does that count?"

"Do you think it was my dad?"

"I hope so. Otherwise, I may have something to worry about."

Annie called the florist, but she stonewalled.

"I'm sworn to secrecy," she said. "I will say it was a gentleman."

***

Her grandmother's frugal tendencies made for a cool house, but good sleeping. When the alarm jarred her out of pleasant dreams, Annie did not want to come out from under the warmth of the worn cotton quilt.

Instead, she cuddled in dreamy reflection and went over her exchange with the mysterious Virginia Taylor. When she asked one of the nursing assistants about Virginia, she was more intrigued than ever.

"She's eccentric, but it's not dementia. She does everything by the moon phases, always has," said the young woman. "Baths, visits, doctor appointments, everything is by the moon."

When Annie asked her grandmother about Virginia, she was vague.

"Sounds familiar, but I can't place her," Beulah had said.

Annie wanted to know more about her father's family. She'd had so little contact with them. Her father wasn't interested in maintaining those relationships, or any in Somerville for that matter, so she'd had no connection to any of them as a child. His parents were dead, so there were no grandparents. He had a sister Annie had met once or twice, but they'd had some kind of falling out years ago and she had moved away. The only other relatives left in the area were distant. Meanwhile, Annie had been gone for ten years, living in New York. Now that she was home, she had to admit she had a desire to know more about them, as if somehow knowing them might shed light on her father's complicated personality.

Annie hoped her father would come for Thanksgiving. She knew well enough the number of times he disappointed her, but he might actually come through this time.

The snooze went off again and she forced herself to get up. Wrapped in a thick terrycloth robe, she slid into her fuzzy slippers, and slipped on her engagement ring.

The front porch was her favorite spot in the early mornings

to enjoy her coffee. As fall edged into winter, those opportunities would diminish, making days like today even more precious.

The recent rain batted away many of the dying leaves and there was now a rich, woodsy scent filling the air.

Distraught mama cows called for their calves and disrupted the normal early morning quiet. For the second time this week, she had heard about the moon phase when Jake decided to wean the calves while the moon waned into the last quarter. If there was anything to it, the mamas would cry one day versus the typical three days. Annie hoped it was true. The cries put her on edge.

An emergency siren pierced the bawling. While common in her former life in New York City, it was unusual to hear such a thing all the way out here, nearly three miles from town.

A flash of red lights flickered through the trees. Annie's heart skipped and her legs went limp as it seemed close to the Wilder driveway. *Not Jake, please.* The sound grew louder now, closer, but the road was not visible from the porch. Could something have happened to her grandmother inside to cause her to call 911 while Annie was out on the porch? Annie stood frozen, unsure of what to do next. It went silent and Annie knew where it had stopped.

Annie opened the door and heard her grandmother call down.

"Where'd that siren go?" Her grandmother stood at the top of the stairs in her nightgown, the curls of her gray hair sticking out willy-nilly.

"I think it's at Joe and Betty's."

"Oh mercy," Beulah said. "Wait on me, I'll get dressed."

While she waited, Annie called Richwood Manor and left a message saying she would be late.

"Let's take my car," Beulah said, and handed Annie the keys.

Annie sped down the driveway, gravel crunching and rocks pinging against the wheel well. For once, Beulah didn't criticize her speed.

"Oh no," Beulah said when the parked ambulance came into view.

They went through the small living room to the kitchen, where the scent of frying meat hung in the air. Betty Gibson lay on the floor, sweat beaded on her forehead, white-faced, her right hand clutched on her chest. Her eyes, wide and frightened, focused on Joe, who knelt beside her. The brightly-colored muumuu she wore spread out on the worn linoleum.

Paramedics bent over her. The sole of one of their shoes had a slimy substance on the bottom, which Annie recognized as vomit. A few feet away, a pan lay on the floor, unbaked biscuits scattered here and there.

"Beulah," Joe said, his voice a mix of fear and anguish. Beulah grasped his hands without saying a word. Bacon still sizzled on the stove and Annie turned it off.

The paramedics worked with calm intensity. They attached electrodes all over Betty's body, inserted an IV, slipped something under her tongue and placed an oxygen mask on her face. She visibly relaxed under the care.

The squawk of a radio, then "myocardial infarction" and "cath lab requested." Within a few minutes, Betty was loaded onto a gurney, Joe still holding her hand, and carefully moved to the ambulance.

"We'll drive you," Beulah told Joe. "You don't need to drive yourself."

"I might need my truck," Joe said in a quiet monotone, and let go of Betty's hand as the EMS workers maneuvered through the doorway.

"Jake can bring it later," Beulah said. "Let us get you there and we can call your kids."

Joe nodded and they got into Beulah's car while the paramedics loaded Betty into the ambulance. Annie backed onto the road and waited for the ambulance to pull out, then followed.

Joe groaned from the back seat. "She got up this morning and said something wasn't right. I was back in the bathroom when I heard her hit the floor."

"You need to call the kids. Do you have your phone?" Beulah asked. Annie watched in the rearview mirror as Joe searched his pockets, then shook his head.

Annie pulled her phone out and handed it to Beulah.

"Give me the numbers and I'll call," Beulah said. "We'll have them meet you at the hospital."

Once they arrived, Beulah went in with Joe to help with paperwork in the emergency room while Annie called Jake.

"Hey," Jake said. Hearing his comforting voice made her eyes sting.

"Betty's had a heart attack and we're at the emergency room now. Joe needs his truck here, if you can bring it. I don't know where the keys are; I think we left the house unlocked. If you can get inside, he also needs his phone."

"Got it," Jake said. "Be there as quick as I can."

"Be careful," Annie said, and imagined Jake driving too fast down the curvy, country road.

Jake was there by the time Joe finished the paperwork. He squeezed Annie's hand and then went to Joe, holding out the truck keys and phone, handing him a small bit of control in a sea of chaos. Joe looked up at Jake, his eyes blinking in gratitude. Jake put his hand on Joe's shoulder and squeezed.

Annie caught Jake's eye and motioned him to the hallway, where they found a small waiting area.

"What happened?" he asked.

Annie relayed the events of the morning. "Doesn't sound good," he said. Annie started to cry and buried her face in his shirt. He wrapped his arms around her, making her feel safe and protected.

"All this mess with Grandma," she pulled away to look at him. "If Betty doesn't make it, she'll feel awful," her voice broke.

"I know. I probably need to do Joe's chores for a while, either way. Can you drive me back to the farm?"

"Yes, good idea."

***

Annie dropped off Jake, updated Colleen, and was back in the waiting room with Beulah and Joe in time to see Joe and Betty's daughter, Peggy, crumple into her father's arms. They squeezed hands and exchanged hugs before they settled in for silent, prayerful waiting.

Finally, a doctor appeared and called for the family. Annie and Beulah barely dared to breathe. Annie wondered if Betty had already passed or if she was fighting for her life. When Joe and Peggy came back several minutes later, Annie knew from their faces that Betty was still alive.

"We had to give permission for bypass surgery," Peggy said. "They're taking her to Lexington."

Beulah nodded. "I'll go back to the house and clean up the kitchen. Call us when you know something."

"Thank you, Beulah," Peggy said. "There's been no better friend to my mother than you."

Her grandmother patted Peggy's hand. "I'll be up to the hospital in a bit."

"Do you want me to drop you at the Gibson's or the house?" Annie asked her when she ended her call with Evelyn.

"Take me home first. I need to get myself together, and then I'll go over and clean up."

"I can help."

"You go on to work. Evelyn's going to help, then I'll ride up with her to Lexington."

Chapter Seven

IN A SMALL community like Somerville, news such as this traveled like wildfire. Still, Annie wanted their close friends to hear it first. There was Lindy Childress, the young lawyer who had become her best friend in town. She likely already knew since her father, Tom, was dating Jake's mother. Tom was Evelyn's—boyfriend? Using that term didn't seem right to refer to someone in his fifties. Man-friend might be more appropriate.

After a lengthy conversation with Lindy, Annie called Woody Patterson, the forty-something bachelor farmer who took part in their Sunday dinners, and left a short voicemail. Her last call was to Scott and Mary Beth Southerland, the recently married preacher and his schoolteacher wife.

It was difficult to concentrate after the events of the morning, yet she badly needed focus for the pressing tasks at hand. She had little overall guidance from Colleen, the facility director. A job description did exist, but it was filled with such legal jargon and presumptive words that the director had tossed it aside on her first day and gave her a simple directive—engage the patients in mind, body, and soul, and value their lives.

The job had no specific structure, schedule, or routine like she'd had at the airline. She was able to work as she needed, putting in forty hours during a combination of traditional work hours, evenings, and weekends, if necessary. The clientele was quite different as well. Instead of harried passengers with little time to spare, she had twenty-four patients who faced the paradox of long days at the end of seemingly short lives.

The December activities calendar was due to be posted. It was already late. The facility director had explained that December, of all months, needed to be filled to the brim with options of every type. It was a hard month for elderly residents. Many had either no family or family members who lived far away, and the looming holidays magnified the loneliness that was tolerated most of the year.

Annie stared at the blank calendar and realized she needed help from one special resident in particular. She filled two cups of coffee in the break room, checked the time, and headed for the library. Vesta was in her wheelchair, parked at the antique table, two books open in front of her.

"How's business?" Annie asked.

Vesta looked up from her book, her almond eyes bright and clear for her ninety-something years. Vesta had been a school librarian most of her life, both prior to racial integration and after, and she had taken over the operation of the library as soon as she moved to Richwood. More than that, she was the "unofficial mayor of Richwood," as the director called her, and Annie had good enough sense to check in with her before making any broad strokes.

"Good morning, Annie," she said, and accepted the coffee Annie handed her. "It's been a busy morning. Cold weather is good for books."

"Do you have Thanksgiving plans?"

"My nephew Jerome and his wife Vivian will take me to their house. Vivian is not a good cook, but she's very hospitable. With all their grandchildren running around, I'll be ready to come back here for some peace and quiet. What are your plans?"

"We'll gather at Evelyn's for dinner. She and Tom Childress are seeing each other, and I think Evelyn wanted to host, especially with this being their first holiday together. Jake and I will probably go to the movies, but he'll be busy on the farm catching up with projects since he'll have some time off from the bank."

"How is Jake managing the bank job and the farm?"

"Busy, but the bank consulting is a good income supplement, especially since he is getting started with the farm."

"You seem troubled." Vesta closed the books in front of her.

"Betty Gibson had a heart attack this morning." Annie shared the details. "They moved her to Lexington for the surgery."

"Lord, please heal this woman," Vesta said, her head tilted back and eyes closed. "But if you don't, we trust her into your sweet arms."

"Amen," Annie said, reaching across to squeeze Vesta's hand.

"Have you heard anything on the historical marker?"

Two weeks had passed since she and Vesta had submitted paperwork and requested a marker identifying the significance of the old stone house. The marker was meant to honor Annie's ancestors as the owner of the first stone house in Kentucky, and Vesta's ancestors as the slave laborers who helped build the house.

"Nothing yet," Annie said. "It could be two to four more weeks before we hear anything."

Vesta folded her hands and put them in her lap. "My, how I enjoyed that day out a couple of weeks ago when you took me to see the old place. We may not see such a mild day again until spring. The trees still held such magnificent color and the way the sun washed through the leaves and cast a golden hue on the limestones was breathtaking. I do hope I live to see the dedication."

"I can't imagine it without you. It'll be better in the spring after the bad weather breaks. Only three or four months away."

Vesta smiled. "I love the optimism of youth."

There was a comfort with Vesta that made Annie feel somehow as if she had known her since childhood. Yet, their paths had crossed only weeks ago when Tom Childress recommended Vesta as a local historian. The discovery of a shared connection through their ancestors in the late 1700s made Annie believe there might be such a thing as blood memory, and now a recognition all these years later of this mystical bond.

"Vesta, I need your help. I'm working on the December calendar and noticed some things are already on the schedule that happen every year, including the Sunday afternoon musical programs, the Christmas carolers on Wednesday evenings, and the Christmas hymn sing on Christmas Eve, followed by a visit from Santa and Mrs. Claus. It seems heavy on the music side, so I was thinking of adding some lectures, readings from Christmas poems and stories, and maybe a couple of outings if weather permits. What do you think?"

"We want to strike the right tone: a balance of activities, plenty for everyone no matter their interests, and as much intellectual stimulation as they can take," Vesta said. Her eyes danced with the prospect. "I'll come to your office after I finish here and we'll look at the calendar together."

***

Annie was preparing to meet with Vesta when she noticed a voicemail from her grandmother.

There was palpable relief in her grandmother's voice. "Betty made it through the surgery. But she'll be in the hospital for a few days, then there'll be a long road of recovery after that and some lifestyle changes. Evelyn and I came back home since they've got a passel of family up there right now."

Annie dialed Jake. "She made it through the surgery."

"Mom called me. Good news," Jake said.

"Where are you?"

"Over at Joe's, checking cows. Have you talked with Colleen?"

"Not yet. I'll do it as soon as possible. Maybe she'll agree to early March? Then we can move into the stone house."

"Too far away. We can live here in the cottage."

There was silence on the other end of the line for a few seconds before he spoke. "Seeing Joe facing the loss of his wife—" his voice trailed off. "It made me think we shouldn't waste a minute."

She toyed with the silver cross around her neck, the one Jake had given her when she'd turned sixteen. They'd already missed so much time together. What he said was true. As long as she lived, she would not forget the anguish on Joe Gibson's face. For all her faults, he loved Betty completely and the prospect of losing her devastated him.

"Let's talk tonight," Annie said. "I'll make dinner at your place."

She pushed the conversation out of her mind and cleared the paperwork from her desk. Unpinning a large wall calendar, she laid it on her desk while she waited for Vesta.

They had lots of days to fill for the residents, not to mention planning for the following year. Gray, cold winter months needed bright, fun activities to keep the residents upbeat. A wedding in the middle of it all felt impossible. Yet, she also felt the urgency Jake expressed. Something changed this morning when she saw Betty lying on the floor facing the doors of death.

Life held no guarantees.

Chapter Eight

BEULAH DROPPED HER purse by the back door and removed her coat, glad she had cleaned Betty's kitchen early in the day and that Evelyn had driven her to Lexington and back. With all those turning lanes, stoplights at every corner, shrill sirens, horns honking, and the thick traffic, she had felt like she might have her own heart attack before they made it to the hospital parking garage.

Once they parked in tight spaces in a multi-tiered concrete structure, they trotted across the busy street on a covered walkway high above the city traffic. It seemed like a mile to the correct wing and floor of the hospital. Her father had once told her she had no business up in Lexington, and Beulah believed it. The city was plumb exhausting. She collapsed into the recliner and raised the footrest.

In the end, the news was good. Betty should recover with no long-term damage. Beulah replayed seeing Betty prostrate on the kitchen floor. What if Betty had died this morning, leaving Beulah still holding onto her anger? No one was ensured another dawn; yet she still felt hurt over the whole mess.

"Lord, help me let go of this. Help me love her, even though I'm still mad as the dickens at her," she murmured before falling into a deep sleep.

Sometime later, the portable rang out. Startled, she reached wildly for it.

"Beulah," the voice on the other end of the line was tentative, as if he had known she was sleeping.

"Pastor Gillum," she said, her brain fuzzy and dull from sleep. "I was taking a little rest."

"I'm sure you need it, and I'm awful sorry to bother you," he said. "I just came from the hospital. Joe seems to be doing well and we've got meals lined up for them for the next two weeks after they get home."

"Good," Beulah said, and carefully lowered the footrest. "It was a terrible scare, but it sounds like everything will be okay."

"Yes," he said, then hesitated. "There's something else I wanted to speak with you about. I know you weren't interested in doing the community potluck, but with Betty out of commission, we're in a terrible fix. Would you be willing to step back in this year? To be honest, Betty hadn't even bought the turkeys yet, and I'm not sure what else she'd gotten done, so it could be a whole lot of work left to do."

For goodness sakes. The irony of the potluck falling back in her lap now when she didn't even want to do it anymore nearly made her laugh out loud.

"There's another option I should mention. The Presbyterians are offering to do it this year. The meal's come to be our best local outreach and I hate to give it up entirely, but maybe it's best if you're not interested in taking the job."

"I will be happy to serve, Pastor. Since it is a community event after all, why don't we invite the Presbyterians to partner with us?"

"Well now, that is a fine idea. Fine indeed."

Now that she was up and moving around, Beulah wanted a little pick-me-up. There was leftover pumpkin pie and homemade whipped cream in the refrigerator, and she had thought about them the entire drive home from the hospital. It was not possible to have pumpkin pie without a cup of fresh coffee, so Beulah filled the basket, added water, and plugged in the percolator.

"Beulah?" Evelyn poked her head in the back door.

"Come in," Beulah said. "I didn't see you drive in."

"I'm trying to exercise more, so I walked over. Have you talked to Joe or Peggy since we left?"

"She's heavily sedated, but seems to be doing okay," Beulah said, automatically pulling down another plate for the pie.

"My word, what a day."

"What a week! Annie said her father called and he's coming to see her."

"I hope he does," Evelyn said.

"I do too, but if I had a penny for every promise he made, I'd be rich as Croesus."

"I reckon she's excited," Evelyn said.

"Over the moon. He's acted like it might be for Thanksgiving. We'll see."

"At least now she has Jake," Evelyn said. "He knows as well as anybody how flaky her dad can be, and he'll be there for her even if Eddie doesn't come through."

Beulah shook her head. "Evelyn, seeing Betty on that floor, well, it made me so ashamed of letting my anger go so long. I'm still torn up over it."

"Bless your heart, and hers, too. She's been awful peevish."

"I reckon she's not out of the woods yet." Beulah sliced two pieces of the pumpkin pie and set them on the table.

"No pie for me," Evelyn said. "But I will take a cup of coffee."

"You love pumpkin pie," Beulah said. "I've got fresh whipped cream."

"I'm trying to shape up a bit more. Beulah, this whole dating thing is turning me upside down." Evelyn sat down at the kitchen table. "Tom mentioned taking a trip in early January to the Caribbean for a law conference with some other couples. You know that means swimsuits, and I can hardly bear the thought of him seeing me in one right now. It's one thing to be dating at twenty-something. It's altogether different at fifty-something."

"Well, traveling does bring about intimacies you don't normally have in everyday life," Beulah said.

"He is a gentleman, of course, and has already booked us separate rooms; but you do learn a lot about a person when you travel together, so I thought it might be a good thing to go. If only I could avoid the swimsuit."

Beulah tried to remember the last time she'd worn one. Land sakes, it was probably more than thirty years ago when she and Fred had gone to Gatlinburg and rented a cabin with a Jacuzzi tub on the back deck.

"Well, our churches are finally going to work together on something," Beulah said.

"You don't say. Is it the potluck?" Evelyn held her coffee cup up to her face with both hands and peered over the top conspiratorially.

"It is. Pastor Gillum called to see if I would step in. They've offered to help, so it seems the right thing to do."

"Will wonders never cease," Evelyn said.

They sat in silence for a few minutes, lost in the comfortable presence of a long friendship.

"Do you have any idea what kind of recovery Betty will have? I wonder who will stay with her during the day while Joe's working. Both Polly and Peggy have full-time jobs, and baby Frances takes up all of Penny's time," Evelyn said.

The same thing had crossed Beulah's mind while sitting in the cold sterility of the hospital waiting room. It seemed human nature for everyone to flock around when a crisis first happened, but when Betty really needed help going to the bathroom and doing daily house chores, everyone scattered to the four winds.

"I'll be glad to stay as much as I can," Beulah offered.

"Maybe we should let the family work it out first, and then we can fill in where needed," Evelyn said.

It was a good plan and Beulah felt satisfied. Or maybe her satisfaction came from the last bite of pumpkin pie with a big dollop of whipped cream on it.

***

After Evelyn left and the pumpkin pie goodness sank into memory, Beulah sat in the kitchen drinking her coffee and thinking how this day had started like every other. Yet in a matter of moments, death clutched at her neighbor.

It took her back to that terrible time over two years ago when Fred died. It, too, had started like an ordinary day. They had gotten up early and eaten breakfast as if they would have a thousand more together. Beulah couldn't remember what they talked about that morning. It was nothing unusual, and yet, if they had known, the things they could have said to each other. He put on his straw hat and went out to plow the field. With a list of errands a mile long, she had left for town, never dreaming it was the last time she would see her beloved.

Later that morning, Joe Gibson saw the tractor turning circles in the field and called 911. He managed to climb onto the tractor where Fred had slumped over the wheel and turn it off at a great danger to himself. Beulah had been driving home on May Hollow Road when the ambulance flew past her and turned into her own driveway. All the rushing in the world hadn't helped Fred; the heart attack was massive and quick. He hadn't suffered one bit, the coroner said, and for that she was grateful.

The wall phone rang out again, disturbing her reverie.

"Beulah, what's the update on Betty?" Woody Patterson was on the line, the forty-something bachelor who took frequent Sunday dinner with her and Evelyn as rotating hosts.

Beulah told him what she knew.

"Reckon I can do anything for Joe?" he asked.

"Jake's taking care of the cattle for him, but I'm sure he could use some help doing something. Why don't you call Jake, since he knows more about Joe's business than anybody?"

"All right, then," Woody said. Beulah waited for him to close out the conversation with a "talk to you later" or "I'll let you go now," but he didn't.

"Okay," she said, and waited.

"Yep, good news on Betty."

"Woody, is there something on your mind?"

"Well, now that you brung it up, there was something I want to ask. It's about Stella," he said. Of course, Stella. The distraught soul from Chicago who had stumbled into their lives last spring, rented the old stone house, and accidentally started the fire that nearly destroyed the home that had been in her family for generations. In the process of setting things right, Stella and Woody had met in her own living room. Sparks had flown again, but of a blessedly less literal sort.

"I was wondering if, well, you could show her a thing or two about cookin'."

"I reckon so, if that's something she wants to learn. Or is this your idea?"

"Beulah, it's an awful mess. I never thought much about it since most of the time we go out. Last weekend I went up to Chicago for an early Thanksgiving dinner at her house. I like to have starved to death. She brought out sliced turkey breast lunch meat and cooked it in the oven, so it was dried to a crisp. The boxed stuffin' was soggy. It was the worst meal I've ever seen nor heard tell of. I don't know if there's any hope for her, and I can't marry a woman that don't cook. Eatin's too important to me."

Beulah sighed. "Now Woody, don't go throwin' out the baby with the bath water. You know Stella grew up in foster homes. She's not had anyone to teach her. You bring her down here and let her stay with me for a bit and I'll help her."

Good heavens, had she offered to have another houseguest? Only weeks ago, she had another houseguest under her feet all day when Rossella DeVechio was thrust upon her while Annie and her New York City friend, Janice DeVechio, went to Italy in search of Beulah's nephew, Benito. Janice's mother-in-law strained the limits of Beulah's hospitality

"Thank you, Beulah, thank you. That's what we'll do. You might've saved my potential marriage. Will next week be all right? I mean I know it's Thanksgiving and all, but that might be a good time for her to learn."

"Well, Woody, let's see how this goes with Betty first. I might need to help out over there for a while."

"Now Stella can help if you need her. She's a good worker and she'd like to go on and move down here. We might hitch our wagons together if she can get this cooking down pat."

"Woody, you need to remember no one's perfect and sometimes you have to take the good with the bad," Beulah cautioned, and remembered Woody's one attempt to marry years ago ended with him leaving a woman at the altar.

"Aww, now Beulah, she is perfect, except for this one thing. But it's a big thing. It's one of them 'non-negotiables,' if you know what I mean. I'm not sayin' she's got to be Betty Crocker. If you can help her with fried chicken, gravy and biscuits, I could prolly live on that if I had too."

Poor Stella. Beulah shook her head, glad her ancient phone didn't allow Woody to see her face. Did this woman have any idea what she was stepping into?

"Let's see how this week goes and we'll set a time for her to come down."

"I'd be much obliged. Talk to you later."

Beulah refilled her coffee cup and sat back down at the kitchen table. Change was coming to May Hollow Road and Beulah was square in the middle of it. It was as if she was on a beach watching the swell of a rising wave, and no way to avoid the overwhelming soak of salt water.

Annie and Jake engaged; Tom and Evelyn talked of trips to the Caribbean together; Woody and Stella headed toward wedded bliss, pending her ability to cook, and now, Betty's heart attack.

Not to mention all the changes she faced. Now that she had gotten used to Annie being around, her granddaughter would move into her own home and make her own family. As happy as Beulah was for them, it left her feeling a little blue at losing Annie and now, possibly Evelyn.

Evelyn's visits had grown slightly less frequent with Tom Childress taking more of her time and social life. What if they married and she moved to town where Tom had a beautiful antebellum home within walking distance of his office?

That left her with Betty and Joe. Who knew what this health crisis meant for the rest of their lives. Beulah had even heard of personality adjustments after heart surgeries. Of course, a little personality alteration might be good, since Betty had such a bad habit of gossiping and had sure been downright nasty lately.

Beulah drained the last of her coffee and put the mug in the sink. The truth was, she detested change because it was unknown and it made her feel out of control. Routine was what she needed and liked. Predictable days with the comforts of daily chores, solid relationships, and the assurance of a sun that would set and rise again were things she enjoyed.

Change might be coming, but God would see her through. There was the sweet anticipation of meeting Benito and his family soon, right here in Kentucky. In only a few months, Annie would marry and their Italian relatives would come for the wedding, seeing all the places Ephraim loved. The very thought made her heart leap with excitement.

She also had her love of cooking and the pleasure of enjoying good food. Desserts in particular, although she could hardly admit out loud how much she enjoyed her sweets.

Yes, at least she had these things.

Chapter Nine

FROM THE KITCHEN, Annie watched Jake make a teepee with pine cones and then place the logs around. It was a picturesque domestic scene, portending of things to come. Shelves filled with Jake's books framed both sides of the fireplace, and in front sat a brown leather couch and distressed-wood coffee table Jake had built for his house in Cincinnati. A flat-screen television hung above the mantle, but they rarely turned it on when together. It was a cozy space, a room she planned to replicate in the stone house with the great fireplace in the living area.

She stirred herbs into a mixture of balsamic vinegar and olive oil, then drizzled it over arugula, romaine, and butter lettuce. Black bean soup with chunks of ham steamed in a pot on the back burner.

It had become their evening routine to eat in front of the fireplace instead of at the small kitchen table.

"It's ready," she said, carrying cups of soup and salad on a tray to the coffee table.

Without saying it, they had both decided to wait for the serious discussion until after dinner, so they made small talk while they ate and enjoyed the crackling fire. Finally, dishes cleared, they settled on the couch.

"All right, you said you had some ideas about the wedding. Tell me what you're thinking," Annie said.

Jake ran his fingers through his hair. "Here's the thing; I'm ready to make this official. I want to come home to you every evening and wake up beside you every morning. I want to see you in nothing but one of my shirts." He grinned at her mischievously. "The sooner, the better, in my opinion. If we went down to the courthouse tomorrow, I'd be happy. But I know that's not what you want, so maybe there's a compromise. Really, I'm good with whatever you want, ceremony-wise. Unless you want to put off the wedding, in which case we have a problem."

"Don't tease about that, not after what we've been through," she said, and shoved him gently.

"Seriously, if you're going to pull this runaway bride thing, let me know now, so I can put on my running shoes. I am faster than you, remember," he said.

"How did I get you? I can't imagine anyone else in the world who understands my craziness, my dysfunctional family, my—"

"Your beauty, your strength, your determination," he interrupted. "Now, tell me what you want and let's see how we can make most of it work."

"Well, I *could* tell you what I want—" her voice trailed.

"I hope you do," he said, reaching for her hand. "But for now, what kind of wedding do you want?"

She sighed. "Grandma wants Benito and his family here in the spring when everything is pretty and they can spend time outside, seeing the places where Ephraim spent his time. The Gianellis will be here for the wedding, so I assumed we'd do both at once."

He nodded, encouraging her to go on.

"I want a honeymoon—"

"So do I," Jake interrupted, pulling her closer to him again.

She laughed. "So that leaves between Christmas and early March before you get busy with the farm. I haven't talked to Colleen yet, but it's so soon after I started. I may not get the time off. Besides that, there's your job at the bank. Aren't you tied up until you end your contract at the end of February?"

"I can take time off and extend the contract, so that's not a big deal. What else?"

"There's Dad. I want him to be there, but his work schedule

is so erratic. It's impossible when he's on a job." Her father contracted out to oil companies, traveling to job sites for months at a time. When he wasn't working, her father chose to live in Spain for a reason she had never really understood. Annie believed long periods of idleness had contributed to his drinking habit and his penchant for younger women. No matter his faults, he was still her father, and she desperately wanted him to be there on her special day.

"Maybe we can get married when he comes for the visit?"

"Next week? That doesn't leave time for Benito and Angelina to get here from Italy. I also want to say our vows in front of family and friends as witnesses. I want others to be a part of our commitment to one another. Small and intimate is fine. But I don't want to hear our vows echo off the high ceiling of the county courthouse with people we don't even know signing the marriage license. Afterwards, I want to celebrate with our family and close friends. We made it back to each other after all these years apart. Don't you think it's worth a party?"

"You're right, I know that. But I can't help being impatient. You mentioned Italy for the honeymoon, but does that still stand if it's winter?"

"It'll be cold then, but it's still Italy."

Jake nodded, his blue eyes nearly glowing in the light of the fire as he stared, seeing something beyond burning embers. In a few minutes, he turned back to her.

"Who should we invite?"

It was Annie's turn to look at the fire for an answer. She had always envisioned a large celebration with extended family and a host of friends. As she imagined the actual solemn ceremony, the list narrowed fairly easily.

"Grandma, Evelyn, Dad, Lindy, Janice, Benito and Angelina for sure. Your sister, and your grandmother, too. That's the heart of it. Beyond that, Scott and Mary Beth, the Gibsons, Woody and Stella, and some of our friends from New York and Cincinnati."

"How about this; what if we get married in Italy, later this month or early January? Take the core group with us, that way Beulah gets to meet Benito, then you and I can honeymoon there after the wedding. Your Dad doesn't have to leave Europe since Italy is a short flight from Spain, making it easier on his schedule. Then we plan a big celebration in the spring, here, so Benito and his family can come and see Kentucky and we get to celebrate with all our extended friends and family who didn't attend the wedding."

"The expense, Jake," she said. "How could we afford that?"

"We have a huge advantage with Benito knowing the area. He could suggest lodging and where we could have a dinner after the wedding. Mom can pay for her own flight over, and so can Tom and Lindy. Janice flies for free with her job. That leaves us to help Beulah."

"It will depend on being able to take the time away from my job and Dad's availability," she said. "Wait! We can't get married in a Catholic church. We're not Catholic."

"We'll find another place and see if Scott and Mary Beth can go so Scott can officiate. If not, we can surely find somebody to perform it over there. It might not work, but it's an idea. By the way, did you find out who sent the flowers?"

"The florist won't say a word. I called Dad, but didn't get him. It has to be him. I can't imagine anyone else."

***

Annie sat under the buzzing white lights in her office and stared at the Richwood activities calendar. She had fallen under the spell of Jake's solution for the wedding plans in the romantic firelight last night, but now with the harsh reality of daylight, everything coming together seemed like a pipe dream.

Two weeks was needed for a trip like that, with preparations before the wedding, the actual festivities, and the honeymoon after. It might be squeezed into ten days if needed, but that was a lot to ask.

Annie had a meeting scheduled with Colleen the next morning to go over the December calendar. If she liked it and was pleased with her work, then that might be the time to make the request. All she could do was say no, and if she did, they were back to square one.

Annie's gaze fell on the bouquet of yellow roses on her desk. There had been no word from her father, so she dialed the number again.

"Eddie Taylor," he said, in a brusque voice.

"Dad?"

"Yeah, Annie, good to hear from you." He sounded distracted.

"I received some beautiful yellow roses." She waited and hoped.

"What's that?" he said.

"A bouquet of flowers. Did you send them?"

"Not me. Listen, I'm not going to make Thanksgiving. Been invited to a Cowboys game that day, box seats and all that. Too good to pass up. I'll call you when we're headed that way."

"Dad—" she said to an empty phone line.

She slumped over her desk and rested her head on folded arms.

***

"Vesta wants you." A woman in bright yellow scrubs poked her head in the door at the end of the day.

Annie gathered up her satchel and turned off the computer and overhead light.

"You know you don't have to send those nurses running for me. I always stop by your room before I go home."

Vesta met her gaze with a pretended stern look. "They're nursing assistants, not registered nurses. You've been here long enough now to know the difference."

Annie smiled at her, sat, and dropped her satchel to the floor beside the chair.

"I meet with Colleen tomorrow morning to go over the calendar and then it'll be posted unless she has some changes. It all came together with a couple of substitutions, but we were able to keep the same topics for the lectures."

"Excellent," Vesta said, closing the large print Bible that lay in her lap and placing it carefully on her bedside table. "How's Betty Gibson?"

"Making improvements, but still in ICU. She should come home by the weekend if all goes well," Annie said. "Can I ask your advice on something?"

"Of course," Vesta said. "I'm always happy to offer an opinion."

"Jake and I are talking about getting married sooner rather than later. Maybe even by the end of this month or early January. I'm still so new and I didn't discuss any time off with Colleen when I took the job. Without pay, of course, but do you think there's any way she'll say yes to a week or so for a wedding and honeymoon?"

Vesta smiled, her eyes lighting up. "Where are you going?"

"We're thinking about Italy for both. I have family there and my father's in Spain, so it makes it easy for him to get there. We could stay for the honeymoon afterward," she said.

"Surely you're thinking about more than a week. Why, you won't have but a few days after you arrive, get settled, and have the ceremony before you have to turn around and fly back."

"I know," Annie said. "But it's so much to ask this early."

"Colleen is fair, but she can be tough," Vesta said. "Instead of bringing her a problem, bring her a solution."

"Like?"

"Who can step in for you and lead the activities while you are gone? Who will make sure the outside folks show up for lectures or performances? Make it easy for her to say yes."

"You're brilliant, Vesta. I love you," Annie kissed the elderly woman on the cheek.

"Now don't go on with all that nonsense," Vesta said, but her smile betrayed her stern tone of voice. "Let me know what happens after the meeting."

"You'll be the first to know," Annie said from the doorway. She found herself smiling all the way down the hallway and when she turned a corner, she nearly bumped into Lonnie Caldwell.

"I'm so sorry," she said, as he grabbed her arms and steadied her.

"If I said you had a beautiful body, would you hold it against me?" Lonnie grinned.

"Cute, Lonnie, but not original. The Bellamy Brothers said it first." Annie moved around him.

"Hee, hee," he chuckled. His eyes were on her when she glanced back.

Good grief. She was used to a bit of ogling as a flight attendant, but she hadn't anticipated it in an assisted living facility.

Chapter Ten

LINDY CHILDRESS SAT across from Annie in the living room of the antebellum home where she lived with her father. Annie was curled in a corner of the couch while Lindy stretched out on a chaise lounge, each with a glass of chardonnay and a plate of cheese and crackers on the coffee table.

"Oh Annie, I'm so sorry," Lindy said after Annie relayed the conversation with her father. "What does Jake think?"
"He's still hopeful he'll come. I think he's more concerned about who sent the flowers."

"Who would that be?" Lindy reached for a piece of cheese.

"I have no idea. I've been so distracted with everything else, I haven't thought about it. Now I have to tell Grandma Dad's not coming. Every time I bring him up to Grandma, she gets this look, like she's smelling a rotten egg. I don't know why I even told her he might be coming for Thanksgiving. I should have waited until I knew for sure. Now she'll get this other look, the one that looks like she knows everything—which she does, by the way. She knows he never does what he says. I should know that, too, so why do I fall into the same old trap?"

"Because he's your dad and you want him to act like one," Lindy said.

"Here's my prediction; he'll go to the Cowboys game where someone will invite him to Las Vegas for the rest of the weekend. He'll gamble away whatever money he's made betting on the Cowboys game. People like him—he's lots of fun—so over a few drinks, someone will invite him to their villa in Mexico, where he might actually remember to call me and say he's run out of time and needs to head back to Spain from Mexico. He's so sorry and all that, etcetera, etcetera." Annie could feel the heat in her face as she worked herself up.

"Eat some cheese," Lindy said.

"What?" Annie said.

"Eat cheese—it has a calming effect," Lindy pushed the plate toward her.

"Are you serious?"

"Totally. It's the casein," Lindy said.

Annie took a deep breath and popped a slice of Gouda in her mouth.

"I get so mad at myself. I know better than to get my hopes up," she said.

"It's never wrong to hope. People can change."

"I think it's more than this; it's this whole wedding thing. I had all this time off and didn't want it and now when I need it, I may not get it."

"Surely Colleen has a heart; this is your wedding, for goodness sakes."

"Vesta says I need to present her with a solution. Someone who could help fill in the gaps while I'm gone so it doesn't fall back on Colleen. Any ideas who?"

"I wish I could do it, but I hope to be in Italy with you. If you get two weeks, I could help out in the evenings or on the weekend when I get back home while you're on the honeymoon. When do you meet with her?"

"Tomorrow morning."

Annie watched as Lindy's wheels turned. She knew everyone in town, their kids, grandkids, cousins, and in-laws. If anybody could think of someone to help, it was her.

"Not a soul comes to mind," Lindy said, finally, and picked up a cracker.

"It's hopeless," Annie said, sipping her wine.

"If she agrees to two weeks, I am willing to do whatever I can after I get back from the wedding. We're actually slow during the holidays and Dad will probably be all for it since it's a form of community service. I still have to work some, but if I have the events ahead of time, I can schedule around them."

"Lindy, that's something I could offer if you're serious about it."

"Sure, offer that and maybe it will help," Lindy said.

"It's the week after Christmas, so I can't imagine Dad having to work then, although there'll probably be some other excuse. Then all we have to do is convince Grandma to take an overseas trip. She doesn't even have a passport yet. Are we crazy?"

"Certified."

"I need to come to terms with not having the wedding of my dreams."

"Welcome to my world. The wedding of my dreams got dashed when the groom married someone else."

Annie sighed. "I am being ridiculous. I have the man of my dreams. Forget the wedding. County courthouse, here we come."

***

Annie called Jake on the way home from Lindy's.

"Are you at home?"

"I wish. Still doing chores for Joe. One of his heifers got her foot caught in some barbed wire, so I'm doctoring her. She'll be okay."

"I'm stopping by to use your laptop, but I also wanted to tell you something."

"All right, I'm all ears."

"I think you're right, we should go ahead and get married in the courthouse. We can have a party later in the spring. That really does make the most sense."

"Are you serious?"

"Totally. This is all so silly. What really matters is us being together, and the sooner the better. There's always time for a party later."

"Annie, you don't know how much I've wanted that, but I can't let you do it now."

"What do you mean?" She got out of the car and slipped into the dark cottage.

"I know what you really want. Granted, it's hard to pull all this together and there's a lot of moving parts. But I don't want you to look back and regret not having the wedding you wanted. That'd be selfish of me. So, let's keep to the plan."

"I love you, Jake Wilder."

"I'm counting on that," he said.

Inside Jake's cottage, she turned on a lamp and opened the laptop.

First, she emailed her father. Writing was sometimes easier for her to communicate with him due to his penchant for taking over a conversation. She could at least make her request and he could do with it what he willed.

Next, she emailed Vincenzo so he could translate her request to Benito.

Springing an overseas trip on Beulah, amidst everything going on with Betty, was risky. If Benito was in agreement and the way was clear on their end, it might pave the way for Beulah, and make the prospect irresistible.

Annie asked if the week after Christmas was okay for them to come and have a small wedding. Then she inquired about a place to have the ceremony and possible lodging accommodations nearby so the family could be in the same village. Annie remembered the hotel, La Chiusa, where she and Janice had enjoyed staying when they searched for Benito only weeks before. It was charming and comfortable, so she suggested that to the Gianellis. After reading and re-reading what she had typed, she hit send.

***

Annie studied Beulah's *Farmer's Almanac* while she brushed her teeth, holding it open to the pages on the phases of the moon. According to the Almanac, when the moon was full, everything on Earth pulled forward, upward, just as the gravitational force pulled the tides. When the moon was a crescent or new, everything went down, or backward. Jake weaned the cows during this time. It was still hard to imagine how that affected a conversation, but who knew? Hopefully, Virginia Taylor was ready to talk.

A few hours later, Annie passed through the activities room and checked on morning exercise class. Lonnie Caldwell winked at her, but seemed more interested in the young teacher encouraging them to move their arms and legs.

Virginia wasn't in exercise class, so Annie went to her room and knocked on the door.

"Come in," Virginia said.

"Are we close enough to the new moon?" she asked.

"Jes' right," she said, and patted the bed. Annie sat, glad there was an hour before the next activity.

Virginia turned in her chair and faced Annie full on. Deep brown eyes seemed to take her measure before the older woman smiled.

"I'm not crazy, if that's what ye might be thinkin'. Written all over your face, jes like your mama. Never could hide a thing, that little one."

"You knew my mother?"

"When your daddy courted her, he brung her around some. She was awful pretty. Course, he was right handsome hisself."

"How are we related?"

"I'll start from the beginning, like a good story should. My people were from Evarts, in the mountains. There was coal and scrappin' a livin' off the hills. We made our living selling ginseng roots, 'sang' as we called it. From a young age, it came clear I had the gift of spotting sang, so I became a help to my family. I only got schoolin' when sang wasn't in season. My given name is Virginia, but soon I was called Gin because of my work. When I was fourteen, my mommy died and poppy got mean on the likker. Those years were hard on me. We wasn't much on markin' birthdays, reckon I was about eighteen, tho I can't be for certain—Duke Taylor came through town with some other men on state business about the local mine. I spotted him and he put a bead on me at the company store. Duke called me his 'diamond in the rough.' I didn't know then he's married, but by the time I did know, we's in love and he was my ticket out of the hills. He divorced his wife and we was married. I's tired of workin' like a dog for my daddy."

Annie nodded, mesmerized by the mountain-melody of her voice.

"I moved up here and everythin' was new. Indoor plumbin' with hot n' cold water. As much food as we wanted 'cause Duke had a good job with the mining agency. Pretty clothes fer me and a nicer house after a while. Duke had a way with people. Politiken he called it. He'd shake hands, friendly as can be and people liked 'im. He weren't that a-way at home. It was like there's two of him. Then he took a run for the statehouse and won. All that power went to his head." Virginia tapped her head to make the point. "He took money from people and got things done fer 'em. Bribes, they said, when he got caught."

"He went to prison," Annie said. "I heard about that. He was my father's uncle."

"That's right. He went to prison and fell for a pen pal. He divorced me. It shouldn't 'uv been a surprise since we started up that-a-way. It's no good end when you start bad."

Annie nodded, understanding and compassion flooding her heart for this woman.

"What did you do after that?"

Virginia grinned. "Only thing I knew to do. Hunt 'sang."

"Around here?"

"There's some to be had, but I made trips deeper in the mountains. I always left the seeds though. That-a-way it'd grow back. It's no good taking the root if you don't leave the seeds. Then there'll be none left fer the future."

"You made your living that way?"

"It's how I'm a-payin' for this place," Virginia smiled.

"You are an entrepreneur, Virginia."

"Ye didn't know your daddy too good, did ye?"

"Well, no, not much at all as a child. I've spent more time around him as an adult, but he lives in Spain and has for a while, so it's not easy to get to know him."

Virginia nodded. "I knew him as a little feller. He was always a runnin' from somethin'. His daddy was hard on him. Bad on the likker like my daddy. I always felt for the little feller. His daddy threw his mommy up against a wall one time. I seed it just after. Her head was bleedin' something fierce. She died two weeks later of a stroke. We all knowed it was her husband what killed her.

Nobody said nothin', though."

Annie felt a sharp pain in her heart at the image of her grandfather throwing her grandmother up against a wall, an injury that led to her death. It was a few seconds before she could speak. "Did my father see that happen?"

"He seed it. I reckon he was six or seven at the time. He didn't have much of a daddy after that. Kindly raised himself. I didn't have no children of my own and tried lovin' on 'im, hopin' mebbe he'd take to me. He seemed afraid of gettin' close to anybody."

Annie felt her throat close up and she could hardly speak.

"I don't mean to hurt ye," Virginia said, her voice tender. "It's why the moon had to be new. Emotions run high on a full moon."

***

Colleen Whitley sat erect at her computer and looked at Annie over her glasses. "Are you early or am I late?"

"Neither, I hope," Annie said, and noticed the prickly tone in Colleen's voice.

"All right, let me close out of this and we'll see what you've got."

Annie laid out the calendar on the director's desk.

"Would you like me to walk through each activity?" Colleen didn't answer. She was already scanning the calendar.

"We had him speak recently," the director said, and pointed to a professor Annie had confirmed. "Can you cancel him for someone else? It's better to have variety."

"Okay, sure. Vesta thought he was really popular with the residents, but I can find someone else."

"You'll need a backup plan for this outing. If the weather's bad we can't risk it."

"All right," Annie said, and scribbled a note on her legal pad. "I'll come up with an in-house activity."

"Can you be a little more creative with the music? Churches are willing, but if we had something a little more professional, like the college music students, that lends a more sophisticated air."

"No churches at all?"

"These two have good choirs. Let's wiggle out of this one," Colleen said, and scratched out the church name.

Annie felt her heart sink. She had been on the phone with that particular choir director for thirty minutes as she expressed how much their church loved performing at Richwood.

"They want so much to help. Can I use them in another way?"

"Crafts or game night," she pushed the calendar away. "All right, it'll do."

"Any thoughts about January?" Annie asked.

"You can start working on it, but the new director will have the final say. I'm leaving at the end of the year."

"You're leaving Richwood?"

Colleen looked down at her hands. It was as if a hard mask fell away and she struggled to gain control over the quiver in her lower lip. "Actually, it was my request. My husband was diagnosed with ALS recently. I need to be in Louisville, close to family. I'll be taking a position with another home in our corporate family."

"Lou Gehrig's disease," Annie said. "That's awful."

"He won't get better. It's a matter of how fast it will progress. They can slow things down a little, but there's no cure."

"I'm really sorry," Annie said.

"You have no idea how sorry I am. He's only fifty-four. We had so many plans," she said, a bitter tone in her voice.

"Is there anything I can do to help in the transition? Or help you in any other way?" Annie could think of nothing else to say with such heavy news.

"The new director will start the job here on January 2. So, there won't be any time that Richwood will be without a director."

"That will provide continuity for the residents," Annie said, and realized her chances of taking time off were down to zero.

"This affects you, too," Colleen said. "The new director is part of the family who owns the company. His wife is also an activities director. They work together as a team."

"I'm losing my job?"

"I'm afraid so. They wanted me to offer you a position in Indiana, but I told them you are rooted to the area."

Annie nodded. "Yes, I want to stay here, but thank you."

"I'm sorry, Annie. With some time and experience you would have made a good activities director. Please consider volunteering. I know the residents, especially Vesta, have really taken to you."

"As long as Vesta's here, you can count on my involvement at some level," Annie said. "This is nothing compared to an ill husband. I'm the one who is sorry your family is going through this."

"Thank you. I am still a bit in shock myself. We found out last week."

"That is a shock. I can't imagine. So, my last day is December 31?"

"That's right. Of course, if you need time off to look for another job, that's understandable."

"Actually, I do have a request. I'd like to get married the week after Christmas. I am happy to stay through Christmas with no time off."

"Of course. December 24, it is. That's the least I can do."

"Thank you," she said.

"One more thing. I haven't told Vesta about the upcoming changes yet. I'm going to wait until after Thanksgiving. Please keep that between us for now. My plan is to bring down the new director and his wife in early December so we can make the announcement together. I think having the residents meet them will help with the uncertainty."

"I understand," Annie said, and wondered how she would keep something so significant from Vesta, who saw right through her every expression.

Chapter Eleven

PARSING OUT THE turkeys among the Baptists and Presbyterians was an unexpected trial. The Presbyterians wanted to deep fry their turkeys, something Beulah had never heard of before. She had lain awake the night before the potluck, imagining the Baptist turkeys lined up all nice and golden brown with butter, and the Presbyterian turkeys charred to a black crisp. However, she was not prepared to fight the entire presbytery over turkey preparation. If their birds flopped, it was their fault.

As it turned out, all her fears were for naught. The deep-fried turkeys were gnawed to the bone, while the Baptist turkeys provided the leftovers the Somerville Baptist Youth Group delivered to the shut-ins that evening.

Beulah added pecan pies, like she had always wanted to, and they were eaten in equal measure to the pumpkin pies. She'd found orange tablecloths to cover the fold-out tables, but the faded little cornucopias and pilgrims still fanned out in the middle of the tables. One step at a time. All in all, the community potluck went off without a hitch, thanks to the ecumenical spirit of all the volunteers.

Ernestina Chadwell would be proud, she thought. Through

the whole painful episode of the last week or so, she had learned a lot about letting go. There was truth in Betty's words after all; she did have a tendency to be a little bit controlling when it came to the kitchen. Maybe even more than a little bit.

The day had worn her out, standing on the concrete floor of the family life center kitchen for hours. While she had hoped to visit Betty on Monday after the potluck, it was Tuesday before she actually made the trip, thanks to Jake, who had a meeting in Lexington and dropped her off right at the door of the hospital.

Beulah pushed the buzzer on the wall outside the ICU unit. The door clicked open and she made her way to room 402. Joe faced the door from a chair in the corner and his expression brightened when she entered, setting Beulah at ease. He stood up and moved toward the edge of the bed, reaching out to pat an exposed arm.

"Guess who's come to see you," he said to his wife of over forty years.

Betty's curly blonde hair was unwashed and flattened against the crisp, white hospital sheet. Clear oxygen tubes looped from her nose. The room's scent was a mixture of body musk and antiseptic chemicals.

"Hello, Betty," Beulah said, and moved close to the bed.

Betty turned her head slightly and her eyes lit up when they rested on Beulah.

"I sure am glad to see you looking better," she said, and tried to keep her voice from shaking.

"Beulah," Betty said in a soft voice.

"Betty, I'm awful sorry for everything. I don't ever want to let anything get in front of our friendship again," she said.

Betty's eyes narrowed, as if she suddenly got sleepy, and her lips murmured soundless words.

"What's that?" Beulah asked and leaned over the bed. Joe stood up and leaned in with her.

Betty moved her lips again, but no words came out.

"She said she's sorry, too," Joe said. Betty's eyes popped open and she cut them sideways at Joe. The effort was wasted, since he turned his back on her and sat down in the seafoam green vinyl chair. When he looked back at Beulah, out of Betty's line of sight from the hospital bed, he winked.

Betty Gibson had never once managed to utter the words "I'm sorry," so why in the world did Beulah think she would now?

"Well, I accept your apology, Betty. Now let's move on from this."

"They pried my chest open like a tin can," Betty said, suddenly finding her voice. "But I'm all fixed up, they say."

"You look good," Beulah said. The lie slipped right out of her mouth as if she were a slick-tongued lawyer. Who looked good laid up in a hospital bed?

"Joe's took good care of me," Betty smiled faintly, her straight white teeth exposed for a moment. "Thank you for seeing to him that morning. It was a terrible fright."

Beulah nodded. "You would've done the same for me."

Betty nodded. "I've tried to be a good neighbor."

"You get some rest now. Is there anything you need done at the house?"

"The girls are taking care of things. Pray for me, Beulah. You know they've put me on the cardiac diet and right here at Thanksgiving. I'll be eatin' turkey off a hospital plate; better than bein' dead, I reckon. I don't know how I'll feed Joe when I get home, what with me having to eat healthy and him eatin' whatever he wants." Betty's bottom lip trembled.

"Now, now," Beulah said and patted Betty's shoulder. "Let's cross that bridge when we get there. You concentrate on getting well so you can get out of here."

Betty nodded, obedient as a child.

"I'll see you real soon, all right?" Beulah said, and turned to go, catching Joe's eye.

"I'll walk out with Beulah and get some coffee," Joe said, following her out of the room. They moved down the hall in silence. Joe pulled out a small chew of tobacco and stuck the wad in his jaw, right as they passed a sign reading *Tobacco Free Campus.*

"Doc says she might go home this weekend if all goes well," Joe said.

"Land sakes, that is fast. Do you have help lined up?"

Joe worked the tobacco in his jaw and took his time answering. "Peggy's working on it. Seems they've got weekends and nights covered, what with Missy able to stay with us at nights for a while, but the day time is when we really need help with me working. She was going to call you to see if you have any suggestions."

"Evelyn and I will be glad to help as much as possible," Beulah said. "We'll ask around about someone to help during the weekdays."

Joe stopped and looked at Beulah, his eyes soft with gratitude. He reached for her hand and held it in his rough, weathered hands.

"Thanks for coming, Beulah," he said.

***

Jake dropped Beulah off at the back door and she took extra care as she stepped across the jagged limestones, still cautious after her knee operation last summer.

A little care in watching her step was nothing compared to what Betty Gibson now faced. *A lifestyle change in diet and exercise*, she imagined. Betty loved sweets about as much as Beulah and had been told by her doctor she needed to lose weight several months back. Betty had laughed at the advice, saying her body had settled on a number and there was no budging it.

Betty's Kentucky nut pies were famous in town and had won the blue ribbon at the county fair for over twenty years in a row. Except that one year when one of Betty's jealous fellow homemakers injected salt water into Betty's pie right before the judging, but that was a special circumstance.

It was hard to imagine making a pie without eating a slice.

Truth was, Beulah's doctor had recommended she lose a few pounds a year ago, too. She had tried for a time giving up sweet tea, but she found herself as grouchy as a bear and went right back to it after a miserable week. Fad diets failed the test of time and she didn't want to go down in size and then right back up again, buying a new wardrobe and then bursting out of it again. No, it had to be a discipline a body could keep from now on, a depressing thought.

With all that had happened to Betty in the last few days, it did make Beulah think about her own lifestyle. She never smoked and never did drink until that week recently when

Janice's Italian mother-in-law came to stay and brought all manner of wine into the house. She had done a little partaking to be sociable, but that was it. There had been her daily morning walks, but when her knee had gone bad, that exercise had flown out the window. Her appetite had not diminished, nor had her love for sweets. Now that she thought about it, it was probably time for a medical check-up like Annie suggested.

Beulah grabbed the metal pot scrubber and attacked a pan she'd left soaking in the sink while she turned over the possibility of new eating habits. It was two days from Thanksgiving, the on-ramp for a month-long careen down the road of gluttony.

At the end of the sugar euphoria there was January, the blessed month of second chances. Yes, that was the best time to begin such deprivations. The Lord surely wanted his flock to celebrate his birth, and how in the world did a celebration happen without food? Either way, it wouldn't hurt to run in for a check-up after all this rigmarole.

Although Beulah hadn't noticed the sound of crunching gravel, a banging commenced on the back door. Drying her hands, she went to open the door right when Woody poked his head inside.

"Can I come in?"

"Of course, come on."

Woody had a habit of showing up at meal times, but this was too early for supper.

"Would you like some tea?"

Woody folded his long, lanky frame into a chair. He wore faded overalls over a flannel shirt and his wiry red hair was ruffled from the November wind.

"Beulah, I know you said to wait until next week and all, but me and Stella, we've got a problem," he said.

She waited, hoping to goodness they weren't in the family way.

"Stella's rent is paid through the end of this month, which brings us to this weekend. She's trying hard to get out of debt and do everything Jake's advised her to do. We got to talking, and since she's on a month-to-month, there's no harm in her going ahead and getting out of her place here in a few days, especially since it's Thanksgiving and she was coming on down here for the weekend anyway. See, we can leave her stuff there and get it next week, then she don't have to pay rent in December. So, we's wondering if you wouldn't care to let her move in this weekend? Now, she can help do anything you need her to do. She wants to earn her keep as long as she's here, and if you can teach her a few things about cooking, we'll go on and get hitched sometime after the first of the year, so it won't be forever."

Beulah sat still, hardly knowing how to respond. She knew Woody Patterson was raised up rough. Still, it was awful presumptuous of him to ask such a thing from her. It wasn't that she minded giving cooking lessons for a week or so. But this was beyond hospitality. He was asking her to let Stella move in with her for an undetermined period of time, a dangerous gamble with Woody's track record on following through with marriage.

Then she thought of the conversation she had with Joe Gibson about needing help taking care of Betty during the weekdays. While she and Evelyn could certainly be on the schedule the next few weeks, there was no way the both of them could handle every day, all day. Stella could do it, and that left her and Evelyn to fill in and prepare meals for Joe. In fact, the meal preparations could serve as Stella's cooking lessons.

"Well, I know it's an awful lot to ask," Woody said. "If you need to say no, I'll understand. I could move her into my house, but I was hoping to do the right thing here and not get the cart before the horse for once." His blue eyes opened wide under raised, wiry eyebrows.

Beulah nodded. "I'm thinking it through Woody, but it might work. Joe'll need help with Betty, there's no doubt about that. I reckon I could provide her a room and board if she's willing to do light housekeeping, fetching things for Betty, seeing to her comfort, and making sure she gets her medicines."

"Oh yeah, she's good at that. She did organizing and cleaning at her library job. When can she start?"

Beulah wasn't sure it was a great idea to negotiate all this with Woody instead of Stella, but if she was as eager as he was, it might be the answer to a prayer not yet prayed. As far as living with her, there still needed to be boundaries and house rules, and a deadline of when Stella would move out.

"All right. I'll agree to have Stella live here awhile, but let's you and me agree that she'll need to move out by the middle of January. Either you all can get married by then or she can find a place to live and a job. In exchange for her working the weekdays at the Gibson's, she can stay here until then and I'll provide her room and board. I don't know how long Betty will need help, but I think for a few weeks, anyway. We'll see she gets time off to go to job interviews if she gets something lined up. Of course, if she gets a job and moves out before then, there's no obligation to stay with Betty, but we'll be counting on her these first two weeks for sure."

Woody shot up out of his chair and hugged Beulah, nearly knocking the breath out of her.

"Mercy sakes," Beulah said. "Just keep your end of the bargain." Woody saluted and made his exit.

Beulah sighed and picked up the phone to call Joe Gibson. It was done now and she wouldn't go back on her word. She hoped to goodness it was the right thing to do.

Chapter Twelve

"I'M SORRY," JAKE said and pulled her close. Annie had been holding back her emotions since the meeting with Colleen, but in the safety of his arms, she let everything go, including telling him about the visit with Virginia.

"It explained so much with my dad. I am grateful she shared what she did, but that on top of losing my job, another job. Two in a less than a year." She pulled away and looked at him. "I thought I had a purpose after all these months of floundering around." She wiped her eyes and moved next to the blazing fire. "I'm sorry for Vesta, too. I felt like we were a team and it gave her new energy, at least that's what she said, and now that's all being torn apart."

"You can still volunteer and spend as much time with Vesta as you want," he said.

"I know, and I will, but it's not the same. I need to earn a living, and I would like to do something meaningful. Those kinds of positions are limited in a small town. It's not like I have the whole of Manhattan to scour for employment. At this point, Lexington may be the best option." She sank back onto the couch. "Then there's two hours in the car every day going back and forth, and to top it off, I don't even have a car. I'm still borrowing your SUV."

"Look, the good news is we're clear for the wedding, and that's a month away. You have a job until then. Let's not try and figure it all out right now. After we get back from the honeymoon, the old stone house will be ready for painting. That will keep you busy until we figure out the next step. Until then, I can keep on consulting at the bank. I could do it a little less than I have lately, but keep on doing it for a year or so. Especially if I had your help."

Annie sat up. "Are you thinking I could help on the farm?"

Jake scratched his chin. "I don't know exactly, but you know I've been thinking about my dad's dairy barn and how to incorporate that into what we're doing rather than convert it into something else."

"You want me to milk cows?"

He laughed. "I was thinking goats, actually. Not that you would do the milking necessarily, but maybe do something with the milk that we could sell, cheese or something. We'll figure it out. You have a roof over your head, food to eat, and no debt. That's more than most people in the world have."

***

Vesta had gone home with her nephew for Thanksgiving on Wednesday, which, thankfully, freed Annie from her questioning gaze. One penetrating look from Vesta's almond eyes would destroy her resolve.

It was a quiet day around Richwood with many of the residents gone for the holiday. Those remaining would be fed a full course, Thanksgiving meal on Thursday, celebrate the Hanging of the Greens on Friday, and enjoy choral music from two local churches on Saturday. Annie was on-call in case something went amiss, but she was free to be off since the volunteers had run the programs for many years in a row.

Annie had yet to tell her grandmother about losing her job. Beulah was consumed with preparations for the Thanksgiving meal and getting the guest room ready for Stella. On Wednesday evening, she found her grandmother spooning sugared pecan topping on sweet potato casserole, and the time seemed right.

"Grandma, you're not going to believe this. Or maybe you are. I lost my job at Richwood."

"Good heavens, what happened?" Beulah turned to look at her, wide-eyed.

"It's nothing to do with me personally. The director is leaving and the new director works as a team with his wife. She'll be the new activities director. They're actually a part of the family who owns the facilities. I didn't do anything wrong, if that's what you're thinking. Simply unfortunate circumstances."

"I didn't think you did anything wrong, for goodness sakes," Beulah said. "It surprised me, that's all."

"It surprised me, too. It's supposed to be kept quiet until next week when they can make the announcement to the residents," Annie said. With Betty Gibson out of commission, the gossip danger was low, but still, she wanted to keep her word to Colleen.

"I won't say a word." Beulah sighed. "I'm sorry for you, I know you liked it."

"I know. I'm sorry, too."

"Maybe there's something else better. You never know what's around the corner."

"Jake might put me to work on the farm, who knows. When does Stella get here?"

"Tonight. I gave Woody a key in case it's after we've gone to bed."

"I moved my stuff to the bathroom down here so it opened up a little space."

"I should have asked you about all this. It came up so suddenly." Beulah dropped the spoon in the sink before she turned to face her granddaughter. "What time is your father coming tomorrow?"

"He's not. I don't know when he's coming or even if. I'm sure that's no surprise to you."

"I'm sorry he won't be here."

"Are you really?" she pushed, waiting for *the look*.

"Sure I am, for your sake. I'll admit, I've had a few surprises today, but that's not one of them."

"Yeah, I know. I think I'll go out for a run."

"At this hour? It'll be dark in thirty minutes."

"I'll be back by then. I'm only running to the old house."

"Be careful on that road. Someone may not see you at dusk."

***

Maybe Jake was right, she thought as her breathing settled into a rhythm. Not working opened up the time for them to travel to Italy for a wedding and a honeymoon without the pressure of what wasn't getting done at work while she was gone. It allowed them to settle into life together in Jake's cottage while she painted the inside of the old stone house and helped move along all the finishing touches. Then there would be packing up and moving. Jake still had some things stored in one of the outbuildings, and she had things stored in the attic of her grandmother's house. Now she'd have the luxury of nesting time.

The idea of doing something with the farm sounded appealing. She liked the thought of working with Jake, of both of them pulling toward some greater goal together.

"What's your dream job?" Janice had asked her in one of their mindless chats as they waited in the airport on their recent trip to Italy to find Beulah's nephew.

"Being a flight attendant was my dream job," Annie had answered, and it was true at the time. The forced grounding changed her mind, though, and when the job was offered to her later in the summer, she turned it down. Now there was Jake, her grandmother, and their friends in Somerville. She was rooted here in this place where generations of family members had lived. Now there was an opportunity to make something new, to truly create what she desired.

Annie turned down Gibson's Creek toward the old stone house, away from the danger of the country road now that dusk gathered. She had gone longer on May Hollow than she intended, lost in her thoughts and the good feeling of blood and oxygen pumping through her system.

She loved people and being around them, for all their quirks and flaws—the same thing she had loved about being a flight attendant. Every day was new with a whole new set of passengers, so there was a mystery to what the day might bring, both good and bad. How could that be incorporated into farming on May Hollow Road?

Annie's mind went to Italy as it so often did. The poplar Italian *agritourismos* provided an authentic farm stay with a breakfast, and sometimes dinner, from the farm's produce. The idea intrigued her—could that translate into some type of farm tourism here?

Annie stopped running on the bridge over Gibson's Creek and stretched her legs and her back. The old stone house was visible now with most of the leaves gone off the great sycamore trees that lined the creek. As much as she liked Jake's small cottage, she was looking forward to this place being her home, a place where she could still feel her mother's presence, even if that presence lived only in memory induced by the landscape and house.

If all went well, they could move in before spring, when she could plant a lavender garden outside the kitchen door as her mother had so long ago. There were other plants she could reproduce from her childhood, all the ones her mother loved, like frog belly, lamb's ear, and bleeding hearts. There used to be a snowball bush to the side of the house, the blooms she used to decorate the tops of her mud pies. The fence that separated the drive from the cow pasture needed mending and painting, another job for the spring.

A truck was parked to the side of the house and a light was on inside. In the dusky evening, she could make out the truck's lettering—*B&B Heating and Air*.

Annie pushed open the front door to the old stone house. The smell of fresh wood greeted her and she shut the door and stood for a few moments, taking in the smells of renovation. It was far better than the smell of charred wood that greeted a visitor a few weeks ago, after it had been damaged in the fire in late summer.

"Hello," she called out.

"Annie?" a man responded from the kitchen in a voice that had a familiar drawl.

Annie turned the corner and in a millisecond, her heart skipped a beat as her past rushed full into the present, a tidal wave of recognition. Brett Bradshaw stood before her with his shock of blond hair, strong features, and wide smile.

"I hoped it might be you," he said.

In the second it took for her to respond, she flashed to those years before. Dark blonde hair plastered to his forehead, dressed in pads and the blue and white Somerville High School uniform colors. It was the way he looked when he came off the football field. Now, he was dressed in coveralls instead of football gear, but he had the same blonde hair, the same smile with full lips, with the addition of lines around his eyes that hinted at humor and wisdom.

"Brett?" she finally said. "What are you doing here?"

He laughed and opened his arms for a hug. She hugged him and then stepped back.

"Wow, it's so good to see you."

"I had the advantage over you," he said. "My dad and I own a business together and we do work for Jerry Baker. When I found out it was your farm, I offered to take the job, hoping I'd see you."

"You did?" she said and laughed. "Gosh, I don't think I've seen you since—"

"We broke up," he said. "Yeah, I know. But I've kept up with you. New York and all, and I heard you came back this summer."

"Yeah, lost my job. I actually just lost another one, if you can believe that," Annie said.

"You'll find something else. You were always so smart and confident," he said, his brown eyes serious.

"Well, thanks. And how about you? Are you married? Kids?"

He shook his head. "Divorced. She left me for a guy at work. Three years ago."

"Oh, I'm so sorry," Annie said. "That must have been so painful."

"It was, but you learn a lot when you go through something like that. You're seeing Jake Wilder, I hear."

"Engaged, actually." She put out her left hand to show off her engagement ring.

"Wow, that's a beauty. He's a lucky guy."

"We're both fortunate," she said. "Look, I didn't mean to interrupt your work. I need to head back before it gets too dark."

"Wait a minute. I'm almost done. I'll run you home," he said.

"You don't have to do that," she said.

"It's on my way and I was getting ready to leave anyway."

"Well, okay, if it's no trouble," she said. It had gotten dark fast, as her grandmother had predicted.

Brett helped her climb into the tall truck, and when he slid into the driver's seat, the memory of so many dates in high school washed over her. Annie touched her running pants as if they might magically transform into her cheerleading outfit, and then she looked at Brett and saw in her mind the all-state high school football player, tousled hair still damp from the after-game shower. He caught her gaze and smiled.

"I'm glad to see you, Annie. I've wanted to tell you I'm sorry for how things ended with us."

"That was such a long time ago," Annie said. "We were teenagers. All is forgiven."

"You are as beautiful today as you were in high school," he said and smiled. "I can't wait to tell Dad I ran into you. You were always his favorite."

She blushed. "Tell him I said hello. How is your mom doing?"

Annie could see his face change in the dusky light. "She passed away right before I moved home. It's part of why I came back once the divorce went through. Dad needed me around, so now we're two bachelors living with each other and working together every day. It gets a little close at times, but we get along pretty good."

"I didn't know your mom died," Annie said. "I'm so sorry. She was always so nice to me."

"She was a real lady. She liked you, too. In fact, she gave me a hard time when I broke up with you for Jennifer."

"I know. She wrote me several times after that," Annie said. The truck turned into Beulah's drive and Annie saw Jake's farm truck parked next to the back door.

The truck stopped. "It was really good to see you, Annie. I'm glad you're doing so well."

Jake came out of the house and went to open her door.

"Thanks, Brett," Annie said. "Maybe I'll see you around."

Jake helped her down and looked past her to the driver. Annie saw a glint of hardness pass over Jake's face when he recognized Brett, but then it disappeared and he smiled at him and leaned across the seat with an extended hand.

"Jake Wilder, long time no see," Brett reached out and they shook hands.

"How you doing, Brett?"

"Mostly working," he said. "We're doing the job at the stone house. Thought I'd give Annie a ride since it's dark. I'll get on my way now. Later, man."

Jake nodded and watched Brett leave.

"That was a surprise," Annie said. "I had no idea he was the HVAC guy. He was there when I ran over to the stone house."

"You shouldn't have been out running after dark," Jake said. His hard tone stung her.

"Jake, I lived in Manhattan for ten years. This is Somerville. I know how to take care of myself."

"I know you do. I didn't mean it like that."

"Why am I feeling like I did something wrong here?"

Jake took her hand. "I'm sorry. You didn't do anything wrong," he said. "It's me. I don't trust that guy."

Chapter Thirteen

ON THANKSGIVING MORNING, the mild weather allowed Annie to enjoy another spell on the front porch swing. She inhaled the coffee scent before taking that first delicious sip. What was it about coffee that made the day seem so fresh and new and full of possibilities? It was like a rich cup of second chances. The nostalgic smell transported her back to those safe mornings in the old stone house when the local radio station blared country music on the transistor in the kitchen. Coffee bubbled in the percolator and her mother fried eggs at the stove.

"You need a full belly so you can have a clear mind," she had said every time Annie resisted eating breakfast. "Be grateful we have food to eat—so many people don't."

That was long after her father was gone and before her mother's illness. Those blessed ordinary days before life changed drastically. After losing her mother at twelve, Annie shuffled through the next two years in a state of numbing routine. She had moved in with her grandparents, made decent grades, and showed up for the Somerville Baptist Youth Group activities as required by her grandparents. While other girls recounted the woes of middle school, Annie could hardly remember those years.

By the time she turned sixteen, the numbness had worn off and a new thirst for life grew inside her. Jake had always been her best friend but she sensed his feelings toward her were changing. He gave her a necklace for her sixteenth birthday and asked her to the homecoming dance. When Brett Bradshaw asked her to the same dance, she dumped Jake for Brett, telling herself Jake's invitation was simply out of friendship. For two years, Brett was at the center of her world while Jake played baseball and pursued his own interests.

Brett broke it off with Annie when they went to college. Now it was flattering to think he had been keeping up with her. Then a thought struck her. *Could Brett have sent the yellow roses?* An even stranger thought came from the blue. *Did he want her back after all these years?*

"Isn't it cold out here?" Beulah opened the front door.

"A little chilly." Annie pushed up from the swing. "Do you need my help with anything?"

Beulah pulled her cardigan closer around her cotton work dress. "Not now, but we'll need help getting all the food carried over to Evelyn's later. Was Stella up when you came down?"

Annie followed her into the warmth of the house. "Her bedroom door was shut, but I didn't hear any sign of movement. I never heard her come in last night." Beulah sat at the kitchen table.

"It was around midnight," Annie said. "I was lying awake and heard the floor creak." Annie poured cereal into a bowl.

"Couldn't sleep?"

"It took a while. I ran into Brett Bradshaw last night, and I guess it made my mind go back to high school memories."

"Where'd you see him?"

"He's working at the stone house, doing the heating and air."

"I thought he went off to marry a girl in Ohio," she said.

"Divorced."

"Uh-huh. Well, I wouldn't give him too much thought."

"I'm not, but it's hard not to go back in your mind when you see somebody from your past. Don't you have any old boyfriends around? I mean, I know you and Grandpa started dating young, but wasn't there a sweetheart or someone from elementary school?"

Beulah held her coffee in both hands and stared out the

window. "There was a boy I liked when I was about thirteen. His name was Billy McAlistar. We passed notes and met at the theater downtown one Saturday afternoon, but it never amounted to much."

"What happened to him?"

"I have no earthly idea," Beulah said.

"Maybe we could track him down."

"Heavens no. I don't spend time going down memory lane with old boyfriends. There's not much good to come of that."

"That's not true," Annie said. "Jake's a good example."

"You have me there."

Annie smiled at her and wanted to tell her grandmother about their wedding plans, then hesitated. She needed everything to be lined up first so there was no way for her grandmother to wiggle out.

"Grandma, with all that's happened, I forgot to tell you about talking to Virginia Taylor. You might know her as Gin."

A flood of recognition brightened Beulah's face. "Of course. *Virginia*. All I've ever heard her called was Gin. She was married to Eddie's uncle when the sting operation happened and he got sent off to prison. Folks said she was an innocent mountain girl. I figured she had gone back to the mountains once they divorced."

"She was back and forth, but she made her life here. She's an interesting person; I think you might like her. There are some things about my dad that she told me." She could count on one hand the honest conversations Beulah had about Eddie Taylor. It was a subject they both avoided.

"What was that?" Beulah asked and leaned back in her chair.

Annie went on to tell her, word for word, what Virginia had said.

"Oh, my," Beulah said. "I knew his daddy was a drunk and his mama died when he was young, but I didn't know the rest of it."

"We're all responsible for our behavior, but it does explain some things, don't you think?"

"I reckon it does."

"All right, well, I'm going over to Jake's. Is there anything you want me to take to Evelyn's this morning? Or I can come back later and help you load up everything."

"You can take the pies, but the rest needs to come out of the oven right before. Can you be here by one o'clock?"

Annie nodded and picked up the pie carrier. "See you in a bit."

***

"*Buongiornio*, Annie," Angelina wrote. "I check with La Foce for cost. Has much history from Second World War. If open in December, I let you know. Checking also options in our village. We will make happen week after Christmas."

Annie smiled and clicked out of her email. She had turned the problem of telling her grandmother about the trip over and over in her mind. Beulah would resist, she knew that. As much as Beulah wanted to see Annie marry Jake, and as much as she wanted to see Benito and his family, for her, the idea of traveling to Italy for the first time at her age was like riding a rocket to the moon.

The extent of her grandmother's wanderings consisted of North and South Carolina, the mountains of Tennessee, and one trip to the beach in Florida. She'd also accompanied her father up to Chicago a couple of times as a girl, taking cows up to the stockyards. A nine-hour flight, the time change, and an unfamiliar culture was a lot to bite off. Annie also needed to expedite a passport for her grandmother as soon as possible.

Should they announce their plans today at Thanksgiving and let everyone get used to the idea at the same time? If Beulah got caught up by the excitement of the others, that left little opportunity to back out. This strategy was not without risks. Her grandmother hated surprises, and this was definitely a surprise. But if it secured her for the trip, it was worth it.

She called Jake.

"Where are you?"

"In the back field. There's a cow in trouble. Can I call you back?"

"Sure," Annie said, but when she ended the call, she was too excited about her idea to wait. Cutting through a small wooded area behind the cottage, up a hill, and into the back pasture, Annie scanned the field and spotted Jake on the far side, down on his knees looking at something.

It was an odd scene, with both Jake and a cow staring down at something on the ground. As she came closer, the small, stillborn body of a tiny calf came into view, still covered in afterbirth.

Jake looked up as she approached.

"What happened?"

"I don't know. This is the third cow that's lost a full-term calf in the last week."

"Would Joe have any idea what caused it?" Annie asked.

"He doesn't know."

"I'm sorry. Is there anything I can do to help?"

"This is farm life," he said.

"It's getting close to meal time. It's Thanksgiving," she said gently.

"I won't be long."

Annie turned and then stopped in her tracks. "I almost forgot why I came," she said. "Why don't we spring our wedding plans on everybody today during Thanksgiving? Make the date official?"

Jake gathered the calf in his arms and carried it to the back of the side-by-side. "That's the best news I've heard all day," he said.

***

Stella Hawkins, the plump woman with flyaway red hair, sat in a frayed green robe and pulled apart one of Evelyn's gooey cinnamon rolls.

"Everything okay in the guest room?" Annie said.

"Everything is wonderful. The bed is so soft; I don't think I've ever slept in such a nice bed." Stella pushed her wire-framed glasses up on her nose. "I hope I didn't wake you all when I got in last night. I offered to help do something, but Beulah handed me this cinnamon roll instead."

Annie smiled back at Stella, remembering the first time she saw her. Back then, Stella's shoulders slumped as if the weight of disappointments had grown so overwhelming she could no longer stand tall.

Beulah turned from the sink and wiped her hands on a dish towel. "I think it's all done, other than the baking. I'll need everybody to help load the car and take it all over to Evelyn's in a bit."

"Beulah, do they know when Betty will be home? I'm ready to go to work anytime," Stella leaned forward in her chair. Annie could see the young foster child with unruly red hair and glasses, eager to please, and her heart warmed toward Stella even more.

"Don't be too eager," Annie said. "Betty Gibson will wear you out."

"Annie, you'll scare Stella to death," Beulah said. "Betty's a little childlike, that's all. You have to learn how to handle her. Be kind, but don't give in to her pouting."

The phone rang and Annie snatched up the receiver and handed it to Beulah, stringing out the long, curly cord.

"Happy Thanksgiving," she said. "Yes, she's here." Beulah passed the phone to Stella. "It's Peggy, Betty's oldest daughter. You can take it in the dining room."

"When will Betty come home?" Annie asked.

"The family is pushing for today, although if I was them, I'd let the hospital handle her as long as possible. But it's hard on Joe going back and forth. Either way, Stella won't be needed until Monday when everybody has to go back to work. Then she'll have her work cut out for her."

Chapter Fourteen

BEULAH LOOKED AROUND Evelyn's dining room table with that peaceful contentment that followed a good meal and good fellowship. Evelyn sat at one end of the table with Tom at the other. Annie was to his right, then there was Jake and Lindy. Next to Beulah sat Woody, and Stella was down by Evelyn. In her view, eight was the perfect number for table conversation. It allowed for seat-mates to visit, but was small enough the entire table could participate in one conversation as well.

Topics had ranged from Jake's farming operation, Stella's move down from Chicago, Tom's caseload, the health of Evelyn's mother, Lindy's dating woes, a discussion of Nubian versus Boer goats, a rehash of the community Thanksgiving potluck, and finally Betty's health and projected arrival home in the evening. All this was conducted between bites of turkey roasted to perfection, gravy, mashed potatoes, sweet potato casserole, green beans, yeast rolls, and seven-layer salad. Stella had relaxed into the hum of conversation as if she had been a member of their little group for years, and Beulah was pleased to see it.

Beulah was also pleased she had made a doctor's appointment the prior day for a checkup next week, since she was sure she was overdoing it today. Somehow the thought of taking one step toward better health mitigated the effects of the upcoming desserts. Evelyn plugged in the percolator, and in a conversation lull, Annie spoke.

"I have some news to share. First, the not-so-great news. I lost my job at Richwood." There was a collective groan. "They're telling the residents on Monday, so it's best not to say anything in the community until then."

"I'm so sorry, Annie." Evelyn's eyes were full of compassion.

"You've had your share this year," Lindy sympathized.

Annie looked at Jake and smiled.

"There's a silver lining to all this," Jake said and nodded at Annie.

"My last day will be Christmas Eve, which works out great, since we are getting married December 30."

A cheer went up and Tom slapped his hand on the dining room table.

Beulah was thrilled, but her mind was racing to Benito. *Could he travel to Kentucky on such short notice?* It wasn't the prettiest time of the year to see his ancestral home, but that meant she got to meet him so much quicker than waiting until the spring. *What needed to be done to the house and farm in order to prepare for the wedding? Could they pull it off that fast?*

"We need to call Benito and Angelina so they can make plans," Beulah said. "Where will you do it? It'll be too cold to have an outdoor wedding like Scott and Mary Beth."

All eyes turned back to Annie and Jake.

"We've already talked to Benito and Angelina. They'll be there," Annie said.

"Wonderful!" Beulah clapped her hands together. "I'll need to get the house ready."

"They can stay with me," Evelyn said. "I've got empty bedrooms."

Annie looked at Jake and something passed between them that stopped Beulah from saying another word.

"They'll be there, not here. We've decided to have the wedding in Italy."

In Italy? The words ushered in surprise and disappointment. Her granddaughter was excluding everyone from attending the wedding. Worse still, the very reason for Benito's visit to Kentucky was being snatched from her.

"We're going to Italy!" Lindy squealed as joy spread over her face.

"That's right," Annie said, and glanced at Jake.

"We want you all to go with us," Jake said. "All you have to do is buy your ticket over and we'll take care of everything once you get there."

Beulah looked down at the crumbs on the tablecloth. This was crazy talk. How in the world could everyone afford a ticket to Italy? She always pictured Annie getting married right here in Somerville at the church. It was time to speak up and stop this madness.

"You have to get married at Somerville Baptist. Your ancestors laid the cornerstone of that church. I always thought—" she stopped talking when she saw the angst in Annie's face.

"Grandma, we want you to go with us. I know it's not what you envisioned, but it will be an adventure we can share together."

"Benito and Angelina, they want to see Ephraim's home, and—" Beulah's voice trailed off. She felt herself on the edge of crying, and it embarrassed her.

"We're planning a big barbecue in May to celebrate the wedding and let all our friends meet our Italian family," Annie said. "We knew you wanted them to come in spring."

"Beulah, just think, you get to see Benito's home and then he will come here to see yours," Evelyn said.

Beulah nodded, trying to process this whirlwind of information.

"I think it sounds lovely," Evelyn smiled at Tom. "I've always wanted to go to Italy."

"Me too," Lindy said. "I'll start looking for cheap flights."

"I spent time there during college, but I've always wanted to go back," Tom said. "Besides, I can't let my two girls travel without me," he gave Evelyn an affectionate look, and it somehow made Beulah feel left out in the cold.

The whole idea was ridiculous. It was as if a locomotive gathered steam and they all jumped on board without a thought as to where the train was headed.

"Well now, I sure do appreciate the invite," Woody said. "But

I'm not much on foreign speaking places. No disrespect, but I'll wait right here for the barbecue come spring," he said. "But you can count on me to help with that."

"Me too," Stella said. "I better stay around here and do my job first. I'd be happy to help with the barbecue."

On that note, the train sputtered a bit and all eyes were on Beulah.

"Aren't they Catholic over there? How do you get married in a Catholic church?" Beulah asked.

"We'll find a venue outside of a church, and we're going to ask Scott and Mary Beth to go so he can perform the ceremony. We'll do the legalities here before we go and the ceremony in Italy. I'm hoping Dad can make it, since it's only a couple-hour flight. I'd like him to give me away."

The wistful lilt in Annie's voice betrayed her disappointment in Eddie not being there around the table today, breaking Beulah's heart. There was a deep void for a fatherless child that even a grandfather could not fill at times. Now that Fred was gone, it seemed natural for Annie to turn to her biological father, but Fred should be there to give her away in his rightful place as the man who raised Annie, not Eddie Taylor. But what was she thinking? Even if Fred were still living, he would no more travel to Italy than he would Mongolia.

"I don't know," Beulah said. "This is all so sudden. How many days?"

"We'll try to leave on December 26, so we can all enjoy some time with Benito and Angelina before the wedding. I'd recommend you stay until New Year's, depending on flights, and spend the rest of that time with Benito showing you around Tuscany. Grandma, Benito wants to take you to Siena and Florence, to show you all the places he knows and loves, like how you want to show him Kentucky."

"He thinks I'm coming?" Beulah asked.

"More than that, he's counting on it," Annie said. "So are we."

"Well for heaven's sake," Beulah said. "I can't stay at home."

***

Beulah craved busywork so her mind could digest the wedding trip Annie had sprung on them yesterday. Normally, she turned to cooking. With all the Thanksgiving leftovers sitting in the refrigerator, plastic boxes stacked, that seemed pointless.

Instead, she dragged out her Christmas decorations. Over the years, she had gone back and forth on Christmas decorations, some years going "whole hog" as Fred would say, and other years favoring simplicity with the nativity, the tree, and a wreath on the back door. When Annie was home, it had been easier to decorate for her, but since she had lived in New York, Beulah had done less. With Fred's passing over two years ago, she didn't even have the heart to put up the tree, and the house's only nod to the season was the manger scene.

As a matter of priority, Beulah always placed the nativity on the mantle first, a tradition her mother started. It was also the last decoration she put away, a reminder of what the season was all about. She laid the baby Jesus in the manger, then stepped back to admire the scene. The shepherd's staff lost its crook one Christmas when a feral cat shot in the house and bounced helter-skelter over the living room and knocked the nativity onto the floor.

Stella joined her and cleared off the table in the front window and made room for the artificial tree, with its ancient fake branches and wiry needles. Every year she had thought to replace it with a new discounted tree after Christmas, but who was in the mood to buy a Christmas tree in January? Once her spindly tree was covered in ornaments, lights, and a star, it looked fine enough.

With both Annie and Stella living with her, it was time again to be festive, so she brought the sorry old tree out for one more Christmas. With the light of day shining on it, she peered into the branches and realized it was even worse than she thought.

She had to make do this year. Every penny for the next month would be saved for the trip. She had in mind to pay for a couple of the dinners in Italy and to pay for her own plane ticket, as much as Jake had assured her he wanted to cover that. She would not be mooching off her future grandson-in-law, nor would she suck the life out of her new nephew, Benito. After all these years, she wanted to give back to him—not take.

"This tree will work all right, don't you think?" Beulah said, and stood back to admire it.

"It's magically beautiful," Stella said.

Beulah chuckled, appreciating Stella's ability to roll with the joke, but then she saw her face. Stella was serious.

"Have you had many Christmas trees before?" Beulah tried to sound casual. She picked up a wad of lights and handed it to Stella to untangle.

"There was one," Stella said.

"When was that?" Beulah asked, her voice gentle.

"When I was with my Georgia foster mother. Her name was Mama Jean and she was the one person my whole life who I truly knew loved me. We had a year and a half together before I aged out of the system, but she was so filled with love. No matter how much I pushed her away, she came back with arms open. I finally gave in to her and let her love me. That Christmas we had a tree and it was the most beautiful thing I had ever seen, I guess because of how I felt on the inside. I could see the beauty more than ever before."

"Is she the one who died last year, the one that brought you south?" Beulah was careful how she worded the statement, knowing Stella hadn't simply been coming south. She was intent on ending her life in the one place she had been happy, a small town in Georgia. Instead, she ended up in Somerville and her plans were derailed.

"We kept in touch for a long time after I left to go to college up north, but her biological daughter never liked me. I think she was a little jealous. When I found out she was gone, it hurt me so bad to know I had missed paying my respects. Even more, that she wasn't in this world anymore, the one person who had really loved me."

"That was a dark time for you," Beulah said.

"Then I ended up setting the stone house on fire after you all had been so kind to me."

"We wouldn't have known your story if that hadn't happened. We wouldn't have found Benito's letters."

Those blessed letters from World War II, sent from her brother Ephraim to their parents. They brought to light his love affair with a shopkeeper's daughter while he was stationed in

Naples. Shortly after, he was killed in the battle of Anzio. His young girlfriend discovered she was pregnant, and her parents wrote Ephraim's family in the only language they knew, Italian. The letter was put away in a box along with a picture of Elena, sent to them from Ephraim's personal effects and other letters he had written to them prior to his death. When Annie's friend Janice translated the letter, the long-silenced knowledge of Ephraim's love and his son came into light.

"Yes, Stella, it was all meant to be," she said.

"So, here we are," Stella said and plugged in her end of the light string. The glow lit up her face. Beulah leaned down and connected her lights.

"Here we are."

Chapter Fifteen

THE SOMERVILLE BAPTIST Church had a long center aisle with wooden pews on both sides, referred to as the "piano side" and the "organ side." It was popular for weddings because of its grand central aisle, and Beulah allowed herself a moment of grief over Annie not marrying in the place where her family had laid the cornerstone.

Beulah took her seat, six rows back from the organ, accompanied by Stella, in her family pew. The May name was engraved in a plaque on the side of the pew, a result of her daddy shelling out a donation when the old ones were replaced.

"I'll not be a back-row Baptist," her daddy had said. "We'll sit near the front or not at all."

There were times when she found a visitor in her pew, and when that happened, she remembered the Lord's command to prefer others over ourselves. So she eased herself into the pew behind or in front.

She was an advocate for church members having their regular places. It helped Pastor Gillum know who was missing on a Sunday. Beulah had been thrust into widowhood and solitary living, so the accountability was appreciated even more.

There was a faction of young folks advocating the "mix and mingle" approach, sitting here and there and everywhere, in order to know one another better. Beulah bit her tongue when this nonsense came up. After all, potlucks were the time to get to know one another, not worship.

Annie and Jake had taken to Scott Southerland's church, Grace Community, with its folding chairs and live band, but that was not Beulah's style. She preferred the Baptist Hymnal, the old-time preaching of Pastor Gillum, a start time of eleven and the regularity of the invitational hymn ending exactly at five minutes before noon. She did have Sunday dinner to host, at her house or Evelyn's, and a preacher could say everything that needed to be said within the traditional twenty minutes of sermon. Evelyn had an even better situation with the Presbyterians, who always ended at eleven forty-five, but they did make an earlier start of it.

Beulah and Stella had barely settled into the pew when three ladies from the Women's Missionary Union, a group Betty chaired, descended on them like a flock of barn swallows.

"How is she?"

"Has she gotten home yet?"

The questions flew at them like arrows, but Beulah answered each one with a final assurance. "Betty's home now. She'll make a full recovery, the doctor said."

The organ started playing, a signal for everyone to quiet down and go back to their seats. The ladies scattered, but not before giving Beulah a squeeze of the hand or a sympathetic look. She was as close to Betty Gibson as anyone in the church, and that made her the receiver of sympathy, although she felt a twinge of guilt about that with all that happened over the potluck.

The song leader stood to the side of the pulpit. With a glance to the piano and a flourish of arms, the piano and organ went into a rousing version of "I'll Fly Away." Beulah felt a lump in her throat, and the fear she had pressed down threatened to burst open.

Of all the hymns that could have been sung this morning, why this one? *What does it mean?* She listened with a rare intensity to the song lyrics:

Some glad morning when this life is o'er,
I'll fly away;
To a home on God's celestial shore,
I'll fly away (I'll fly away).

I'll fly away, Oh Glory
I'll fly away; (in the morning)
When I die, Hallelujah, by and by,
I'll fly away (I'll fly away).

Did this mean the plane would crash and she would fly away to glory? Good heavens. The thought made her head spin. It wasn't that she was afraid of dying, it was the manner of death. She never imagined herself leaving this world in a heaping mound of charred metal, or worse, nosediving into the Atlantic.

Was there any other way to see Annie married and meet Benito? There were ocean liners. *Did people travel by sea anymore?* Maybe she could cancel her flight and book passage on a boat. Yes, she would look into that tomorrow. If boats were good enough for Jesus, they were good enough for her.

She felt an anxiety that threatened to drown her. Beulah bowed her head and murmured prayers to request the peace that passed all understanding. A couple more songs and Beulah's spirit settled as she prepared for the sermon. Pastor Gillum pushed his large girth up from the chair on the stage and went to the podium. His full head of white hair swooped low over his forehead but miraculously stayed in place, even during his most animated sermons.

He opened his Bible.

"Our sermon today comes from Psalm 23. I'll be talking about the valley of the shadow of death. We all face death, either the death of a loved one or one day our own death," he paused and Beulah's mind raced.

It *was* a warning sent straight from heaven. She sat up in the pew and listened with all her might.

***

Sobered from the sermon, she drove to Evelyn's house in a daze. It was as if the Lord had delivered a clear message to her and now there was the dilemma of how to respond. Was she meant to avoid the flight altogether and seek other means to cross the ocean? Not go at all? Or face her destiny head-on?

She parked her car and went in the back door. Evelyn had on an apron and was busy with pulling things out of the oven and dishing up vegetables into bowls.

"Afternoon," Evelyn said, glancing over her shoulder. "How was the service?"

"Just fine," Beulah said. "They're all concerned about Betty. I think some are going over this afternoon to take some food for the week."

"You look a little piqued. Are you feeling all right?" Evelyn studied her face before Beulah could turn away.

"I'm fine, maybe a little tired today."

"Don't worry about staying to help clean up. You've had your hands full lately. You should go home and take a nap."

"Yes, I believe I will." Other than the dinner meal on Sunday, she tried hard to rest the remainder of the Sabbath, staying out of the kitchen as much as possible.

Beulah set about pouring sweet tea in the glasses. Evelyn's dining room table was set and ready.

"We should have traded Sundays with you hosting Thanksgiving," Beulah said.

"Oh, it's fine. You know, sometimes I think it's easier to go on and host a couple of things in a row once the house is all clean."

Beulah debated telling her friend, but there was little time before the others arrived. Instead, she settled for small talk and set the tea pitcher on the buffet.

"Evelyn, have you and Tom talked about going to church together?" Tom was as ensconced in the Methodist church as Evelyn was in the Presbyterian.

"No, although I'm sure we've both thought about it. I suppose we can keep going to our own churches, although I prefer to share that part of our life if we continue."

"What can we do?" Lindy asked, Annie and Jake following her into the house.

"Grab a dish and put it on the table," Evelyn said. "We'll do family style this week." Beulah always served family style with heaping dishes of meat and vegetables on the table when it was her turn to host, but Evelyn sometimes served buffet style, with all the items lined up on the kitchen counter and guests filling their plates.

Tom entered the room as the last dish was set on the table. Beulah couldn't help but see Evelyn's face light up with what could only be described as delight. It warmed her heart. Tom was handsome, in his late fifties, and a pillar in the community. He served as county attorney but was also active in his church and in preservation groups both local and statewide. Practicing what he preached, he and his wife had restored one of Somerville's finest historical treasures, an antebellum home. That was before she was felled by a brain aneurysm in her home a few years ago.

Jake greeted his mentor and potential stepfather before both men pulled out chairs for the ladies, and then everyone sat down. Evelyn asked Tom to say a blessing on the food, which he did in his mellifluous courtroom voice.

"Where're Woody and Stella?" Lindy asked, and passed the rolls to Beulah.

"Enjoying the day together before she starts taking care of Betty," Annie said.

"Woody wants me to teach Stella how to make fried chicken, biscuits, and gravy," Beulah said.

"Sign me up for that lesson," Jake said.

Annie nudged him with her shoulder. "I thought you liked my salads and hummus."

"I love your salads," he said. "But a little fried chicken every now and then wouldn't hurt."

"Speaking of fried chicken, I wonder how Betty is doing with her new diet," Evelyn mused.

"I stopped by this morning before church," Beulah said. "Joe's having a hard time with her. Moody as can be and resisting this new diet." Beulah shivered at the thought of a cardiac diet with all that low-fat, low-salt food.

"Did you all see the news this morning?" Tom asked.

"Awful," Annie said. "I can't imagine what happened."

"Terrible," Evelyn said. "Do they suspect terrorism?"

"What happened?" Beulah said.

"A passenger plane went down en route to New York from Paris," Tom said. "The wreckage is somewhere off the coast of Iceland."

Beulah dropped her fork and it clanged on her plate.

"Grandma, are you okay? You look pale," Annie said and pushed back her chair.

Lindy grabbed her hand and squeezed. "Are you choking?"

Jake got up and Beulah imagined he was about to grab her around the waist and perform the Heimlich.

"No, no, I'm fine," she sputtered. "I'm okay."

Annie caught her eye and gave her a studied look, as if she were seeing her for the first time. Beulah looked away from Annie and motioned everyone back to their seats.

"I don't know what it was," Beulah said, telling another blatant lie, and right after church.

Chapter Sixteen

VESTA SAT PRIMLY in her wheelchair in front of Annie's door when she arrived on Monday morning. One look at Vesta's face told Annie she knew the secret.

"I'm so relieved that you know." Annie dropped her purse and shed her coat.

"Well, I'm beside myself," Vesta said. "I will write a letter of complaint and get everyone's signature."

"I heard they're really nice folks," Annie said. "She's a former school librarian."

Vesta cocked her head. "A librarian, you say?"

Annie sat on the edge of her desk. "She'll be better than me, Vesta. I was shocked at first, but after having the weekend to think about it, it's the best thing. There are no issues with me taking time off now."

"Now you'll have to find another job." Vesta smoothed out the folds on her skirt. "I won't see you as much."

"You might see me more. Colleen says the new director wants me to stay on as a volunteer and help with the library and book club in particular. So, you're stuck working with me."

Vesta clasped her hands together and grinned. "Well, that's something to be happy about."

"In the meantime, my main job is to make sure December goes out with a bang and get the standard things in place for the new year. She'll want to have input on next year's schedule, but we have complete control over the library. Have you had breakfast?"

"I was waiting on you to arrive," Vesta said. "But I don't eat much these days, anyway."

"I could use a cup of coffee. Let's go to the dining room." Vesta agreed and lifted her feet onto the foot pads of her wheelchair.

"How's the house coming?" Annie handed her a cup of coffee from the urn in the dining room.

"Good, except my high school boyfriend showed up right before Thanksgiving in the form of our HVAC contractor. It's a sore spot for Jake. They were rivals in high school, more than I even knew at the time."

"A triangle," Vesta said.

"Eggs?" Annie waited, the spoon in midair, until Vesta nodded her agreement.

"You should have some yogurt, too. You need the calcium and the probiotics."

"I suppose, but at least give me one with fruit in it. I can't stand the plain."

"No triangle," Annie said. "He apologized for breaking up with me, which I thought was kind of nice." Annie carried the tray over to a table while Vesta wheeled her chair close. "What about you? Did you ever have a serious boyfriend?"

Vesta's brown eyes looked beyond Annie, as if she were seeing the ghost of another person.

"I was engaged once, a very long time ago."

"What happened?"

"He died in a farming accident."

"Oh, I am so sorry."

Vesta sighed. "It was a long time ago and there's not much to say about it. We were sweethearts at church and had an understanding. No one could afford rings back then, but we planned to marry as soon as he saved up enough money. He hired out to a man who raised corn so he could make the money for us to get married. It was harvest time and he got his arm caught in a corn picker. They got the machine stopped, but he lost his arm and too much blood."

Annie shook her head. Words failed.

"It was a long time ago. In all the years, I never found another man who could compare to Clarence. My education and then my job became my focus after that, and I was content. Now, that's enough of dwelling on the past. I didn't live to be this age looking back all the time. I'll finish my yogurt and we'll get to work on activities."

Annie drained the last of her cup of coffee and got up.

"In book club this afternoon, we're discussing a fine book of poetry by a young man from over in Washington County. Do you know some of these people have never heard of iambic pentameter?" Vesta's laughter tinkled like fine crystal bells.

"Unbelievable," Annie said, and pushed Vesta to her room.

***

Lately, Jake had so much extra work to do that it had eaten into their time together. Between cow problems, tractor repairs, and taking over Joe's chores, all on top of working a day job, he often didn't get in until bedtime. Tonight, she had a couple of errands after work, but she hoped they could spend the rest of the evening sitting by the fire.

Jerry requested she choose the wood flooring from some samples at the stone house, but on her way, she saw her grandmother's car parked in the driveway of the Gibson bungalow, and a prick of guilt made her slow down. She had not seen Betty since the day she had the heart attack. With her grandmother to dilute the visit, now was as good a time as any.

Annie turned the SUV around and parked. The front door was open, so Annie let herself in and followed the voices down the short hall. Joe, his daughter Peggy, Stella, and Beulah all crowded into the small bedroom. Betty was propped up in bed in a pink nightgown, her blonde curls pushed back by a sequined headband.

"Annie," Betty cried. "Oh honey, come here and give me a hug."

"I'm glad you're okay," Annie said.

"Law have mercy, I almost left here. Thanks to Joe hearing me fall. That was the first time he paid attention to me, but thank God he did. Do you want to see where they cut me open like a can opener?"

"Oh no, that's okay. It looks like the bandage is nice and secure."

"Cracked my chest open and it hurts somethin' awful," Betty said, and then burst into tears.

"Now, now," Beulah said, and patted her shoulder. "Is it time for your pain medicine?"

Peggy looked at her watch. "Not yet. She needs to wait another hour." She turned to face Betty. "Settle back and rest, Mama. We'll let you be quiet for a bit while we're in the living room. Ring this bell if you need anything." Peggy snugged a small bell next to her mother's hand.

"Miss Betty, I'm leaving now, but I'll see you tomorrow morning." Stella stroked her hand.

Betty nodded, meek as a kitten, and lay back against the pillow.

Annie followed the others to the living room.

"She's been emotional," Joe said. Annie noticed dark circles under his eyes, his face showing the strain of the hospital stay.

"They say it's normal," Peggy said. "I'll stay tonight so Daddy can get some rest. Stella, thank you so much. You've been a lifesaver. Missy will be here to relieve you tomorrow night."

Stella nodded and slipped out the door.

"Beulah, I can't thank you enough. Having Stella here is wonderful," Peggy said. "But we should pay her something."

"I'm sure she wouldn't mind a little gas money since she's looking for a job, but she's not expecting anything since she's got her room and board covered," Beulah said.

"We can do that," Joe said.

"Well, I hope Stella can stand it," Peggy said. "Mama's a handful."

Laughter broke the heaviness of the mood and Annie said her goodbyes, leaving her grandmother to settle in for a longer visit.

At the stone house, Annie pulled next to Brett's truck. It was after six o'clock and she was surprised he was still here.

"I was hoping to see you," he said when he met her in the foyer.

"What's up?"

"Jerry left the wood samples in the kitchen. I'm putting a few things away, but I'd like to see which one you like."

Annie nodded and found the samples on the floor. Brett came in a few seconds later and stood next to her. He stood so close she could feel the heat from his body.

"I like that one. What do you think?" she said.

"Good choice," he said as she picked it up. Brett took the wood from her and placed it on an upturned bucket. "I'll see Jerry tomorrow, and I'll make sure he knows which one you like."

"Thank you," she said. "I guess I better go. Jake's probably wondering where I am."

He nodded and held her eyes for a moment. "Annie, I told my dad about seeing you and he said to tell you hello. He'd like it if you stopped by for a visit sometime."

"I would like that." Annie stepped backwards, almost tripping over a stack of wood trim. Brett reached for her arm and steadied her. "Got it, thanks," she said. "All right, see you later."

She felt like a teenager all over again. It had crossed her mind to ask Brett if he sent her the roses, but that would invite an awkward conversation. No, much better to let him finish his work, move on, and forget about the past.

At Jake's cottage, a new black Suburban was parked next to his farm truck. There was barely room for the small SUV, but she squeezed it between the fence and the Suburban. She noticed Kentucky tags on the unfamiliar car, then heard raucous laughter coming from the cottage. A woman's voice and more laughter.

She quickened her pace. A man's voice, not Jake's, then more laughter. Annie threw open the door and saw a strange tableau in Jake's small living area. A woman with long, dark hair framing an exotic face was perched on the armchair in tight fitting, brightly colored clothes. Jake was standing near the fireplace, cigar in one hand, poker in the other, facing the woman. Smoke hung heavy in the air and Annie's eyes finally rested on the man sitting in the armchair.

"Dad!"

"There's my beautiful girl."

Annie went into his arms and inhaled the familiar mixture of tobacco, vanilla, and bourbon. She wanted to stay in that warm embrace, but he released her and returned to the armchair. He looked good, even younger than when she'd seen him last. Salt and pepper hair, dark moustache, barrel chest and muscular arms.

"Annie, I want you to meet Sofia."

"So nice to meet you," Sofia said, a heavy Spanish accent to her English. "I hear so much about you."

I haven't heard a word about you, Annie thought, but reached for her proffered hand and returned the greeting. Jake leaned in and kissed her, shooting her an apologetic look.

"I thought you were going to call?" Annie said, and sat down on the couch across from her father.

"Well, I decided to surprise you. We checked into a hotel in Rutherford, called Jake, and drove over. You're looking good, sweetheart." He gave her an appraising look. "Jake tells me you've got the wedding all set in Italy. Fine place; I've spent several vacations there on the Amalfi."

"We thought that'd be easy for you to reach from Spain. You said the week after Christmas is okay. Will that still work?"

"Of course."

"I want you to give me away," she said, feeling a little self-conscious of this pronouncement in front of Sofia.

"Are we going formal or will a dark suit suffice?" he asked, the hint of a tease in the lines around his eyes.

"A dark suit will be fine," Annie said. "How long can you stay here?" Annie was trying to work out in her mind how she could ask time off from work now. She wanted every minute she could get with her father.

Eddie leaned back in the armchair. "Couple days or so. We'll see," he said. "I've got some business tomorrow. I thought I'd take you both to dinner tomorrow night in Lexington. How's that sound?"

"It sounds great, but I'm sure Grandma would love to have you over for supper as well," Annie said. *Love* might be too strong of a word, but she knew her grandmother would do it.

"No, no, I don't want to put Beulah out," he said, and took a deep puff on his cigar.

"What about tonight?" Jake said. "We can round up something here."

"We're meeting a cousin of mine soon, having dinner with him, so don't go to any trouble."

"I didn't realize you kept in touch with any family members," Annie said. "Who is it?"

"You don't know that side of the family, do you?" he asked, and studied her. "It's just as well. There aren't many of them anymore. We're a dying breed," he said with a half-smile, and looked at Sophia. She took her cue and giggled.

Annie realized he didn't answer the question, but she didn't press.

"I'm being a bad host. How about something to drink? Cheese and crackers?" Jake put his cigar down on an ash tray Annie hadn't even known he owned.

"What's in your liquor cabinet?" Eddie asked.

"There's a little bourbon, although we're mostly wine around here," Jake said.

"What kind of bourbon?"

"Makers Mark?"

"Perfect. Double, straight up."

"Sofia? Annie?"

"Red wine for me, please," Sofia said.

"I can help," Annie said.

"No, stay there and visit. I'll get you a chardonnay."

"Just a small glass," Annie said. Somebody in the room needed to keep her senses.

"Sofia, are you from Spain?" The woman was in her mid-to-late thirties, Annie guessed, far closer to her own age than her father's.

"Si, Malaga. I meet Eddie at Pete's." Pete Barnes was a former Briton who owned the local bar where her father and other ex-pats hung out in Malaga.

"How is Pete?" Annie asked. "Last time I was there, his wife recently passed away."

"He's got a new wife. One of Sofia's friends, as a matter of fact."

Jake produced the drinks and then brought in a plate of cheese, crackers, and olives and put it on the coffee table. The presentation lacked style, but in this case, substance was more important. She gave him a grateful smile.

Eddie took the bourbon, sniffed it, and took a drink. "Kentucky's best," he said. With a cigar in one hand and bourbon in the other, her father leaned back in his armchair, ready to hold court.

"Jake, did I tell you about the time I was kidnapped in Yemen?"

Chapter Seventeen

ANNIE MET LINDY at Bill's Diner for lunch where they scooted into the vinyl-seated booth across the street from the Childress law office. Lindy's pixie face glowed between shoulder length blonde hair.

"Dad, Evelyn, and I are all booked," she said. "The flights arrive on the morning of December 27 and we come home on January 3."

"Perfect," Annie said.

"Same as usual?" The waitress placed glasses of sweet tea in front of them.

"It's hard to get anything but a burger at a burger joint," Lindy said.

"No reason to branch out," Annie agreed. "Hold the fries for me, though."

"What's this?" Lindy said.

"I do have a wedding coming up. I shouldn't even be drinking sweet tea, but at least I'm cutting back some," Annie said.

"How's it all going?"

"Coming together, but here's the big news: Dad's in town."

"In Somerville?"

"Staying in Rutherford, but he has some business around here today. He was a little vague about it last night. He's taking Jake and me to dinner tonight. Grandma's on pins and needles, but unless he stays past tomorrow, I'll doubt they'll even see each other."

"I'd love to meet him," Lindy said.

"I'm afraid he might ask you out; that'd be embarrassing and weird."

"Being your stepmother might have its advantages," Lindy teased.

"Don't make me sick," Annie said.

Lindy's eyes focused beyond Annie and widened.

"Annie, don't look now, but that hunky Brett Bradshaw is here. Didn't you date him in high school?"

"Brett's here?" she said. Annie scanned the diners and her eyes met his. He smiled back and left his table.

"Is this still your haunt?" he said to Annie. "Customer now instead of a waitress?"

"I can't stay away from the place. I'm addicted to the grease. But, it's all changing soon," she said. "This is my friend Lindy Childress."

"Brett Bradshaw," he said, and took her extended hand.

"I know, I was behind you in school, but you played football if I remember right," Lindy said.

"And you're a lawyer," he said. "I've heard your name." Brett smiled at Lindy, then turned back to Annie.

"Well, I gotta go. Nice to meet you, Lindy. Good to see you, Annie, as always."

"Is he single? He is still so good looking," Lindy said.

"Divorced, but I don't think he's dating anyone. It never came up, so I'm not sure."

"Well, if it comes up again, I'm available. Unless that's uncomfortable for you."

"It'd be more uncomfortable for Jake. He doesn't like him."

"It's because you dated him. They might be best friends if they knew each other under different circumstances."

"You think?"

"Sure, that's how men are."

"Then have at him."

***

Jake helped Annie into the car. "Where are we meeting them?"

"I told your dad we'd pick them up at the hotel on the way."

"We should be driving his Suburban," she said.

"I think we are."

"Ah, I get it. You're the designated driver. I'm sorry, Jake. Welcome to my father's vortex."

"I like him, Annie. I really do. He's got some great stories. Besides, after he has a couple of bourbons, I'd much rather be the one driving."

"I can tell he likes you, too," she said. "You let him smoke in your house. That was a test, you know. Dad's all about the tests—he pushes to see what kind of mettle you have. You keep going like this, he'll invite you on a wild boar hunt in Spain."

"Sounds like a new adventure," he said.

"Speaking of new adventures, I ran into Brett today when Lindy and I went to lunch. She'd like to go out with him. What do you think?"

"About you running into him, or Lindy going out with him? I think he's still hung up on you."

Annie smiled and cocked her head. "Are you jealous, Jake Wilder?"

"Not the least bit. But I will punch him out if he tries getting too close to you."

"Maybe I can divert attention to Lindy. You wouldn't like them going out either?"

"Nope."

"All right, we'll change the subject. How was your day?" she asked.

"We heard back from the veterinarian. The cows died of botulism."

"How did they get that?"

"Hay. It might have come from animal feces, we don't know." Jake ran his fingers through his hair. "We had to buy hay this year, and we got it from a reputable source. It looked good, but maybe it was contaminated."

"You know, Vesta told me she was engaged once, but her

fiancé died in an accident with a corn picker."

Jake winced. "That used to happen a lot."

"It made me think about you and all the things that are dangerous on the farm," Annie said.

"This is coming from a flight attendant?"

Annie smiled. "Flying is far safer than farming. Speaking of flying, have you heard anything back from your sister about coming to the wedding?"

"They have a standing skiing trip after Christmas with Chuck's family. They'll be here in full force for the barbecue. She said she'd call you later this week."

"I wish Suzanne didn't live so far out West."

"It's her home now, and her husband's business is thriving. I don't see her coming back anytime soon. I do miss her, though."

"What about your grandmother?"

"We have her full blessing as well, but she'll wait for the spring barbecue, too."

"At least we have two events to anticipate."

"What about Janice?"

"She's supposed to call me soon, but there are some complications she's trying to work out. I can't imagine getting married without her there. What about Scott and Mary Beth?"

"I talked to Scott about the legalities, and we're official once everything is filed here. They can go, but it will be a quick trip for them so they're not away from the kids too long."

"Understandable. At least they can make it. Oh, I got an email from Angelina today. The place she recommended for the wedding is booked. I guess the holiday time is popular for weddings. She's working on another idea."

"Here we are," Jake said. "I'll drop you off so you can go up to the room. Meet you back down here."

In a few minutes, they settled into the rented Suburban with Jake driving. Her father sat up front while Annie and Sofia took the second row of seats.

"We're going to Dudley's," Eddie said. "Short Street."

"I know the place," Jake said. "It's the best in town."

"We are celebrating," Eddie said, and looked back at her with a grin. "It's not every day my girl gets engaged."

Annie smiled. "It's special that you came to see us."

"Are you kidding? I had to get here once I heard the news. It was a cause for celebration."

That, along with business in Dallas and a Cowboys game, she thought. It reminded her of a question she'd been meaning to ask.

"Dad, what kind of business did you have in Somerville today?"

"Nothing important, a little legal matter that needed attention. Jake, kick up that speed. Let the big horse rack," he said.

Jake caught her eye in the rearview mirror and winked at her. He sped up.

"That's right. Son, you never get anywhere staying under the speed limit."

***

Dudley's on Short was a culinary institution in Lexington. Annie and Jake had eaten there once before and the atmosphere was that of a cozy living room, with perfect lighting, good art, and fine local food. Her dad had done his homework, and she appreciated the gesture.

Her father ordered an expensive bottle of wine, then settled into story-telling mode. With prompting questions from Jake, he told of his many travels, his love of Spain, and his community of friends in Malaga. When dinner arrived, he ordered a second bottle of wine, then launched into tales of his gambling wins and losses and the women he had loved. Her mother was noticeably absent from the list. Sofia wasn't on the list either, but didn't seem to mind. Sofia sat quietly throughout the meal, laughing at the appropriate times, batting her eyelashes at Eddie when he cast a glance her way, and politely answering Annie's questions.

Annie was torn between watching her father, still amazed that he was here, live and in person, and watching Jake. It had seemed impossible to do, but she was falling even more in love with her fiancé by watching the way he listened to her father. Jake, of all people, knew her father's history as well as anyone. Despite the fact that her father's stories grew more outlandish as the evening went on, he sat respectfully and listened intently, honoring her father, and in turn, honoring her.

As her father, and the evening, wound down, they finished with coffees and Dudley's famous crème brûlée, Kentucky style with a bourbon glaze. The check was brought to the table and her father reached for his wallet. He leaned to one side and then the other as it became evident his pockets were empty.

"I'll be," he said. "I must have left it back at the hotel."

"No worries, I'll get it," Jake said, reaching for his wallet and dropping his credit card onto the check plate.

"I'll return the favor when you come to Spain," her father said. "Are you a hunting man?"

"Quail, when I get the chance," Jake said.

"I'll set it up when you come. I know a good place."

The valet brought the Suburban around and Jake gave a generous tip to the young man. As they neared home, Annie interrupted the hunting conversation.

"Dad, are you around tomorrow? I'm sure Grandma wants to say hello."

"Heading out early tomorrow, but give her my regards," he said as Jake pulled into the hotel parking lot and handed her father the keys.

"So, I guess the next time we see you will be the wedding?"

"Right around the corner," he agreed.

"It's been so good to see you," she said, and kissed him on the cheek.

"You're a first-rate girl, Annie. You picked a fine young man here. He'll do fine," her father said, and grabbed Jake by the shoulder. "Come on, Sofia."

"Thank you very much," Sofia said. "So nice to meet you."

***

Annie was ready to replay the evening with Jake on the way home when she saw a missed call from Janice.

"Go ahead and call her back," Jake said.

She dialed the number. "Janice, is it too late?"

"It's fine. Jimmy's out on a call and the kids are in bed. We can't wait for the barbecue. We'll bring Mama DeVechio, but we'll rent a place in town."

"You will not. Grandma would love to have your mother-in-law stay with her," she said.

Janice laughed. "Are you sure about that?"

"They did make peace at the end," Annie said, laughing too. "But what about the wedding?"

"Annie, I don't see any way I can do it," Janice said.

"You have to be there. You're my matron of honor," Annie said, not caring that she sounded like a disappointed child.

"We can't afford it. My buddy pass only takes care of two people. The kids are out of school for Christmas break; Mama DeVechio is working now at the restaurant and can't take care of them. My sister's out of town that week. I don't see any way to make it happen," she said.

A wave of sadness washed over her. Janice, of all people, needed to be there. She had taken Annie to Italy, helped find Benito, served as translator, and coached Annie through her commitment fears that threatened to destroy her future with Jake.

"Oh Janice," Annie said, and looked at Jake.

"Don't make me cry," Janice said. "I've been putting off this phone call as long as I could."

"I understand, I do. I can't help being disappointed," Annie said, and mustered resolve in her voice.

"Me too," Janice said. "I wanted to help translate, too."

"I'm not worried about that. Vincenzo and his family speak English well. I want you there because you're my best friend and you're an important part of this whole thing."

"I know," Janice said. "I will be with you in my thoughts and prayers."

Annie clicked off and turned to Jake. "She can't do it. No one to take care of the kids."

"I'm sorry," Jake said.

"We're doing the right thing, aren't we? I mean, is this too complicated? Several people can't come, and we don't have a place for the actual ceremony. One of the reasons this was attractive was to make it easy for Dad, and he's as reliable as a hole-riddled boat in a choppy sea. Maybe Italy's not meant to be."

"I have a feeling your dad's going to be cagey no matter where we hold the wedding. He doesn't seem to plan very far out. It'll all come together, don't worry." He squeezed her hand.

Chapter Eighteen

"I CAN'T THANK you enough, taking me in like this all of a sudden and teaching me these things," Stella said as she wiped flour onto her apron. Fried chicken sizzled in the iron skillet.

"It's been my pleasure. Now, turn each piece so it cooks evenly, but don't splash that grease out. I've got many a burn from frying chicken."

A great clamoring and thumping on the closed-in back porch announced Woody's arrival. "Is that fried chicken? Aww golly! I can't wait."

Stella looked at Woody. "I'm doing it all by myself."

"Hot dog," Woody said, the color flushing his face. He had the look of a man in love, but Beulah wasn't sure if it was Stella or the fried chicken that was the object of his affection.

"I heard a squawking in your chicken house when I came in, Beulah. Now that it's getting dark earlier, you might have had a possum slip in there. Thought I'd better go check on it."

"Can you shut them in while you're out there? Annie sometimes gets home late. And don't be too long. All we have left is the milk gravy and then it'll be ready for the table."

She turned to Stella. "Now, you've got your grease hot. Sprinkle the flour in, but keep stirring. Don't stop stirring."

Beulah could tell Stella was going to have some lumps in her gravy by the way the flour mixed, but gravy took practice.

Stella did as she was told. "Now we add the whole milk. Don't fool with that 2 percent stuff. Milk wasn't made to be stripped of its fat."

Stella moved the wooden spoon around and around. "Let's put it on medium heat and you keep stirring. Once it starts thickening, we can turn it down."

"Do I smash down these little lumps?"

"That'll help, but don't stop stirring. Gravy takes practice, but it'll still eat good."

After dinner, Woody pushed back his plate, leaned back in the chair, and grinned.

"Ladies, that was some meal and I thank ye kindly."

Stella blushed with the praise.

"I guess I better go on home, now," he said, and looked at Stella with a question in his eyes.

He got up and Stella stood, too. As if the awkwardness of the moment was too much, she sat back down.

"Stella, why don't you see Woody out? I believe he'd like to say goodbye."

"Oh yes," Stella said, and bumped the table with her hip.

With Stella, Annie, and Evelyn all courting heavy and Betty laid up with a heart attack, Beulah felt a little sorry for herself as she drummed the kitchen table with her fingers. It wasn't the dating, but she missed the long conversations and fellowship with her friends. It almost made her miss Rossella DeVechio.

Almost.

***

Beulah flipped mindlessly through a hunting magazine in the waiting room. Why had she eaten such a big meal last night, knowing she had to go see the doctor the next day? And so late?

Could the doctor tell how much fat she had eaten the night before from the blood they had taken when she arrived? After fasting all morning, she was hungry as a bear again.

Beulah chastised herself for the bad decision, then nearly jumped out of her seat when her name was called. After another extended wait in the cold examination room perched like a bird on the table, Dr. Bright entered the room and studied a chart through his reading glasses.

"Hello, Beulah, how's that knee?" He put down the chart and felt around the kneecap.

"It works good," she said.

"Should last you for another fifty years." An obvious joke. "Let's check your heart." He took out his stethoscope and listened to her heart and then put it on her back. He looked in her eyes and ears, down her throat, and up her nose. He poked and prodded her abdomen and checked her reflexes.

"All right," he said. "Let me help you down." He extended his hand and she slid gingerly off the examining table. "Have a seat right here."

Beulah settled herself on the padded chair while Dr. Bright sat across from her.

"Beulah, your sugar levels are higher than I want them to be. We call that pre-diabetic, which means if you don't change anything, you'll develop diabetes. I don't want to see that happen, so we need to turn this ship around now and head the other way. I recommend you cut way back on the sugar. I'd also like to see you drop ten to fifteen pounds."

"What does that mean, exactly, to *cut way back*?" she asked.

"I'd like to see you cut it all out for a while. Go cold turkey. But if that's too hard, start mixing your sweet tea with unsweetened tea. Cut back on desserts. Watch your consumption of potatoes and other simple starches. I want to see you back here in six months to check out your numbers again. Everything else looks good, but we need to get that sugar level down. Any questions?"

"Well, yes, I do." She gathered her thoughts and plunged in. "I'm going on a trip, flying overseas, at the end of this month, and I'm, well, I'm awful nervous about it." There. She had voiced her fear out loud to another person.

"A common fear. Behind death and public speaking, I believe," he scribbled on a prescription pad. "I know you don't like to take medicine, but I want you to take this pill about an hour before you get on the airplane." He ripped off the paper and handed it to her. "It's for anxiety. It will relax you and take the edge off your fears. I also recommend you wearing compression hose to help with circulation and swelling. Other than that, you should enjoy your trip."

A few minutes later, Beulah left the sterile examining room with its bright white lights and antiseptic smells and felt slightly rejuvenated by the cool air and sunshine outside the doctor's office. It was a beautiful day, but the news from Dr. Bright depressed her. How had it all boiled down to a nerve pill and no sugar?

***

"Evelyn?" she said, and pushed open the back door, decorated with a live green wreath.

"In here," her friend called from the small room off the back hallway. "I was on the computer," Evelyn said, and appeared from around the corner. "Come on in."

"Am I interrupting?"

"Not at all. I was looking at swimsuits for women over fifty," she giggled. "I pulled mine out and realized it was ready for the rag pile."

"It's hard to think about a swimsuit in December. They're predicting snow next week."

"Do you know we leave for the Caribbean three weeks after Italy? I don't know when I've done so much traveling. I feel breathless about the whole thing, as if I am in someone else's life now. Sit down, please."

Evelyn poured Beulah a cup of coffee without even asking her if she wanted it.

"Dr. Bright told me I have to cut back on the sweets or else I might get the sugar."

"Oh, no. I was going to offer you a cinnamon roll, but I guess you better not."

Her mouth watered at the thought of Evelyn's cinnamon rolls.

"Well, I was thinking that maybe I should have one last roll now that I know I have to cut back," Beulah hedged.

"I agree. Start tomorrow. You need a little time to adjust," Evelyn said.

Beulah's mood lifted as she watched Evelyn dish out a roll onto a plate.

"Are you having one?"

"Not this time. I'm cutting back, too, so we can both be miserable together," Evelyn laughed. "This is my last pan of cinnamon rolls until Christmas, so enjoy. Now tell me, is Annie's father still in town?"

"Supposed to have left today," Beulah said.

"Did you ever see him?"

"Not once. He had some legal business in town, and he spent both evenings with Annie and Jake. I'm glad of that, anyway. It shocked me that he even came to town. I hate to say it out loud, but I suspect this legal business had more to do with his reason for coming than seeing his daughter. I reckon I always suspect the worst, but with Eddie Taylor, it's a fair bet."

"I do hope he makes the wedding. I know she's counting on it."

"On that note, you know we're going to have to tell Betty about Italy," Beulah said.

"I've been thinking about that. She'll feel left out," Evelyn said.

"They wouldn't have gone anyway. Joe can't be away from the farm, not with Jake gone."

"No, but she'll pout about it. I think you should do it, Beulah. She takes everything a little better from you, anyway. She called me crying last night. I got on the phone with Joe and he said she had already called you doing the same thing."

"I don't know what we're going to do with her. I talked to Stella about putting up her Christmas tree and getting the house decorated. Maybe that will lift her spirits."

"I'm not doing much decorating this year. With two trips after Christmas, I don't want to add putting away Christmas decorations in the midst of it."

Evelyn's idea of Christmas decorations far exceeded anything Beulah did on her biggest years. Evelyn draped greenery down the staircase bannister, placed wreaths on every door, decorated a large Christmas tree in her formal living room, and smaller trees in the other downstairs rooms.

"It's hard to imagine this house without it being decorated to the nines," Beulah said.

"It's strange for me, too, but I have a strong sense of letting go this year, a shedding of sorts. Maybe it's dating Tom, but somehow, I feel on the verge of a new chapter and I'm re-examining all the things I used to do in light of it."

***

"Italy?" Betty cried as soon as Beulah entered the Gibson's small living room. "Beulah, when were y'all going to tell me? I'm not dead yet."

Stella slunk low in the couch next to Betty's La-Z-Boy, her face flushed red. She looked up at Beulah and mouthed the words, "I'm sorry."

Rats. She had forgotten to ask Stella not to mention it.

"Everybody's going around planning a trip to Italy and here I am laid up with my chest cracked open and can't go and my best friends in the world not even telling me about it."

Beulah sat in a chair on the other side of Betty and took the hand not filled with a wad of tissue.

"Betty, we knew you couldn't go and we didn't want to upset you in the middle of your recovery. We planned to tell you, of course we did, but you've had such a hard time with all this."

Her friend deflated, like the air going out of a balloon. "I reckon so," she said. "But I coulda stood it. I don't like not knowing things."

There never was a truer statement, Beulah thought. "Well, you know it now. We were planning to tell you, and that's the truth."

"Truth, truth. I'll tell you what's true. You don't know what it's like to have your whole world shook up. Not only do I have a cut right down the middle of my bosoms, I'm constipated all the time now. A stick of dynamite couldn't move me. How is that possible, I ask you, with all the vegetables I'm eatin'? Every meal is a plate full of rabbit food. I can't have nothin' I like no more; no vienny sausages, no bacon or fried chicken. None of the good stuff I've eat all my life. I feel like my life is over, and that's the truth."

Beulah pulled in a deep breath.

"Betty, if you're so fired up to know the truth about everything, I'll tell you. You're not the only one on a diet. I've got high sugar and can't have sweets; Evelyn's trying to fit into a swimsuit; Annie's trying to fit into a wedding dress. You're the only one that's had her chest cracked open, I'll grant you that. But you're alive and you've got a man who loves you and daughters who are sacrificing every moment outside of work to take care of you. You have a roof over your head and land to grow food. You even have Stella here during the day to see to your every need. Betty Gibson, you're a whole lot better off than most of the people in the rest of the world, and I suggest you quit feeling sorry for yourself and direct that energy to getting back on your feet."

For the first time in Beulah's life, Betty Gibson was speechless. Both Stella and Betty stared back at her with wide eyes and open mouths. She pushed back her chair and left. There was not a word more to say.

Chapter Nineteen

THERE WAS A bouquet of yellow roses on her desk. No card, once again, but Annie knew it had to be Brett. He had admitted to keeping tabs on her. It was flattering, but the gesture made her realize his intentions needed to be addressed. She was engaged to Jake, and Brett should know whatever they had at one time was over.

Annie picked up the roses and carried them to Lonnie Caldwell's room.

"Lonnie, I brought you some flowers that you can distribute to all your lady friends."

"They're beautiful," Lonnie said. "Are you sure?"

Annie nodded. "I brought some green floral paper we had left over in the craft room. Pick out one or two and wrap the stems in this. Here's some ribbon as well. Your ladies will love them."

"Well, now, don't you think of everything," he said, amused with her creativity.

"You better take one of these," he said, and pulled out a rose. "You are my most special girl, after all," he said, and winked again.

"Lonnie, whoever you're with at the moment is your most special girl and we both know it. But thank you just the same."

"Thanks to you, my dear, and thanks for thinking of me."

***

Jake was herding goats that had ventured into a neighbor's orchard. After that, he had to repair fences where the goats had escaped. At least Joe Gibson was around to help and happy to have an excuse to be outside the house.

Annie had dinner with her grandmother and then went upstairs to read before going to bed. She kept reading the same sentence over and over, finally putting the book aside. She thought about the flowers, which led her to think about both Brett and Jake. As a teenager, she desperately wanted to leave Somerville, to live the life her mother had not, and dating Jake meant staying put. So, she picked Brett, the football jock who she knew she could never marry and easily leave after graduation.

Marriage and a baby had kept her mother stuck in the tiny town, and she had died before ever seeing a single thing outside of Kentucky. Annie had vowed after her mother's death to see everything she could for as long as she could.

Annie fulfilled her self-promise, traveling the world as a flight attendant. Then, through a providential twist, she lost her job, took stock of her life, and landed home in the arms of the man who had loved her all along.

***

Jake was bringing her lunch, but before it was time to meet him, Annie went by Vesta's room to check on her friend. She found her with several of her AME church family, eating lunch in the dining room and getting updates on all the members. While she waited on Jake, Annie scrolled down her email and clicked on one from Vincenzo, writing for his mother Angelina, which he did sometimes when she had more than she could say in English herself:

Dear cousin Annie,

Please see mamma's reply to you. I will be at your service on your response.

Vincenzo

Cara Annie,

Let me offer another option, not so grand as La Foce. Benito and I live next door to a private chapel. It was part of the original palazzo of Montefollonico. Our neighbor sells ceramics there. If you like, she will allow you to marry there at no charge. All our friends here are so happy for Benito to find his American relatives. It is very simple and rustic, and may not be what you envisioned for your wedding. We can follow with a meal in a nearby restaurant, as you prefer. There is the hotel where you stayed, very nice and clean, if you like for your guests.

Please advise and we will make arrangements, or we keep looking for more locations.

Angelina

A private chapel next door. It sounded perfect.

A knock at the door sounded and she looked up, expecting to see Jake. Instead, the receptionist held a bouquet of yellow roses.

"Is it Valentine's Day around here and I missed it? These came for you," she said and placed the bouquet on Annie desk.

"Oh no," Annie said.

"Not exactly the response I anticipated," the receptionist said and swished out of the office. Once again, there was no card.

"This has to end," she said to herself. "Ridiculous."

She was staring at the roses when Jake appeared with a large paper bag.

"I've got pulled pork," he said, and then noticed the roses. "And you've got flowers. Let me guess: Brett Bradshaw."

"There's no signature," Annie said.

"He's trying to win you back," Jake said, his voice cool. "I told you I don't trust him."

"It's not going to work, even if it is him," she said.

Jake's jaw tightened and she laid her hand on his. "He'll stop trying when he realizes it's hopeless. Besides, I've got great news. Angelina found the perfect place for the wedding. A small chapel right in town. You'll love the price."

Chapter Twenty

ANNIE AWOKE TO the smell of frying bacon and voices chattering in the kitchen below. The morning light filtered through the lace curtains, casting muted sunshine on the faded wallpaper. She let herself imagine for a moment the voices were her mother and grandmother, instead of Stella and her grandmother.

If her mother had lived. It was a phrase she often toyed with in her mind when she missed her the most. If her mother had lived she would be downstairs now with her grandmother, puttering about in the kitchen, making lists for the wedding, managing her grandmother's fears, helping Annie with her fears, and making them both laugh in the process.

A tear slipped out of her eye and wet the pillow. Annie turned toward the window and let the dampness soak into her cheek.

A gentle knock sounded at her bedroom door.

"Annie, Beulah wanted me to tell you it's time for breakfast."

"Thanks, Stella, I'll be right down."

Stella was good company for her grandmother, especially since Annie worked so much now and spent every free minute with Jake. When Annie left for Jake's cottage after the wedding, it was a comfort to know Beulah and Stella had each other for company. As independent as her grandmother was, Annie knew she loved having someone to cook for and share meals with—as long as that person didn't fight for her kitchen. There seemed no danger of that with Stella.

Beulah leaned against the kitchen counter in her work dress and her comfortable shoes of a certain brand worn by women over seventy.

"Good morning," Annie said, and made her way to the percolator.

"Morning," Beulah said. "Sleep well?"

"Like a baby. This regular forty-hour work week is new to me. I've never appreciated Saturday mornings so much." Annie sat at the table with her coffee and folded her legs under her.

She watched her grandmother take the ham out of the iron skillet and add coffee to the grease for red-eye gravy.

"Where'd Stella go?" Annie managed.

"Stella is taking care of the chickens this morning. I needed a couple more eggs."

Annie started. "I forgot."

"It's all right, she likes doing it. After breakfast, Woody's taking her to see his mother today at the nursing home." Beulah poured the red-eye gravy into a gravy boat.

"Sounds like the relationship is moving along."

"Yes, I believe it is. He's been faithful to honor his mother and even though she's not very responsive, I suppose he wants Stella to meet her anyway. Not many people survive a horse kick to the head," Beulah said. "She's been laying there now for all these years."

"Grandma, Angelina found the perfect place for the wedding. It's a chapel right next door to Benito and Angelina. It's being used for ceramics, but they are friends with the lady who owns it and she's agreed to open it up for the wedding. Best of all, no charge."

"Is that right?" Beulah turned from the stove. "Now that is wonderful."

"It seems Benito and Angelina are well loved in their community. Everyone wants to help now that he's found his American family."

***

Beulah's face glowed. "I can't wait to meet them, although I admit I'm scared to death of the plane ride."

"We'll help you with that. Jake booked you in business class, so there's more room. We'll introduce you to the captain so you can see for yourself who is in charge. These big planes have so many back-up systems in case things fail. They're far safer than driving to Somerville."

"I don't doubt it, but when I drive to town, I'm in control of the car, not some unknown pilot."

The back door opened and Annie shivered against the cold air that swirled into the room.

"Good morning." Stella unbundled her coat and her rosy cheeks glowed against her fair skin.

"Morning. How cold is it?" Annie asked.

"Warmer than Chicago," she said. "I know you all think it's cold, but this feels like early spring to me. Here are your eggs."

Beulah took the brown eggs, then cracked them one by one on the side of the iron skillet.

"I'll set the table," Annie said.

"What can I do?" Stella asked.

"Pour the orange juice, then y'all sit down."

"Stella, do you have any family members living?" Annie asked after thanks was given.

"Not that I know about. I went into the foster care system when I was four and both my parents died. I don't have much memory of them or what they looked like, but I do have memories of being safe and loved. What about you, Annie? I know your mother died, but what happened to your father?"

"He left my mother when I was a baby, so I don't have any memories of them together. I guess the responsibility of a wife and child was too much that young, so he left. Really left. He took a job overseas and in most recent years, he's been in Spain."

"Spain?" Stella asked. "What kind of job is that?"

"He's a mud engineer. He works for a company that contracts out his type of work to the oil companies. He lives in Malaga because he likes it there and there's a large ex-patriot community. He could live anywhere, since he moves to different drilling sites where he's working."

"How glamorous," Stella said. "It sounds like something in a book."

Annie thought about her father's apartment in Malaga, a place she had visited three or four times when she worked for the airline. It wasn't glamorous at all. It was a small, sparse apartment in a nondescript building. Pete's bar was on the bottom floor of the building, and his favorite restaurants were all within walking distance.

"Spain is wonderful," Annie said. "Not sure I'd call my father's life glamorous. He was just here, by the way."

"Your father?" Stella said. "I can't imagine that. You're lucky to have a father."

Annie chewed her ham and realized Stella was right. For all his faults, she still had a father.

After breakfast, Annie shooed Stella out the door when Woody arrived, reassuring her that she would clean the breakfast dishes for Beulah this morning.

It was now Beulah's turn to sit at the table and sip her last cup of coffee for the morning while Annie busied herself with the dishes. Her grandmother had always been resistant to a dishwasher, an appliance Annie had made sure they budgeted for in the stone house.

"Grandma, how did my parents meet?"

"Well, goodness, let me think. I believe it was at the county fair that June, right after her high school graduation. Your father swept Jo Anne right off her feet. From the moment they met, they were inseparable. Fred and I didn't like it. Not only because of Eddie's family background—we could have got over that if he was honorable. It was too much, too fast. A body can't make a right decision when you're caught up in a whirlwind. That's what happened to Jo Anne. She fell headlong into the excitement of him and all his big plans and hopes for seeing the world. We tried everything to get them to slow down, but all we did was push Jo Anne towards Eddie." Beulah sighed.

"Labor Day weekend, Jo Anne went out with Eddie that Saturday and didn't come home. We were worried sick. Fred walked the floors all night. I don't think either of us got a bit of sleep. Finally, late that Sunday afternoon, she showed up, without Eddie, to tell us she was pregnant and married. They had gone off to Jellico, Tennessee. Back then, you had to wait three days in Kentucky once you decided to get married for blood tests and such. But not in Tennessee. Jellico was the first town over the state line and it became the site of many a shotgun wedding or elopement."

Annie sat, mesmerized by the story, imagining her mother as a young woman, rebellious and in love.

"So how long did he stay after I was born?"

Beulah looked down at her coffee cup, and then placed it on the table. "He never came home from the hospital. He left that day."

The revelation stunned Annie. "That day?"

Beulah nodded. "Did your mama never tell you?"

"She never talked about it," Annie said. "I've always heard he left when I was a baby, so I assumed that meant a few months into it."

Beulah shook her head. "He didn't leave the area right away, and he did come and visit a few times after you were born. I believe he didn't want to get attached to you. It was all too much for him."

"Wow. How did Mom handle that? I can't imagine Jake leaving me the day I had his child."

"She never told us much, but I don't think they had many good days once they got married. Eddie couldn't handle responsibility like that. I'm sorry, Annie. I don't mean to talk bad of him, it's simply how it was back then. They hardly knew each other. Jo Anne wasn't surprised when he moved out while she was at the hospital, but she was awful sad."

"Claustrophobic," Annie said.

"What's that?"

"That's what Dad said once when I asked him why he left. He said he grew 'claustrophobic.'"

"I'll be honest," Beulah said. "I was a little relieved when he left. We were able to step in and help her without his influence. I figured she'd marry again—some nice young man who could be a proper father to you. But, it didn't happen that way."

"Did Mom ever date anyone else?"

"She went out from time to time while we babysat you, but

nothing lasted more than a couple of dates. She—" Beulah's voice trailed off. "Well, I guess that's enough about this." Beulah carried her coffee mug to the kitchen sink.

"No, Grandma, please don't stop. I want to hear it all."

Her grandmother turned and looked at her, as if to make sure.

"I really do," Annie said. "All of it."

Beulah frowned. "I reckon Jo Anne never got over Eddie. There wasn't anyone else she wanted. And that's why I've always been wary of your father. It wasn't that he left the first time, it was because he didn't come back when she was sick."

"Why would he?"

"Because I asked him to. I had no choice. Jo Anne got weaker and we moved you all over here so we could tend to both of you better. As the disease took its toll, she often cried out for him." Beulah's voice broke at the memory. "I'm surprised you don't remember, but you were in school all day and we kept you busy outside as much as possible. It was agonizing to hear. I began to believe that if Eddie could come one time and hold her hand, it would comfort her before she passed into the next world. I called him and begged him to come. He said no, he was sorry and all, but he couldn't come. Jo Anne died a week later."

Annie felt her chest tighten. She reached for a napkin and wiped her eyes.

"I shouldn't have told you all that," her grandmother said. "I finally granted your father forgiveness, although it did take me a while. I realized later he was simply incapable of it."

"He's had so many opportunities to choose love, but instead he runs away," Annie's voice came out in a whisper.

"Some folks set themselves on a path and can't turn back. If they do, they'll face too many ghosts. So, they keep on a-going."

Chapter Twenty-One

BEULAH DUSTED THE den furniture and thought about her conversation with Annie. She regretted saying so much. Eddie Taylor was Annie's father, after all. Understanding Eddie's history gave reason to things. But in Beulah's mind, reasons didn't equal excuses. At some point, a person had to own up to their responsibility. Eddie had yet to show he was man enough to do that.

The phone rang and she reached for the portable next to the La-Z-Boy. It was Betty Gibson.

"Beulah, I thought maybe y'all might come over tonight and play Rook. I can sit up in a chair and watch, anyway. Of course, I can't eat nothin' good no more, but I can eat bean soup as long as it's cooked with chicken stock instead of fatback. Peggy's making us a big pot, so we can have that tonight. It's our normal night out at the Diner anyway, so I figured you didn't have plans."

So, she was forgiven her outburst. Accepting the invitation made everything all right, as it had for all these years whenever a tiff popped up between them. The longest they had ever stayed mad was over the community potluck, and Beulah hoped that would never be repeated.

"I'll make cornbread without sugar. Will you call Evelyn, or should I?"

***

Beulah stepped inside the old stone house and noted the drywall boards that had gone up in places, giving it a more "dressed" appearance. When it was stripped down to the studs, the house had looked vulnerable, like someone who'd lost too much weight. It had been hard to imagine it could recover this well after the fire last summer.

After all the talk about Jo Anne earlier in the day, it made her want to see the place where her daughter had lived for twelve years until she got sick. There were so many memories here, not only of Jo Anne and Annie when she was small, but also her own mother and daddy, and her older brother, Ephraim. Beulah toured the downstairs, then stepped out on the stoop, remembering the day they stood there hugging Ephraim before he left for the service after the terrible attack on Pearl Harbor.

No matter the fears she had about flying over the ocean, she had to make this trip in order to see Annie married, and to meet Benito. Beulah represented the entire family, and they would wish her to be there.

In May, Benito would be here with his family to see his family farm. Yes, his farm, too. The simple thought struck her and she grabbed the doorframe of the house as the weight of those words came down on her.

"This is his farm, too," she said aloud. If Ephraim had lived, they would have shared the inheritance. Since he died in World War II, it had all come to her. Now, Ephraim had a newly discovered heir. Did that mean Benito had a legal right to half the farm?

Never once had that crossed her mind in all the excitement of finding her brother Ephraim's son. Now the question loomed. Did she owe him land, or the equivalent value in money?

The farm was paid off when her parents had passed it onto her. At today's value, half that was a hefty sum; it would drain her savings. Yet, if she owed it, how could she not do what was legally and rightfully due to Benito?

***

"Beulah, what made you think about it?" Evelyn said, and curled her legs up on the couch in a way that Beulah envied.

"Why, I don't know. I was thinking about Benito seeing the farm and where his father grew up, and then it simply hit me. As Ephraim's heir, he's entitled to something."

"Well, the law is a funny thing. I'm sure Tom will look into it for you. He'll need all sorts of facts and things. Any legal documents you might have from your parents."

"I'll get everything to him on Monday. Do you mind mentioning it to him in the meantime?"

"Sure, I'll see him in a bit. Don't worry about it until he has a chance to review it all."

"I'm trying not to, but I don't want to have to sell the farm. I also can't see giving up all my savings with no plan for old age. Or older age," she said with a chuckle.

"Hello?" Annie's voice called from the back door.

"In here," Evelyn answered.

Annie stood in the doorway and put her hands on her hips.

"Grandma? What's that in your bag? *Italian for Dummies* and an Italian dictionary?" She grinned from ear to ear.

There was no privacy on May Hollow Road. Beulah had planned to hide the library books she picked up in town, but had brought the bag inside to show Evelyn some fabric she had purchased.

"Don't get excited; there's something to that old saying of teaching an old dog new tricks. I'd be tickled to master a few words so when I meet him, he hears me speak to him in his language."

"Beulah, that's impressive," Evelyn said, sitting upright on the couch. "I am inspired."

"Maybe we can practice together." Annie sat down on the couch.

"Hold your opinions until I master something, please," Beulah said.

"Maybe we should invite Mrs. DeVechio back down for another week's visit?" Annie suggested.

Beulah cut her a sharp glance. Evelyn laughed while Annie struggled to keep a straight face.

"A few words, that's all."

"Anybody want some iced tea?" Evelyn said.

"I'll have some," Annie said.

"Me too, but it has to be unsweet," Beulah said.

"All right, so what's up with no desserts and the unsweet tea?" Annie asked.

Beulah looked at Evelyn. "You two are always keeping secrets." Annie pretended to be affronted.

"My sugar is a little high, that's all. The doctor wants me to lose a few pounds."

"We're all in that boat, so I'll make mine unsweet as well," Evelyn said.

"Same for me, too," Annie said. "I'm looking for a wedding dress. But I don't want to spend an arm and a leg on something I'll wear one time."

"I've been meaning to talk to you about that," Evelyn said. "You know, I still have my wedding dress. It's very simple and it could be altered if it was even close to something you like. But I don't want to presume anything, so you won't hurt my feelings if it's not your style."

"I would love to see it," Annie said.

"All right, I'll go dig it out of the attic."

Beulah left Annie and Evelyn hunting for the dress and promised to make any alterations needed before heading home to a quiet house. She'd picked up the Italian books on a whim when she passed the public library, but now that she had them, maybe it was the perfect distraction to get her mind off the farm and her financial future.

She read over several of the unfamiliar words used to greet one another.

"*Buongiorno. Come stai?*"

She closed the book and sighed. It was impossible. She had no idea how to pronounce the words, even if she could memorize the spelling. She wished Annie's friend Janice DeVechio, who was fluent in Italian, was there live and in person, so she could hear the words.

Beulah jumped when the phone shrilled.

"Beulah, oh honey, that Stella has been a gift from heaven," Betty said. "I regret every mean thing I said about her."

Betty's voice faded into sobs.

"None of us knew quite what to make of her last summer," Beulah said. "Don't cry now."

Sniffles sounded on the other end of the line. "I know what you said to me the other day is true. I just can't see out of this dark hole."

"Is Joe home?" Beulah wondered if she needed to cross the road. "Have you had your supper?"

Another sob and then silence while Beulah grew more alarmed. She was about to hang up and drive across the road when Betty finally answered.

"I guess you could call it supper. My life will never be the same; this ole diet's no livin' at all."

"Betty, we're all thankful you're alive. It seems hard now, but it'll get better, day by day."

"I reckon so," she sniffed. "I'm awful emotional right now. You can't imagine the thoughts I'm having. They're threatening to put me on antidepressants. Poor Joe, he's about done up."

"Maybe you need something like that to help you for a little while. It doesn't have to be permanent. Only until you see a little clearer."

"Will you come see me tomorrow?" Betty ask in a pitiful, child-like voice.

"Sure I will. I've been every day, haven't I?"

She hung up and sat back down at the kitchen table. The call depressed Beulah not a little. Betty was in a terrible state these days, and she worried her friend might not get better. Their section of May Hollow Road was coming apart at the seams, with everyone on diets, nerve pills, and antidepressants.

She tried to forget about her sugar deprivation, but sometimes the craving came on so strong, she broke down and sucked on hard candy to get a little bit of satisfaction. It was making her irritable, too. She had snapped at Annie over forgetting to put the chickens up last night. She was tempted to go on and take one of those nerve pills meant for her trip, that's how bad she felt. She never dreamed giving up sugar could be so very hard. The worst of it was her telling Annie and Evelyn. If she hadn't told, it would be between her and Dr. Bright. Now, her secret was out and she had accountability, the very thing she had hoped not to have.

On top of it all, they were square in the middle of the Christmas season with all the candy, cookies, pies, and cakes—all the delicacies that she looked forward to enjoying all year.

She needed to take the advice she had given Betty and not fall into a pity-hole. *Focus on something constructive*, she told herself. If she wanted to make sweets, she could. They would simply need to be given away. That was the solution. She could enjoy the process without eating the results.

The back door opened and Annie bustled in with a garment bag.

"Grandma, guess what? Evelyn's dress fits me. With your magical alterations, it should be perfect." Her granddaughter's face was flushed with excitement as she unzipped the long bag.

"Oh my," Beulah said, admiring the long, white gown. "How pretty. I remember when Evelyn wore it. We didn't know her at all, but got the invitation to the wedding up in Lexington, oh so many years ago. It was a fancy affair, with the reception held at the Idle Hour Country Club. I can't believe it's in such good shape."

"It's beautiful," Annie said. "Grandma, did you have a wedding dress?"

Beulah shook her head. "Not like this. Nobody I knew got married like this back then in the country. We were all too poor, I reckon, although no one realized we were poor, since everybody was in the same shape. We went to the preacher's house and I wore my Sunday dress and Fred wore his Sunday suit. That was all there was to it in those days."

"With Mama running off to Jellico, I guess she didn't either."

"I would have made her a nice dress," Beulah said, a wistful tone in her voice. "Evelyn's family was well off and they dressed her in the best store-bought clothes to be had. This was a right fine dress in its day."

"I love it. Although, it's a little tight in the back," Annie said. "I guess I'm a little rounder in the derriere than Evelyn was. She thought you could add a fold here. It needs to be hemmed a couple of inches, too."

"I can take care of that. You'll need to try it on for me again before I go to sewing."

"Want to work on something together?" Annie pointed to the Italian book and placed the garment bag over a chair.

"I'm trying to figure out saying 'How are you?' to start with," Beulah said and pointed to "*Come stai.*"

"Comay sty," Annie said.

"So, the *e* is like an *a*?"

"That's right," Annie said.

"And *stai* is like pig *sty*?" Beulah realized she hadn't even been close on the pronunciation.

"Close enough," Annie said, laughing.

Chapter Twenty-Two

"STAND STILL," HER grandmother commanded. Annie felt all of ten years old for a moment.

"I'm trying."

"I don't want to poke you with this pin. Just another minute."

"Grandma, how about a glass of tea? Or a piece of pie?"

Beulah sighed. "There's nothing I'd like better, but I can't."

"You're awful grumpy these days. It seems like mental health should count for something."

Annie looked down at Beulah, trying not to move in Evelyn's wedding dress, while her grandmother worked at the seam behind her.

Beulah glanced up at her, a pin gripped between the firm set of her mouth.

"There. You can take it off now."

Annie shimmied out of the long dress and put on her clothes.

"Is it this diet, or something more? I know you dread the flight, too."

Beulah took the pin out of her mouth and stuck it in the pin cushion.

"Oh, I reckon it's a little of everything. I'm all out of sorts with what all's happened to Betty and the dread of the trip weighing on me. I don't mean I'm not looking forward to seeing Benito and his family; I can't wait for that. Getting there's the problem. You're probably right about the sugar; I have been grumpy not having my normal sweets."

She sat on the bed and looked up at Annie, a strange expression on her face. "That's not all there is to it. There's something else I need to talk to you about."

Annie felt her legs go weak as she sat next to her. "You're not sick, Grandma?"

"No, nothing like that."

"Is it more about my dad?"

"No, I've said all I have to say on that subject. This is about the farm. You know I planned to leave this farm to you when I die, along with what I have in savings and all."

"Sure, you talked to me last summer, right before your knee surgery. But we don't need to go into all that again, do we?"

"My financial situation may be changing in a drastic way. The reason I have this farm paid for is because my daddy gave it to Fred and me. We've worked it, of course, made money from it and lived off it. Had Ephraim lived, he'd have inherited half of it, maybe even more. This is not the first time I've thought of such things, but with Ephraim leaving no heir, it all stopped there. Now, with this wonderful news of finding Benito, it does change things. It seems Benito would've inherited Ephraim's part. I don't know how these things work out in the legal world, but I have to do the right thing, whatever that is."

"Have you talked this over with Tom?"

"He's looking into it. I got him all my legal documents and he's examining all the facts. I wanted you to know, because it might affect what I told you last summer. You may not have it all."

"It's your land and your money. You need to do with it whatever you think best."

"It all belongs to God—I'm simply a steward, here for a little while. That's even more reason I want to do the right thing with Benito."

***

Annie followed Jake into the barn as he finished his chores. "After what Grandma told me about Dad not coming to see my mother when she was sick, I decided to back off about the wedding. I want him to come, but it made me realize I can't pressure him," Annie said, waiting for Jake as he hung buckets on hooks, leaned shovels and pitchforks in a corner of the tool room, and turned off the light. He took Annie's hand and led her through the dark from the barn entrance to the cottage.

"A good idea," he said. "He may not know until the last minute." It started to rain and they dashed the last few feet to the cottage.

Jake helped her off with her coat and then took off his own. "If the temperature drops, this will turn to snow."

"Snow would be nice. I haven't been here for a snowfall since high school, I guess. We should have a Christmas tree right about here, I think. Evelyn has an extra one we can use."

"How about a real tree?" he said, and stoked the fire.

"I haven't had a real tree since I was little. I can still smell the cedar if I think about it. Grandpa always cut one down for Mama and me, although Grandma preferred the artificial variety. Speaking of Grandma, she's having a time of it."

Jake stood, satisfied with the crackling fire. "Another houseguest too soon?"

"Stella is perfect for her. She steers clear of the kitchen and she's gone during the day. No, it's about the farm."

"What about the farm?"

"She thinks she owes Benito half the farm."

"Because he's Ephraim's son? I hadn't thought about it, but it makes sense."

"Tom is looking into the legal aspects. I hope you weren't counting on Grandma's farm with the cow plan."

"It's Joe's lease and I imagine he'll keep farming it for the foreseeable future."

They sat next to each other on the couch, enjoying the firelight and the closeness when Annie's phone buzzed. "I better check it, it might be Grandma needing something."

The text was from a number unfamiliar to Annie. *Can we talk soon?*

"Who is it?" Jake said.

Annie handed the phone to Jake. "Brett, I assume."

Jake read the text and she felt his body tense.

"That guy has nerve. Sending flowers and now texting? How did he get your number?"

"I have no idea. Jerry must have given it to him. He'll give up when he doesn't get any response. Don't worry about it."

Jake relaxed and leaned back on the couch. "That guy gets under my skin."

"He's harmless, but I kind of like this thing he's bringing out in you, this cave-man-my-woman business," she said, and giggled. "I promise, I'm all yours."

His blue eyes focused on her and softened, and he leaned in for a kiss.

***

Annie pulled into the parking lot of Richwood and passed a hearse coming out.

Oh no, she thought, hoping it wasn't one of her residents. The nursing facility was in a separate wing of the building, and she imagined the hearse came from there.

"Who passed?" Annie poked her head into Colleen's office.

"Emmitt Collier," Colleen said. Annie felt a wave of relief and then a twinge of guilt at the relief. "The Christmas decorations look wonderful, by the way. I've been meaning to tell you," Colleen said.

"Thanks to the volunteers. I pulled everything out and they attacked the boxes like little elves." Now that it was out about the change in management, Colleen was spending most of her time preparing information for the transition and had given Annie free rein to manage her days as she saw fit.

"Do you need me to help you with anything?" she asked.

Colleen looked up from her computer and smiled. "I can't think of anything. With two weeks before Christmas, I suppose we're down to the short rows," she said. "I'm reviewing a press release announcing the changes now."

"Let me know if anything comes up," Annie said.

She reached into her purse for the envelope that arrived in the mail yesterday. If she hurried, there would be time to visit with Vesta before the nine o'clock exercise class.

"Come in," Vesta's clear voice rang out after Annie knocked.

"It came yesterday." She handed the unopened letter to Vesta.

Vesta pushed back from her reading desk and turned the wheelchair to face Annie.

"Kentucky Historical Society," Vesta read aloud. "It's finally here. You didn't open it?"

"You should be the one to read it first."

Vesta pulled the letter out and smoothed it open on her lap, then held it up to read:

> *It is our pleasure to inform you the Josiah May House will be placed on the Kentucky historical register and qualifies for a highway marker. The text below will be on the marker. Please allow eight weeks for the marker to be delivered before scheduling your dedication. Please notify us of the dedication date so we may have official state representatives at the dedication.*

"Did they approve the text as we wrote it?" Annie asked.

"I'll read it to you," Vesta said.

> *The Josiah May House was built in 1789 and was the first stone house built in the Kentucky County of Virginia, prior to statehood in 1792. According to the diary of William Champ, the house was built by Josiah May, his sons, and slaves hired from neighbor John Douglas. The negro slaves queried the limestone and dry-laid it in the fashion of the May's native Scotland. Mortar was later added to the stone, along with a more decorative Palladian window in the early 1800s.*

"Exactly what you wrote," Annie said. "I wish we could have given a name to your ancestors."

Vesta smiled. "No, it's perfect. Douglas is the name we could have given them, but that was not their true name. Their African names are known now only to God, and so the text reads as it should."

Annie nodded. "We'll have to buy the historical marker, but Tom Childress said the local historical society will help raise money. But what about a date? Eight weeks puts it smack in the icy grip of February."

"It's waited all this time, I don't see why we can't wait until spring," Vesta said, and handed the letter back to Annie.

"Spring would be better. That gives us time to finish the renovations to the house and we can open it for tours and refreshments. It'll be a way to mark a new era."

"A new era," Vesta said and smiled. "I like that."

Before going back to her office, Annie stopped by Gin Taylor's room. The moon was waning in the last quarter, which boded well for all conversation.

She found Gin watching a soap opera, but the older woman clicked it off when Annie walked in, a small courtesy she appreciated.

"Ye must have known I needed to see ye," Gin said. "I'd planned to send for ye later today."

"Great minds think alike," Annie said. "How are you?"
"Truth is, a little troubled."

"What's the matter?"

"Your daddy was in town."

"You knew he was here?"

"I hear things from that end of the county. Ye other great uncle passed a few moons back, that'd be my ex-husband's brother. I keep in touch with his widder. She got a little money and the farmstead, rough as it is. Her government draw ain't too good. She needs every bit she can git."

Annie nodded, encouraging her to go on.

"Trouble's brewin' over Eddie's claim on the farm and house as a rightful heir since they ain't got no kids. See, her husband bought it on a land contract and never got around to puttin' her name on the deed. She called me a couple days ago, all in a dither. Seems Eddie's owed some money by his uncle and he's makin' a fuss over some document that gives him rights to the estate. Thing is, I don't doubt he might have such a document. But if he's got a heart at all, he ort to leave an old widder woman alone."

A legal matter over money. Of course. He'd had an ulterior reason to come to Somerville, and it was nothing about his daughter.

"I'm so sorry, Gin."

"I knowed ye would be, but we need some help. Could ye call your daddy and ask him to drop this claim? It would mean the world to her."

Annie sighed. "I doubt anything I say can influence him, but I'll look into it."

"That's all I'm asking. Look into it."

Chapter Twenty-Three

LINDY WAS WAITING for her in their regular booth at Bill's Diner for their standing Wednesday lunch.

"I'm glad you made it," Lindy said.

"I don't have a class until two o'clock today, so good timing," Annie said, and scooted into the seat.

"Ladies, what'll we have?" Bill bounded over from behind the grill and reminded Annie once again of a lovable St. Bernard. "Two weeks is all I have left to ask you that question."

"Deluxe burger for me," Lindy said.

"Salad and water for me." Annie pushed the tempting menu away.

"No burger?" Bill said.

"I'm trying to fit into a wedding dress," Annie said. "Please don't tempt me."

"So, the sale went through?" Lindy asked Bill.

"Yep. Money is in my pocket. They're paying me to keep serving until the contractors can get here the first of the year. It'll have a new look and a new menu," he said, his voice a little wistful. "The Bluebird Café is what they're calling it. All right, salad and burger coming up."

"I can't believe the diner is changing. After serving here in high school, I feel like it's a part of my family," Annie said.

"Bill would keep going if it weren't for Viola's Alzheimer's. But it sounds like the new chef will class up the joint a bit, which may not be all bad." Lindy pointed to the ripped seats and faded artificial flowers in the window sill.

"I kinda like it the way it is, fake flowers and all," Annie said. "At least the food will be healthier. Jake's providing the meat, so that will be helpful for us. Listen Lindy, I need to ask a favor. I know there's all this confidentiality stuff with legal matters, but I need to know about a claim against an estate. It seems my Dad had some other motives for coming to town and I'd like to get the facts, as much as I'm allowed to know, anyway."

"Sure, I can pull the file," she said. "Give me the details and I'll check on it."

Annie relayed the conversation with Gin.

"I'll check on it."

"I should have known all along there was another reason for him to be in Somerville. Why did I think it was me?"

"Because it's natural for a child to hope her parent starts acting like a parent."

"Let's talk about something happy. How's it going with Tom and Evelyn? I've not seen her all week."

"Dad's in love," Lindy said. "I mean, head over heels. He told me last night he's not going to run for county attorney again when his term ends next year. I think he plans to be married by then and wants to be free to travel with Evelyn."

"I think it's so sweet, to find love again in middle age—at any age, for that matter."

"He wants me to consider a run for county attorney in his place. What do you think about that? I'm not sure I could win. It roots me to this place."

"You are rooted," Annie laughed. "It seems like a good opportunity."

"Here's the thing. I came home and lived with Dad because, number one, he had this huge house he was rattling around in, and two, he was still grieving Mom. Now that he's dating Evelyn, I don't think he needs me like he did. Which makes me reexamine what I'm doing. A couple of years ago it made sense to come home and work with Dad. If I'm honest, I also wanted to see where things would go with Rob, and being in Somerville made it easier when he came home."

Annie remembered when Lindy's rock climbing ex-boyfriend came around last summer, flirting and leading on her friend, only to break her heart weeks later with a surprise marriage to another rock climber.

"Now things are different. Dad doesn't need me as much; he and Evelyn might live in our house if they get married. I'm not dating anyone and the potential of finding a future husband here in Somerville is near zero. I wonder if I should look at another opportunity, like Atlanta or even Chicago."

"Lindy, your dad will need you, even if he does get married."

"I know he will, but not like before."

"You're my best friend here and it would make me sad to see you go. On top of that, you may soon become my step-sister-in-law—is that a legal term?"

Her friend's eyes grew pensive.

"I'm not going to do anything impulsive, but I'm at a crossroads."

"You'd make a great county attorney." Annie reached for one of Lindy's French fries. "However, I will support you no matter what you decide. You know if Evelyn and Tom marry and they move into your house, she'll be like any other woman and want to make changes, to make it her own. How will you feel about that?"

"I don't mind, really. I'd like to take some of Mom's things that are special to me, if Dad doesn't care, but either way, I need to move out so they have some room if they decide to get married. If I stay here, I've thought about renovating a loft over in one of the downtown buildings."

"Short commute," Annie said.

"Steps away. A roommate would help—then I could put more into the renovations," she said.

"Somebody will turn up," Annie said. "I never had trouble finding roommates."

"Yes, and you lived in New York, I might remind you. Somerville is not a pool of prospects."

***

On Saturday morning, Annie was bundled up with a thermos

of coffee as she waited outside the back door. Dawn was breaking over the horizon and the air was cold and fresh, exhilarating. There was a pungent earthy smell in the air, a last whiff of fall as the landscape prepared for winter's sleep. Jake's truck crunched on the gravel drive, steam from the exhaust pipe curled up and over the truck bed.

"So where is this special tree?" Annie asked.

"Little ways out of town. It's a short drive, but it'll be worth it."

"Couldn't find one good enough on your own farm?"

"The soil's too good. Cedars do best on rocky land that's not as good for farming."

Annie took a sip of coffee and handed it to Jake. "Did you know Lindy's thinking about leaving Somerville?"

"Why?"

Annie told him about the conversation she had at lunch the day before.

"I can't blame her," he said. "Especially after doing the same thing myself."

"It's got to be hard to be single in a small town. I mean, we never experienced that. We both came back at the same time and found each other, then I pulled you out of Camille's clutches."

"I don't know if you pulled me or I leaped out. Anyway, I agree. It's tough."

He pulled into a farm lane and parked. "Right over there," he said, and pointed to a small but well-proportioned tree.

"It's so cute," Annie said, and hopped out of the truck before Jake could get around to open the door for her.

"Can trees be cute?" Jake grabbed the axe from the back of his truck bed and swung it over his shoulder.

"Of course, anything can be cute."

"Anything?"

She punched him playfully on the shoulder. "All right, let's see your lumberjack skills."

**

They decorated the tree with borrowed lights and shiny, colored balls from Evelyn, since they had no ornaments of their own. The effect was magical in the firelight. Annie cuddled next to Jake on the couch in front of the mesmerizing glow.

"Scott wants to know about our vows," Annie said. "He has a book of standard stuff or we can do our own. What do you want to do?"

"Maybe we pick a standard one and add a bit. As long as I'm promising to love and cherish you forever, I'll be telling the truth."

"We need to pick out wedding bands at Cheney's. Grandma is almost finished with the dress."

Jake stroked her hair as she leaned into his chest. The overwhelming comfort of his body gave her a sense of safety, an ability to feel deeply, knowing there was another with whom she could share the burdens. As much as she tamped down the bitter disappointment of her father's reason for the Somerville visit, it kept bubbling up.

"If Dad did make a claim on this widow's estate, and everything checks out as Gin said, should I call him? Is it my business?"

"Let's get the facts first and then you can decide."

"He's such a slippery fish, and Grandma is about to have a panic attack over flying, it makes me wonder again if we should marry here and wait until the spring for the barbecue. It's so expensive."

"No more than if we had a wedding here," Jake said. "Close to the same cost, but spread over more people. At the end of the day, I like it being more intimate. Then we don't have to worry about any ex-boyfriends crashing the wedding."

"Brett will go away. He called me and left another message. He wants to talk. Do you mind if I have one last conversation with him to clear the air? Does that bother you?"

"I'm not going to say I like it, but do what you have to do."

"I was thinking," she said. "Don't you have a single friend you could introduce to Lindy? A nearby love interest might keep her from moving away."

"I've been thinking about it. Everybody I know is married or getting married. There are a couple of friends in Cincinnati that might be possibilities. But they're pretty ensconced there, and that doesn't help our cause."

"I'm happy and I want to see her happy."

"What happened with Scott's brother? She hit it off with him at Scott and Mary Beth's wedding."

"They emailed a bit, but there wasn't any chemistry."

"Chemistry's not everything," Jake said.

"No, but it's something."

"You're right. It's easy for me to say when my fiancée happens to be someone I can't stop looking at on top of everything else I love about her."

"She's still pining over Rob, I can tell."

"Rob is married—she needs to move on. He made his choice," Jake said.

"She knows that, but in her mind, he's the gold standard for comparison."

***

Annie had expected to be busy with her job and wedding trip preparations, but without responsibilities beyond Christmas, her final days at Richwood slipped into visiting with the residents and running the scheduled activities.

It gave her more time to think about Lindy. There had to be some nice guy who lived in the area. Now that she thought about it, she had noticed a guy who visited one of the residents on a regular basis. He was nice looking, in his mid-twenties, she guessed. If she could get Lindy here one of the days when he was visiting his relative, sparks might fly.

Annie dialed Lindy. "Any word?"

"Yes, I was getting ready to call you. Everything Gin said is true."

"I figured as much. Disappointing, but I'm growing used to that common theme with him. Hey, can you come out here for lunch this Friday? There's a guy who visits his grandfather around lunchtime every Friday. He's about your age and I thought we could meet him."

"Really? What's his name?"

"David Scott." Annie felt a bit like Nancy Drew for sleuthing out his name earlier in the day.

"David Scott? I went to kindergarten with him. He's totally not my type," Lindy said.

"Have you seen him lately? He's not five anymore."

"I saw him yesterday. He's an accountant in the building next door. No way. But thanks for trying."

Annie sighed and hung up. Scratch matchmaking off the list of job possibilities.

Chapter Twenty-Four

BEULAH CRAVED A piece of creamy coconut pie so much it made her skin crawl. The desire was so strong, she had trouble focusing on anything else. Three times she had gone to the kitchen to whip up a pie, but three times she had turned herself around, resisting temptation. In her mind, she went back and forth. The church Christmas potluck was tomorrow and she had every right to make a pie, even if she didn't eat it. In fact, she usually made two. Could she make a pie and not save the filling remnant in the bowl for her own enjoyment? Was it possible to beat meringue and not lick the beaters afterwards?

Of course, she had to make pies. No way around it. She bustled back into the kitchen and gathered all the ingredients on the counter when she saw Evelyn's car pull into the driveway. Feeling as if she had been caught with her hand in the cookie jar, she scooted to the pantry and stuck the five-pound bag of sugar and flour behind the Quaker Oats. She turned the oatmeal so the Quaker stared at the pantry door, as if guarding her treasures.

She smoothed her hair and straightened her work dress.

"Hello," Evelyn said, shedding her coat in the back room. "Are you making a pie?"

Beulah glanced at the kitchen counter and saw the carton of eggs and bag of coconut. *Good grief.*

"I've lost a couple of pounds," Beulah said.

"I've lost five and I'm tickled to death. Who loses weight at Christmas? We should be proud of ourselves."

"Maybe we should celebrate with something sweet?" Beulah suggested.

"We have to hold out," Evelyn said. "We'll be eating pasta and homemade bread with Benito soon and it'll all be worth it."

"I'd rather have pie than noodles, but I reckon you're right." Beulah felt her resolve strengthening. "Has Tom mentioned anything on the farm situation?"

"He wants to meet with you tomorrow if you can stop by after lunch sometime. He's got an opinion for you."

Beulah nodded. "Can you tell me anything?"

"He hasn't told me anything. You know all that confidentiality stuff," she said with a wave of her hand.

"I give you permission to know everything," Beulah said. "Tom surely knows that."

"He does, but he still has to hear that from you, and probably in writing. On second thought, maybe you should have a glass of sweet tea. It might relax you a bit."

"Am I uptight?"

"You're not yourself these days. What's happened to Betty has shaken up us all. It's Christmas, Annie's about to get married, you're going on the biggest trip of your life, and you've got another houseguest on top of trying to lose weight. It's enough to make anybody a little crazy. I wanted to tell you that if it's too much with Stella, she can move in with me."

Beulah thought about the offer to take the shy woman with flyaway red hair off her hands. Truth was, she hadn't been a bit of trouble. Not like Rossella DeVechio, who had fought tooth and nail for her kitchen. In two weeks, Annie would be gone for good—out of her house, anyway. If Stella left too, it would be painfully quiet, and she had grown used to the noise and the presence of another living soul in the house.

"Stella and I have gotten along fine," Beulah said. "She's got a nice, quiet way about her. You should have seen her when she saw the Christmas tree after I decorated it, Evelyn. For a minute, she looked like a little girl, the lights shining in her eyes, and I saw beyond her thirty-something years to the rough childhood she had. I think she's my ministry right now. I want to help her get on her feet."

"What about Woody? Is he treating her well?"

"Here he is," Beulah said, as a truck passed the kitchen window. "You can ask him yourself."

Woody pushed open the back door without knocking.

"Hullo," he said. "Beulah, I put your chicken feed in the storage bin."

Woody was good about bringing her little gifts of chicken feed or tomato starts, or helping with her garden, installing her tomato cages or staking the beans. It was his way of payback for all the Sunday dinners, although it wasn't necessary.

"Speak of the devil," Evelyn said. "Sit down and visit with us."

Woody seems a little down, Beulah thought. *Not his normal, jovial self.*

"Something on your mind?" Beulah prodded.

"I'm glad you two are here," he said, and squirmed in the chair. "I took Stella to see Mama last week at the nursing home." Woody's mother was not in Richwood, the newer, clean, and bright assisted living facility with a nursing arm, but rather the older nursing home that became the end of the line for those patients who were bedfast. The place depressed Beulah, but she visited there at least once a month.

"How did it go?" Beulah asked.

"Not so good, to be honest. Mama told me not to marry Stella."

"How in the world did she do that?" Evelyn asked. Woody's mother was badly brain damaged.

Woody scooted closer to the table. "It went like this. I said 'Mama, I want you to meet Stella. We're thinking about gettin' hitched.' Then I positioned Stella in her line of sight. Mama narrowed her eyes at Stella like this," Woody demonstrated. "Then she closed one eye, like this," he squeezed one eye shut. "I knew right then she was against Stella."

"Maybe she was focusing so she could see her."

"Naw, that was her evil eye. My whole life, all she had to do was slit her eyes like that, drop one shut, and I knew I'd better stop whatever I was doing. Otherwise, a whupping was coming."

"But Woody, she doesn't even know Stella. How can you come to a conclusion based on one gesture that could have so many other explanations?"

"It's hard to explain, I grant ye, but I know Mama. She's been awful protective of me her whole life."

"You're forty-something years old," Evelyn said in a soothing voice. "Don't you think your mother wants to see you settled with someone who will love you and take care of you?"

"Try again," Beulah said. "Take Stella out next time you go and let's see what happens this next time. Maybe there was some other reason for her reaction. You don't want to lose a good opportunity because you mistook a look."

Woody thumped the table with his fingers for a minute and then nodded. "I reckon that won't hurt none. I'll take her out tomorrow when she gets off helping Betty and see what happens."

***

The next morning, Beulah sat in the plush waiting room for her meeting with Tom Childress. She was early, of course, as was her habit. It gave her time to gather her thoughts before a meeting or an appointment, rather than rushing out of breath and headlong into the next thing with no time for thinking. She had stated her request to the secretary and was asked to be seated. Or was she an executive assistant or administrative assistant? Did secretaries even exist anymore?

Beulah thumbed through a magazine and thought about the word. Secretary had come to mean something almost demeaning for women in the workforce who held everything together so an office could run like a well-oiled machine. Yet, in government, to be called the secretary of something or other was the highest office a person could hold in that department. If the Italian language had as many nuances she would be rowing upstream.

She put down the magazine and looked around the comfortable surroundings. A red Persian rug against the dark hardwood, lit by the gentle glow from a lamp. It was a soothing room and helped to calm her nerves, unlike the harsh surfaces of a hospital waiting room with cheap vinyl chairs and fluorescent lights.

"Beulah," Tom said, appearing behind the receptionist. "Come on back."

Tom Childress was a tall man who wore his khaki pants and collared shirt well. He and Evelyn would cut quite a fine figure together with their height and style.

"Please, have a seat." Tom indicated a comfortable club chair positioned at a round table. Beulah sat and put her pocketbook in her lap. She watched as he opened a thick file, put on reading glasses, and studied it a minute while she waited in silence.

"I'm checking to see what we have here before we discuss your concern. We updated your will after Fred passed, so that looks to be in good shape. And, you have Annie listed as your health care surrogate and power of attorney. That all still good?"

"Oh yes, I don't have any changes there," she said.

"I'm glad you have that taken care of. You'd be surprised how many farm people don't address these things until it's too late."

"You know me, I'm practical to a fault," Beulah said.

"Even the most practical of people don't always get around to hiring a lawyer. Now, let's get down to the reason for your visit. Your case is intriguing, Beulah. In fact, I teach a law class and we took it as a case study and examined all aspects of it. Without boring you on all the legal research, we found one precedent in the Commonwealth of Kentucky." Tom paused and took off his glasses. She leaned forward in her seat.

"That's when a case like yours is ruled on by a higher court. It was back in 1991, called Wood versus Wingfield. Basically, the answer is yes. Benito as an heir is entitled to a one-half, undivided share in the original May farm. But he would need to sue in order to contest the will, and he may never do that."

"Sue?" Beulah said. "There's no need for that."

"Now, I know what kind of person you are, Beulah, and that you want to be fair and don't believe in lawsuits and such. I admire that in a person, but I also wouldn't be doing my job if I didn't tell you that if it comes to a suit, that is what he would be entitled to receive. There's also room for discussion and settlement long before that."

Beulah leaned back and clutched her pocketbook.

"Can I get you some water?" he asked.

"No, I'm fine. It's what I suspected."

"Now, here's the thing," Tom dangled his reading glasses over her file. "Based on what you've told me about him, he may not sue. Either way, he does have a legal right, should he pursue it, and there is DNA testing, should you want to confirm he is Ephraim's heir."

"Oh no," Beulah said. "There's no need for that. We know he's Ephraim's son. Besides that, we tracked him down. He didn't come looking for us." Of course, Tom knew all this.

"Now that Benito's been found, the longer time goes on and he doesn't pursue a case, the weaker his claim becomes. When you read the Wingfield case it talks about the concept of *ouster* or what is commonly called *squatter's rights*."

"Squatter?" Beulah said, feeling the blood rush to her face. "Good heavens Tom! How can I be called a squatter after this farm has been in my family for generations?"

"It's simply a way of saying you have rights as the person who has inhabited the land," he said. "I know this must be a lot for you to think about. The bottom line is this: Benito may never pursue his claim. It can be left alone, just as it's been left alone for all these years. Of course, it could crop up again in the future, but like I said, the longer it goes, the stronger your case. You also need to consider your financial position and the prospect of splitting that in half at your age."

Beulah nodded and took a deep breath. There was much to ponder. She wanted to abide by the laws of man in this life, yet there was an even higher standard she was obligated to serve. The farm was a gift to her. How could she hold onto it with closed hands knowing half of it rightfully belonged to Benito?

She knew the answer, yet it opened up so many more questions.

That evening, Beulah made chicken and vegetable soup. She was grateful that at least one of her favorite foods was allowed on her diet. Her skirts *were* a smidge looser. The worst time of it she'd had so far was making the coconut pies for the church's Christmas potluck. Traditionally, Betty Gibson sent over all manner of her candies this time of year, but with her still recovering, she had not been able to make any candy, a blessing in disguise.

Betty's body was healing, but her mental state did not seem any better. Beulah could count on a phone call every morning at ten o'clock between Betty's morning TV shows recounting all the hardships she was facing. Everything from the restrictive diet, to all her aches and pains, to all the ways Joe irritated her. If it went more than ten minutes, Beulah found a reason to get off the phone. Life was too short for negative rigmarole.

Woody's truck rolled in and he dropped Stella off at the back door. Beulah wiped her hands on a tea towel and turned to greet her, anxious for a report on how Stella's job interview had gone.

"I start as a reference librarian right after the first of the year. Oh Beulah, I'm so thrilled."

Beulah clapped her hands together. "Wonderful!" Then she noticed Stella's nose was red and swollen. "What happened to your nose?"

Stella's face darkened. "We went to see Woody's mama again after my job interview," she said. "When I leaned over the bed so she could see me, her arm jerked up and smacked me right in the face. She gave me a nosebleed and I thought for a minute it was broken. One of the nurses got me to lay back in an empty bed while they packed it with gauze and put ice on it. It's not broken, but it sure does hurt."

Beulah peered at Stella's red, freckled nose. "My lands! That was quite a blow."

"At least it was after my job interview," Stella said.

Beulah could not imagine Patsy Patterson moving a muscle, yet she did seem to have some sort of reaction to Stella.

Stella slumped at the kitchen table. "Beulah, I don't know if I want to marry Woody."

Beulah sat back in her chair. "You don't?"

Stella burst into tears. Beulah went into the bathroom and rolled off a wad of toilet paper and handed it to her.

"Now, now, you don't have to marry him if you don't want."

"You all have been so good to me, opening your home and your community. If I don't marry Woody, I won't have that," she sniffed.

"That's not true, Stella. You have a job now and you'll still be a part of our community if you live here. We'll make sure of it. But I thought you liked Woody?"

"I do like Woody, and I was awful flattered that a man, any man, would pay attention to me like he did. But the more time we spend together, the more I realize we're different people. I think I fell in love with all of you all more than him. Maybe Woody was a way into that world, this family I never had. Is that wrong?"

"It's never wrong to make a change before you make a more permanent mistake."

"I don't have a car since I sold it to pay off my debts in Chicago, but I thought if I could find a small apartment I could rent downtown, then I could walk to work and the grocery, even to church. Maybe I can save up to buy a vehicle again. I haven't thought it all through, but I want to stay in Somerville. For the first time in my whole life, I belong somewhere."

"Of course, we want you to stay here," Beulah said.

"I dread telling Betty I got a new job," Stella said. "She's more capable than she lets on, but she'll cry, I know."

"Betty cries at everything these days, so don't add that to your worries. We'll start weaning you off after Christmas so she can get used to doing things for herself. It'll all work out."

Chapter Twenty-Five

"THIS PLACE IS cozy," Lindy said, looking around Jake's cottage. "This is the kind of thing I need, except I'd like it to be walking distance to the office. Does Jake mind us using it for a girl's night?"

"He's out to dinner with some guys from the bank. He loves it because I cleaned it last night, knowing you were coming over," Annie grinned. "Sounds like you're leaning towards hanging around?" Annie said, and tossed the dressing into the salad.

"I'll probably end up here. Somerville is like a magnet. You think you can leave, but you can't. I signed up on one of those online dating sites, so we'll see."

"You did?"

"When you live in a small town, what else can you do? There's no one in my church. I'm not into the bar scene. Do you think it's a bad idea?"

"Not at all. I've heard of lots of people with good experiences. I think it all depends on the guys you get matched with. At least in a small town you can check up on people."

"I filled out this lengthy questionnaire. So now I start getting matches. I can ignore or respond. Maybe it will be fun."

Annie put the food on the coffee table. "Jake and I have a habit of eating here in front of the fireplace on these cold winter nights. This okay with you?"

"Perfect." Lindy sat on the couch. "Did you know Stella and Woody are breaking up?"

"How do you know?"

"Stella called me. She's looking for a place to rent downtown. I'm not sure Woody even knows it yet."

"I'm glad for Stella. I think Woody needs to hire a housekeeper who can make fried chicken and be done with it."

Lindy laughed. "Maybe Stella and I can live together. Do you think we'd make good roommates?"

"She's pretty easy to live with, from my point of view. I think rolling through the foster care system has made her adaptable to any environment." Annie thought about how little she had seen Stella since she moved in. "She's gone during the day of course, and in the evenings, she stays in her room and reads most of the time. I think you'd get along fine."

"Well, I won't require her to make fried chicken," Lindy said.

After dinner, they curled up on the couch, falling into the comfortable talk of good friends.

"Have you talked to your dad about his claim on the widow's estate?"

"Not yet. I keep debating whether I need to mention it or not. On one hand, it's none of my business. But, if I could influence him to do the right thing for once, that would be something. I'm also plain mad at him for acting like he came to see Jake and me when there was a selfish, financial motivation. He has a great job, but he lives big and he gambles, and those are all his choices. To take away the entire financial security of a widow, someone who has little future source of income, that's despicable."

"In his defense, if he has a signed document and he is owed the money, there's nothing wrong with that, legally."

"Legally, but ethically? What am I saying? He's never operated by those rules, anyway."

"It may not do any good to say anything, but if it makes you feel better, you should go for it."

***

Annie found Vesta sitting in the living area with a book open on her lap.

"What are you reading?"

Vesta lifted up the spine for Annie to read and looked at her over the top of her reading glasses.

"*The Odyssey*. Oh my, you are in for it."

Vesta chuckled. "It's quite the adventure." She marked her place with a leather bookmark, then set the book aside.

"Have you thought any more about setting the date for the historical marker dedication?" Annie asked.

"When are you having the wedding barbecue?"

"We're thinking Derby Day." Annie sat down in the chair next to Vesta's wheelchair.

"Why don't we schedule it for earlier that afternoon? That way your Italian family can be there for the dedication."

"I hadn't thought about that late in the spring, but it would be nice to have everyone there and then go right into the party. Are you sure you don't want to do it earlier?"

"I'm sure. I believe our ancestors would like the dedication connected to a wedding celebration," Vesta said. "I've already got a list of who to invite from my side of the family."

"Good. We can send out invitations when we send out the party invites. And they'll all be invited to the barbecue as well."

Vesta's face grew serious. "Annie, the list is in my Bible, should something happen to me between now and then."

"Vesta, don't say that. This whole thing happened because of you. I'm counting on you being there."

"I hope it's God's plan, but just in case, it's in my Bible."

"Understood. Now, it's time for the lecture on old Christmas. If you're ready, I'll wheel you into the meeting room."

After settling Vesta in the front row, Annie greeted the lecturer, made the introductions to the residents, and turned the program over to him.

While he talked, Annie stood in the back of the room next to the door. Lonnie Caldwell sauntered by and brushed against her arm. He turned and winked at her. One of the nursing assistants caught Annie's eye and giggled. Annie shook her head and rolled her eyes.

After the lecture concluded, Annie went back to her office to find yet another bouquet of yellow roses. She fumed the whole way to Vesta's room and placed them on her bedside table for her to enjoy when she returned.

This had to stop. Brett needed to know he could not continue sending flowers, holding a torch, and imagining Jake did not exist. Two difficult conversations needed to be had, one with Brett and one with her father, and the sooner the better.

At the end of the workday, Annie stayed in her office to make the first call, whispering a prayer as she waited for her father to pick up.

"Annie?"

She was surprised he answered and it took her a second to find the words.

"Dad, where are you?"

"Back home now. It sure was fine to see you. That Jake is a real fellow," he said. "Successful and sharp. You did good."

Successful. It occurred to her that his very exuberance over her marriage was selfish. Now she would be another man's responsibility. Not that he had ever helped her much financially, but the weight of any perceived responsibility for her was off him forever.

The thought emboldened her.

"Dad, you mentioned some legal business in Somerville when you were here. What was that about, exactly?"

"A little money that's owed to me. Nothing for you to worry about."

"You see, Dad, it is something I worry about. This claim on your uncle's estate might leave an old woman with nothing to live on. You have a good job and a steady income. That doesn't seem right to me."

"Look here, she's got plenty to live on with social security, but she's not my business anyway. I want what's owed me and I have the document to show for it."

Annie was quiet for a moment. There was silence on the other end of the line as well before she spoke.

"I understand." Her voice chilled through the phone line. "You have all the information for the wedding, right? We'll see you soon, okay?"

"I got everything."

"Bring Sofia."

"Who?"

"Sofia, wasn't that her name?"

"Sure, yeah. We'll see."

Annie felt sick to her stomach. She gave herself a few minutes, took a deep breath, and dialed Brett's number. He picked it up on the first ring.

"I'm getting off work now. If you'd like to meet me at the diner, I can be there in ten minutes. We can talk there."

"Looking forward to it," he said. Annie had debated on where to meet Brett. The diner risked opening herself up to gossip by meeting her old boyfriend in public, but with what she needed to say to him, the public aspect worked in her favor. If they were in private, he might try to make some inappropriate move.

She got there first and slid into a booth. Bill was already gone for the day and the restaurant would close in another hour, so it was empty except for a couple on the other side of the room.

Brett came in and smiled when he saw her. Lindy's word *hunky* came to mind. He was handsome, and seemed to have himself together with the business and all. But there was no attraction for her anymore, and she had to get this across to him. She would be gentle, but firm. A mixture of grace and truth.

He sat down across from her and they ordered coffee.

"Thanks for meeting me. Gosh, this is kind of weird for me. I hope I can get this all out."

"You don't have to say anything," Annie said. "Some things are better left unsaid."

"That's true, but I really need to say this." He took a sip of coffee and cleared his throat. "These last three years have been pretty rough. You know, going through something like divorce makes you look at your life and how you got here. Especially the last few weeks, seeing you and remembering how we were together. I didn't deserve you back then. I was a stupid and arrogant kid, and I am sorry for how I treated you at the end."

"Brett, we were both so immature. Like I said, all is forgiven."

"Well, it made me want all that again. I realized I married the wrong kind of girl, that's why I ended up like I did."

"I'm so flattered by all this. Truly, but I'm engaged to Jake. I love him. We're going to be married soon. You have to stop sending the flowers. You understand, don't you?"

Brett frowned and cocked his head

"What flowers?"

"The yellow roses."

"Annie, I didn't send flowers. Look, here's the thing. I want a girl like you. I know you and Jake are together; it makes all this so much easier since you're happy and everything. I mean, I don't want this to be weird since you and I dated, and since the two of you are friends, but I wanted to see if you could set me up with Lindy Childress?"

Chapter Twenty-Six

ANNIE FOUND LONNIE Caldwell holding court with three giggling ladies in the dining room.

"May I see you a moment?"

"Yes, dear, you may," Lonnie said, giving each of the ladies a squeeze on the shoulder before he joined Annie on the couch in the living area.

"You sent all those yellow roses," she said.

Lonnie cleared his throat. *"And the yellow rose of Texas shall be mine forever more."*

He sang the line in a strong, clear voice.

"Lonnie, I'm not from Texas," she said, not able to stifle her grin.

"No, but you remind me an awful lot of a little yellow rose I knew when I was a young man. She looked exactly like you. Lovely, dark hair and a beautiful figure. I met her when I was stationed in San Antonio and I've never forgotten her. When I saw you as the spitting image, I couldn't help myself."

"You're incorrigible."

"I'm also a lot of fun." His eyes sparkled with mischief.

***

Annie sat next to Vesta as the children's choir from Somerville Baptist sang their hearts out to the aging residents of Richwood Manor, finishing their caroling with a cheerful "We Wish You a Merry Christmas."

When the program concluded, Annie stood up and thanked the choir and then invited everyone into the dining room for cookies and cocoa.

She leaned close to Vesta's ear. "Do you want me to take you in the dining room?"

Vesta shook her head. "I'd like to go back to my room." Annie wasn't surprised at the answer. It had been a big week.

"Jerome and Vivian are coming early tomorrow and I need to rest up," she said, as if she had disappointed Annie.

"I understand. You've been amazing all month. How do you think it all went?" Annie asked.

"The dulcimers are always my favorite. Such beautiful and gentle music. The lectures and the reading of *A Christmas Carol* was also a treat. Didn't he have a lovely voice? Dickens requires a strong baritone, in my opinion."

"Is there anything you recommend changing next year? I can leave some notes for the new director."

Vesta was silent and Annie thought she hadn't heard her. She wheeled the chair into her room and turned it so she could face Vesta. She was smiling back at Annie, her almond eyes bright and shining. "I wouldn't change a thing, it was all so magical."

"What about the Christmas tree craft? That was a little cheesy, you have to admit. Colleen recommended a craft for dexterity and it was all I could come up with on short notice. Having adults glue stars and ornaments on paper Christmas trees was pretty lame."

Vesta's high, tinkling laugh floated in the air. "Extraordinary, all of it. Even the Christmas trees."

"I'm going to miss you," Annie said.

"Miss me? You're having a wonderful Christmas and then flying off to Italy to get married. Don't even think about me or this place. That's an order from the Mayor of Richwood. Do you understand?" Vesta held her index finger up, giving Annie a stern look.

Annie felt her throat tighten. "Just the same, I'll miss you,

Vesta Givens. Have a very merry Christmas. I'll see you as soon as I get home." She leaned down and kissed the old woman's cheek. Vesta's hand went around Annie's head and held her there for a few moments. The emotion choked Annie and she couldn't speak when she finally pulled away and looked down at Vesta.

She was at the door when Vesta found her voice. "I almost forgot," she said, motioning her hand for Annie to come back. Her gnarled hand reached for a bedside drawer.

"We said no Christmas gifts," Annie said.

"This is not a Christmas gift. It's a wedding gift."

Annie opened the carefully wrapped package and brought out a small white cardboard box. Lifting the box top off, an antique cameo with a baby blue background lay on the soft satin folds inside the box.

"Vesta, it's beautiful."

"It's your something blue, and it can be your something old as well."

"And something borrowed, I assume."

"No, this is yours to keep. It was my grandmother's and I thought we should keep it in the family." Vesta smiled. "Do you know where that saying comes from? The old is something significant and sacred to the family and represents what you are leaving behind. Keeping the old item in your new life is a reminder of your heritage. The new item represents the new challenges you are taking on as a married woman. The borrowed item represents the steadfast affection of someone who will be with you during the transition. The color blue represents purity."

"I can't tell you what this gift means to me." Annie clasped the cameo to her chest. "Nor what you mean to me."

***

Annie intended to get home in time to help Beulah with the food preparations, but she found Stella filling the role, apron on and carrying a platter of ham and biscuits to the dining room table.

"Sorry I'm so late," Annie called from the back room.

"The Gibsons let Stella go early, so she's been helping me all afternoon," Beulah said.

"Betty's doing well," Stella reported, picking up a pitcher of tea and a glass. "Her granddaughter is out on school break and volunteered to stay through the weekend. They have family coming in next week, so it looks like I'll have a little time off before I start my library job."

"I should run over and say hello while everyone's there," Annie said.

"We're fine here. You've got another hour before everyone gets here," Beulah called from the dining room.

Annie changed clothes and looked wistfully at her empty suitcase. There was much to do before they got on a plane in less than forty-eight hours.

Across the road, the Gibson house was bustling with energy. Loud and talkative by nature, the Gibson family was made up of daughters and granddaughters who all seemed to want to take the stage. How in the world did quiet Joe survive the hubbub?

The door opened and Annie was swept into the room, handed a glass of eggnog, and passed from daughter to granddaughter until she somehow landed on the sofa next to Betty.

Betty looked better than she had seen her since her heart surgery. Her color was good, her straight, white teeth surrounded by pink-painted lips, and her curly, blonde hair coifed in a new style.

"What about my pretty grand girls? If Hollywood knew what was in this house, they'd bust down the door."

"They are beauties."

"Annie, I'm proud you and Jake are getting married. Beulah doubted it would ever happen, but I knew from day one you two were meant for each other."

"Well, Betty, you always do see these things ahead of everyone else."

"I heard your daddy was in town. Will he still be coming to the wedding? Beulah said he was, but I do wonder." Betty left the question of her father's reliability hang in the air. In the past, Annie would have defended her father. This time, she decided to speak the simple truth.

"I sure hope so."

***

Jake had arrived at Beulah's by the time she peeled herself away from the last Gibson and made it back across the road. Stella and Woody were both there, but not as a couple. Annie observed an awkward few moments in the beginning, but then they seemed to settle into the space and be okay with the presence of the other.

Lindy arrived with an Italian cream cake, and with her entrance, the small party was complete. Tom and Evelyn were in Lexington gathering her mother for the Christmas dinner at Evelyn's house, so they would miss the special fried oysters Beulah had prepared, a Christmas Eve tradition.

The dining room table, last used when Mama DeVechio prepared an Italian feast, was set with Beulah's Christmas plates. Annie and Stella carried platters of oysters, ham and biscuits, mashed potatoes, green beans, macaroni and cheese, and corn pudding to the table. Lindy's Italian cream cake and Beulah's coconut pie sat on the buffet, along with a punch bowl of Beulah's home-made eggnog flavored with a tad of bourbon, another Christmas tradition.

Lindy regaled them with profiles of the potential dates she was matched with on the online dating site. Stella and Woody were all ears and on the edge of their seats. Annie, for one, was happy not to be involved in that discussion and held Jake's hand under the table.

They cleared the dirty dishes and served up slices of cake and pie. Annie poured coffee.

"I'm thrilled we all decided not to give each other gifts this year since we are going to Italy. But Stella and Woody, since you two are staying here to hold the fort down for all of us, we all pitched in and got you each something. If you don't like it, blame Annie and Lindy," Beulah said.

"Me in particular," Lindy said. "But I think you'll like it." Lindy handed each of them an envelope.

"What is this?" Stella's eyes glowed with excitement, then she laughed as she read the note inside. "Did Woody get the same thing?"

"Exactly. Now we're all in the same boat."

"What is it?" Woody said, and stared at the piece of paper as if it were a rattlesnake.

"It's a membership to the online dating service."

"Well I'll be," Woody said. "Can I request a good cook?"

The festive air suspended a second, but when Stella's belly laugh shook her whole body, they all exploded into laughter.

"Now, let's focus on the best gift," Beulah said. "Jake, you have such a nice voice. Do you mind to read out loud the second chapter of Luke? My Bible is right here."

Chapter Twenty-Seven

LATE CHRISTMAS AFTERNOON, Beulah sat with Betty Gibson on the couch in her small living room. They had recounted their Christmas dinners and Betty had moved on to bemoaning her loss of Stella.

"Law have mercy, I sure will miss her. Peggy says I'm able to start doing for myself, but she don't understand how hard it is."

The last part of the sentence was a fervent whisper as Peggy entered.

"The doctor says you need to be doing more, from what I've heard," Beulah said.

"Doctors, doctors, I know my own self better than a doctor. I don't know as I'll ever be the same again. And you all running off to Italy without me in my time of need. I can hardly bear it." Betty sniffled and dabbed at her eyes. Joe sat down next to them in his La-Z-Boy.

"I'm mighty glad you're going," he said. "I sure do look forward to meeting Ephraim's boy when he comes over here. You know, I reckon we're about the same age," Joe mused, tamping vanilla scented tobacco down into his pipe.

"Well, that is something to look forward to," Betty admitted.

"That's right," Beulah said. "We'll have a big barbecue and a historical marker dedication all on the same day. We'll need your help coordinating it all, so you need to get your strength up. The best way to do that is start doing some things for yourself."

"Do you really need my help for the party?" Betty asked, looking like the teenager Beulah remembered back when she first started dating Joe.

"Sure thing. You know, I've been thinking I'd as soon give up that Thanksgiving potluck at church. It's not the same without Ernestina here anymore. Pastor Gillum will need you in top form for that job."

"You're right, I still have some good years left in me," Betty said, and seemed to grow a couple of inches.

"Joe here needs taken care of, too," Beulah said, pushing her luck, but taking the chance anyway.

Betty frowned at Joe while he sucked on his pipe, oblivious to the conversation. "Joe Gibson, put down that pipe. You know you can't smoke around me."

***

The trip was here. With all the festivities of Christmas, Beulah had been too busy to think about it, but now in this last dark night before departure, she lay in her bed and imagined hurtling over the Atlantic Ocean in a metal tube.

Her breathing quickened as she pictured nothing but steel and rivets between her and an atmosphere no human could survive. Delicate wings ready to snap at any bump or jiggle, plunging her whole family into an icy sea. Her heart raced, and she sat up in bed while cold sweat dripped down her back and chest. What if she got sick from the motion of it? Or worse, had her own heart attack up in the air with no ambulance to rush her into an emergency room like Betty Gibson?

She turned on the bedside lamp and reached for her Bible. *Good heavens. What is the matter with me these days?* It was the season of her Lord's birth and yet she had gone three days in a row without reading his words. She opened it and read, the familiar passages relaxing her. When she closed her Bible and placed it back on the table, her mind and heart were a bit calmer.

She was deathly afraid of stepping on that airplane, there was no doubt about it, and about meeting Benito and his family. What if he thought she was some fancy woman with sophisticated airs? Would he be terribly disappointed to find out she was a simple farm woman who spent her life raising a garden, going to church, and tending to her family?

Her decision was made about the farm. But it was going to be an awful financial hardship on her when she returned. Either way, it was the right thing to do.

There was another niggling concern about the wedding itself. It wasn't Annie and Jake, but rather Annie's father, Eddie Taylor. Annie had already reserved a room for him and sent him an email with flight options. She hoped and prayed her granddaughter would not face an awful disappointment on her wedding day.

She recalled her favorite verse, the one she struggled with the most: *Cast all your anxiety on Him because He cares for you.*

She did cast her anxiety on him, but many times she picked it right back up again. That was what she had done all month. *Lord help me in my unbelief,* she prayed, because unbelief was the very root of it.

***

"Don't worry," Annie said as Jake reached for the two large suitcases. "One of those will go back with Evelyn when they leave so we will travel lighter on the honeymoon. It's full of wedding stuff."

"I'm your man," he said. "Anything else?"

"That's it. I can get my carry-on." Beulah and Annie watched Jake carry the suitcases down the steps, his broad shoulders and muscular arms making the load seem light.

Beulah followed Annie into her bedroom as she sat on the edge of the bed that had served as her home base since middle school. When Annie and Jake returned home from their honeymoon trip in two weeks, she would move into Jake's cottage. In the spring, if all went well, they would move into the old stone house, continuing the eight generations of Mays who had inhabited it since the late 1700s.

Annie looked at her with brimming eyes.

"Are you thinking what I'm thinking?" Annie asked.

"That Fred and Jo Anne should be here?"

Annie nodded and Beulah put her arm around her and pulled her close.

"Grandpa should be giving me away," Annie said.

"If he were living, he'd sure be making a fuss about going to Italy with us," Beulah said, and they both laughed.

"He wasn't much on traveling," Annie said. "I could hardly get him to visit me in Bowling Green during college."

"He'll be with us; don't you worry about that."

"Grandma, I'm nervous about getting married. Is that normal?"

"It's as right as rain," she said, and squeezed her hand. "You're facing a big step and the unknown is scary. I've had to realize that myself these last few days. Now, I could use some help making sure I've got everything I need."

Annie followed her across the hall. "All right, we went through your packing list. Did you get the family pictures to show Ephraim?"

"That's right, I knew I was missing something. Can I keep them with me on the plane?"

"Sure, we'll put those in your carry-on bag. Are you ready?"

"Where's Stella?"

"Downstairs waiting on your last instructions," Annie said. She was joking, since Beulah had given the same set of instructions to Stella about five times already.

In the kitchen, Stella stood in a corner, her hands clasped together, as if trying to stay out of the way of all the bustling.

"Now Stella," Beulah said, "don't forget to let the chickens out every morning. Feed and water them, and be sure to put them up in the evening, or else a weasel or raccoon might get in there. Call Joe if the cows get out. Remember to open up the cabinet doors below the sink if it gets down close to zero while we're gone. Those pipes will freeze right up. There's a snow shovel on the back porch. What else? Oh, get the mail and leave it on the dining room table. I'll go through it all when I get home." Beulah studied the linoleum floor for a minute. "I think that's it. Annie said you can call Evelyn's phone if you need anything. She got some plan to make it work in Italy."

"Yes, ma'am. It'll be fine. I'll take good care of the house, and I promise no candles," Stella said.

"Good heavens, I didn't even think about that. No candles, please."

"No, ma'am. No fire of any kind."

Beulah wished Stella had left that last part off. It was another thing to worry about on top of a whole mountain of worries.

"Bye, Stella." Annie hugged her. "Thank you for taking care of everything."

"Check on Betty and Joe, too, please." Beulah extended her hand to Stella. "I do thank you."

Finally, out the door and piled into the car, Jake paused at the Wilder driveway where Tom pulled out behind them with Evelyn and Lindy.

They were off.

Chapter Twenty-Eight

"THIS FIRST FLIGHT will be short," Annie told Beulah. "A quick hop to Detroit from Lexington. We have a couple of hours there and then we get on the flight to Rome. If you decide to take the nerve pill, I would wait for the big flight."

Her grandmother nodded. She was nervous as a cat.

"Beulah, what are you looking forward to most about meeting Benito?" Jake asked.

Distraction, Annie thought. Exactly what her grandmother needed.

Beulah relaxed. "Oh, everything. I want to hug him, for one thing. I want to meet Angelina, his children, and grandchildren. I want to see the farm where he lived and worked until he moved to the village. I want him to see the pictures I'm bringing and to tell him some stories of his father. I want to know what his life was like all these years."

"Remember when you see each other, you kiss him on his right cheek. Always go to the right first. Otherwise, you'll end up kissing on the lips," Annie explained.

"*Buongiorno* is hello," Beulah said.

"Good day, but it works as hello. You could say *ciao* or *buongiorno*. Although by the time we see Benito it will be afternoon. Then you say *buona sera*."

"I'll never remember all of this," Beulah said, and shook her head.

***

They breezed through check-in and security in the small Lexington airport and settled into the commuter plane in what seemed like no time. Annie sat next to Beulah with Jake and Lindy across the aisle, Tom and Evelyn behind them. Her grandmother's white-knuckled grip on the seat made Annie wonder if her advice to wait for the nerve pill was sound. Her grandmother paid full attention to the emergency procedure demonstration and studied the aircraft safety card after the flight attendant finished. Annie smiled, thinking how easy it was to identify a passenger on their first flight.

"We're going to push back now and then we'll taxi before taking off," she told Beulah.

Her grandmother nodded and leaned her head back against the seat and closed her eyes.

"Now we're getting ready to take off. When the nose goes up, you'll feel a lift in the back—that's a good sign. There'll be some bumps but that's all normal and part of the landing gear going up, okay? Do you want to hold my hand?"

Her grandmother grabbed her hand, keeping her eyes shut tight. The plane took off and her grip tightened. Up, up, and then leveling off, her grandmother opened one cautious eye. Annie smiled, avoiding Jake's eyes across the aisle, afraid she would laugh out loud. It was a real fear, there was no doubt.

"You're doing great." Beulah nodded and leaned her head back into the seat. They settled into cruising altitude and in a short time began the descent into Detroit. When the plane hit a few bumps on the way down, Beulah grabbed the armrests, her eyes bulging.

"It's only turbulence," Annie said.

"How in tarnation did you do this for a living?" her grandmother said.

"You get used to it." Beulah nodded and leaned back into the seat again, her hands still grasping the armrest.

Annie looked across her at Jake and he raised his eyebrows. They exchanged knowing looks, and when he winked at her, Annie felt her heart melt again for the hundred-thousandth time. Soon, he would be her husband. The thought amazed, excited, and scared her.

When they touched down, Beulah smiled as if she had won a cake baking contest. Jake got their carry-ons from the overhead while Tom attended to Lindy and Evelyn's bags. Annie hung back with Jake as they walked to the next connection.

"She's a nervous wreck," Annie whispered.

"Maybe she'll relax once we get in the air and she can stretch out," Jake said.

"If she doesn't, it's going to be a very long eight hours."

***

Beulah felt trapped.

Her stomach was tied in knots, the compression hose pressed her legs so hard she looked like a puckered mushroom, and her knees wobbled like pudding. The short ride to Detroit had about sent her over the edge, and now she was looking at multiples of that stressful hour. Who knew an airplane could bounce like that in the air, as if they hit invisible speed bumps?

If she called Woody right now, he could be in Detroit in six hours, pick her up, and be back home in another six hours of hard driving. She would never have to see the inside of an airplane again as long as she lived.

That also meant not meeting Benito. Of course, he could come here in the spring for the wedding barbecue. But what if he chickened out like she was about to do now? Then they would never meet if one of them didn't cross the water.

"Grandma, how about a ride," Annie said, and stood next to a motorized cart driven by a smiling senior citizen.

"I reckon so." Her legs felt like thick noodles.

"I'll ride with you," she said. "Meet you all at the gate."

They zoomed off, the driver making small talk with Annie and beeping people out of the way while Beulah clutched her pocketbook and held on for dear life.

Lord, if you get me home safe, I'll never leave Kentucky again.

They settled into seats at the gate and waited for the rest of the group. Annie took out a bottle of water and handed it to her.

"What's this for?" she asked.

"Drink it. You need to hydrate. Save a little for your nerve pill."

"I haven't decided to take it," Beulah said, a little perturbed at all this bossing around her granddaughter was doing.

"Grandma, you're not the first person to be afraid to fly. As a flight attendant, I saw everything, and your doctor was right to give you something to help you. You won't get addicted by taking one pill for a special occasion. You need to rest. If you arrive exhausted, it makes the jetlag so much worse. You're in Italy such a short time, and if you spend half of it in bed, that's less time to be with Benito."

Benito. She didn't want to miss a minute with her nephew.

Beulah sighed. "All right," she said, and dug in her purse for the prescription bottle. She took it out and tried to open it, but her hands shook.

Annie took it from her and unscrewed the top. "Here."

Beulah put it in her mouth, took a sip of water, and then swallowed. Evelyn, Tom, Jake, and Lindy arrived as she finished off the water bottle.

Beulah waited for something dramatic to happen to her body. If she had an allergic reaction, better to be on American soil. In fact, it might even get her out of this mess.

"Annie Taylor, please report to gate B16," a voice bellowed out over the loud speaker, and Annie hopped up and went to the desk. Maybe it meant the flight was cancelled and they could all go home. Annie came back, a big smile plastered on her face and holding papers in her hand.

"We got upgraded," she said. "New boarding passes. We're all in business class."

"Wow," Tom said. "How did that happen?"

"I think it is a gift from my old boss, Bob Vichy. I'll bet Janice called him. He's the only one I know who could have gotten that done."

"How lovely," Evelyn said. "Beulah, we'll all be with you."

"I've never flown business class," Lindy said.

The happy chatter flowed and Beulah smiled back at everyone, feeling quite serene about the whole thing.

"Let's go," Annie said as announcements blared. Beulah followed along behind the others like a sheep to the slaughter. Except, somehow, she didn't care.

The business class seat was quite different from the tiny chair from Lexington to Detroit. There was a television screen and earphones, a menu, a bottle of water, and a bag with socks, toothpaste and toothbrush, lip balm, and mouthwash.

My, haven't they thought of everything. Beulah tucked the bag into a pocket and pushed a button. Her seat hummed and shifted until it stretched out into a bed. Beulah smiled. *If Fred could see me now.*

"Grandma, we're getting ready to take off, you have to sit up and put your seat belt on."

Beulah looked at her granddaughter. Goodness, she was high-handed these days. Beulah ignored her and lay back on the seat, stretching her tiptoes out as far as she could.

Annie reached across her and moved her into a sitting position. Across the aisle, she heard Evelyn say, "She never takes anything. I was afraid of this."

Beulah pushed the button again and felt the seat recline back.

"Mrs. Campbell," a flight attendant peered down into Beulah's face from up above. "We need you to sit up now so we can take off. Let's put your seat belt on here. I'll let you know when you can lay down, okay?"

Beulah nodded, thinking flight attendants were a bossy lot. It made no sense to sit up when her head lolled around in that position. It seemed much safer to lay back down. She reached for the button again, but Annie clamped down on her hand. Beulah pulled her hand away and placed it in her lap.

Time blurred and soon a tray of food appeared in front of her. She hadn't even realized she was hungry and attacked it with gusto. After the meal, a cart came by with ice cream and toppings, and of course, there was nothing to do but have a fully decorated hot fudge sundae. Afterwards, she lay back, sated with the first sweets she'd had in a while, and slept.

She awoke again to another tray of food, and this time coffee. Morning light was shining through a tiny, oval window and her head felt full of cotton. This was not her bedroom.

Lindy sat next to her now and Beulah realized she was on the airplane. Annie had been her seatmate, or had she? It all seemed blurry. Annie was now across the aisle from Lindy, eating breakfast and talking to Jake. Evelyn stared at her with a silly half grin, as if Beulah had just performed a magic trick.

"You slept well."

"I reckon I did. I don't remember taking off."

"You were pretty relaxed at that point," Evelyn said. "We're about forty-five minutes from landing. If you need to use the restroom, you better go now."

Chapter Twenty-Nine

BENITO AND ANGELINA had arranged for a van and driver to pick up the crowd while Jake and Annie had rented a car they could use afterwards on the honeymoon. In baggage claim, they found a woman holding a sign reading, *May family*. Even though none of them went by the surname of May, it was her grandmother's maiden name, and the name of Benito's father.

Two hours later, they arrived in Montefollonico and checked into La Chiusa, the hotel where Annie and Janice had stayed on their search for Benito a couple of months before. It was colder now, but many of the rooms had fireplaces. She shared a room with Lindy. Beulah and Evelyn shared a room together while Jake and Tom had their own smaller rooms.

They made a plan to take an hour getting settled in, then meet up so a driver could take them to Vincenzo's farm.

Annie was giddy with anticipation, both for her grandmother to meet her nephew and her own wedding. She was also nervous—she was getting married for goodness sake. While Lindy took a shower, she checked with the front desk to see if her father had checked in yet.

No, Eddie Taylor had not arrived.

Annie wrapped up in a sweater and sauntered around the property, taking in the view of the Val D'Orcia under the canopy of horse chestnut trees, where she and Janice had dined with Benito and Angelina in October. Christmas lights crisscrossed the patio and red and green streamers hung from the iron sconces. Although it was cold outside, winter had yet to arrive in full force.

Back in the room, she unpacked her dress and laid the cameo on the dressing table. It was in a room such as this one that she had a turning point in her relationship with Jake when she and Janice were here before. She had been so overcome with fears at that point, so worried that she was like her father when it came to relationships, that she almost threw away all that Jake offered her. With God's help, she was able to see through it and claim the love that she had been given. Less secure men might have given up on her, but not Jake.

"I feel better," Lindy said, her hair wet and wrapped in a towel. "It's amazing what a little water and soap can do after a long trip. Oh, look at your dress."

"It turned out nice, didn't it?" Annie said, and admired the work her grandmother had done.

"It's beautiful."

***

Beulah looked fresh as a daisy and back to her old self when the driver loaded them up for the short drive down the hill to Vincenzo's farm. Annie pointed out the olive groves and the vineyard as they approached the farmhouse, as well as the *cinta senese* pigs that grazed in the pasture on the hillside.

"It's beautiful," Beulah said.

"*Bellissimo!*" the driver said.

"Yes, *bellissimo.*"

"There they are." Annie pointed to the family waiting outside the farmhouse.

Beulah drew in her breath. "Benito," she said, almost reverently.

"Yes, there's Benito and Angelina next to him. That's Vincenzo and his son, Luca. His wife Anna and their daughter, Rosa. I don't know the other woman, so that must be Paola. I didn't get to meet her last time."

"Look at them," Beulah said in amazement. "My family."

Engulfed by kisses and hugs as each one stumbled out of the van, Beulah waited to the end. Overcome with emotion, she needed the extra few seconds to compose herself.

Tom helped Beulah out last, and as soon as she touched the ground, she was in Benito's strong arms. He spoke melodious words in his own language, yet it transcended translation and Beulah understood. Annie heard sniffling all around her while Lindy captured the moment on film, something Beulah would treasure later.

"Paola," Vincenzo introduced his sister to Annie and they kissed. The woman had dark hair, but grayish-blue eyes, like Benito and like Beulah. "We're so happy to meet you," she said.

Inside the farmhouse, the table held platters of cheeses, meats, olives, and bread.

"From our vineyard," Vincenzo said, and poured a small cup of red wine for everyone. "Now, *papà* has practiced English so he could speak to you."

Beulah clasped her hands and looked at Benito as a mother seeing her newborn son for the first time. Annie could not remember seeing her grandmother smile like that since her grandfather was alive.

"I welcome my aunt Beulah, and my family and friends from America, to this happy celebration for Annie and Jake. We are happy you choose here for the wedding. We feel much love and honor." He looked at Beulah, lifted his glass of wine, and drank.

They all drank to the toast, a communion of love and family, of one mind and spirit.

After a three-hour lunch, Benito and Angelina took them for a tour of Montefollonico. Angelina was excited to show Annie the chapel. Vincenzo and Paola went with them while Anna and the children stayed to clean up from the lunch.

"Here," Vincenzo said, and they entered the ceramic shop in the private chapel that formerly belonged to the nobility of Montefollonico.

"It's perfect," Annie said, her voice echoing off the high ceilings. The stone chapel was designed to seat up to a hundred people. It was too large for their small wedding, but they could arrange the small party up front and make it feel intimate.

"The shop owner is our friend. This is her last day before holiday and she will move her tables out of the way, so the altar will be open. We put chairs here. Okay?"

Annie smiled. "It's the best," Jake said. "If she needs help moving anything, we'd be glad to do that."

"No, no, it's okay. We have the whole village offering to help. Everyone knows about your visit and everyone is so pleased for *papà*."

Up and down the cobblestone streets, they looked at the church, the restaurants, the grocery store, the bank, the bar outside the city gate, and the beautiful palazzo gardens. It was a small town and took a short time to see. They ended at Benito and Angelina's house, where they went up the stairs to their living area. Angelina ushered them outside to the terrace where they took in the view of Pienza, then back inside to the warmth of the living room, where Benito built a fire.

"If it were summer, we have wedding dinner in garden," Vincenzo said. "Instead, we host at the hotel for dinner."

"Wherever we have the dinner, it will be fine. As long as we are all together," Annie assured them.

"*Mamma* wants to know if you want to rehearse the wedding?" Paola asked.

"Well, I suppose a little practice won't hurt." Annie looked at Jake.

"*Perfetto*. We practice night before wedding. And we have made the arrangements for dinner that Evelyn requested after rehearsal. It's in a wine cave, down the hill at a famous winery. Very nice. When will your *papà* arrive?" Paola asked.

"Tomorrow, I hope, but I'm not sure. He never told me."

"What do you think about music? We have local accordion player, who is very good and does weddings. Is that okay?" Paola said.

"I didn't even think about music," Annie admitted. An accordion was not the first instrument that came to mind when she dreamed about her wedding, but since there was no piano in the chapel, an accordion was as good as anything else.

"Yes, thank you," Annie nodded.

"And pictures?" Paola asked, pointing to Lindy, who snapped shots of Benito and Beulah. "Can she do that?"

"Yes, Lindy plans to take pictures. Paola, I would like to have some flowers, a bouquet. Do you have a recommendation?"

"*Si*, yes, in Montepulciano. Emm," she said, trying to find a word. "What kind?"

"Something with sunflowers, a simple arrangement."

"Okay, I get for you."

In a corner of the room, Beulah showed Benito the pictures she had brought with her, Paola translating for them. Evelyn, Tom, and Jake sat in front of the fire talking with Vincenzo about the farm and the recent olive oil harvest. Angelina motioned Annie over, and Lindy scooted next to her on the couch.

"They've talked nonstop," Lindy said, and nodded her head toward Benito and Beulah.

"Did you get some good pictures?"

"Tons. Even some video."

"She'll be living off this night for a long time to come," Annie said. "I'm glad you got pictures, but I want to hold this memory in my heart. The warmth and lighting in the room, the soft hum of conversation, the way it feels, even. It's like there's a fog of contentment hanging over the house."

The door buzzer sounded, startling everyone for a moment. Vincenzo disappeared down the steps. They heard a woman's voice speaking animatedly with Vincenzo and then laughter. Annie recognized the voice and stood in disbelief.

"Janice! You made it after all," Annie laughed and hugged her friend before she could take off her coat. "How did you find us?"

"I got to the hotel and they said you all were gone, so I tried Benito's house first. If you weren't here, I was hoping I could remember how to get out to Vincenzo's farm."

Annie introduced Janice to Tom and Lindy, but she already knew everyone else, having been with Annie on the first trip to find Benito.

Janice removed her coat and settled in next to the fire after greeting everyone. Angelina and Paola busied themselves in the kitchen while Vincenzo moved over to Beulah and Benito to help translate. Annie watched the two, imagining what was being said. One minute they both looked very serious, and another minute they laughed, catching up on many lost years.

"How did you manage to get away?" Annie asked.

"Jimmy called his sister and begged. He was tired of seeing me mope around," she laughed. "She took the kids to her house for a few days. I have to be back the day after the wedding, but at least I'm here."

"I'm so glad," Annie said. "Lindy was going to give up being the photographer so I could have someone stand up with me. Now I get both."

"I don't know, you may wish you had hired a professional," Lindy said. "Remember, you get what you pay for."

"So, when does your dad arrive?" Janice said.

"Today, maybe. I don't know. Maybe he won't come at all. You know the history."

Janice nodded. "How disappointed will you be if he doesn't come?"

Annie looked down into the foam of her cappuccino, and wondered how to be truthful and positive at the same time.

"Awfully. It's my wedding and I hope he comes through for me," she sighed. "He also has a history of not coming through for me."

"Hope is good," Janice said. "As long as it's peppered with a good dose of reality."

After a while, Paola brought out some prosciutto, olives, and bread.

"A light supper, before you go back to hotel," she said. "We know you must be tired. If you can stay awake a little longer, you will have a good night's rest."

They ate, talked some more, and then the driver who waited down at the bar picked them up.

"*A domani, cimitero*," Benito said, and Beulah nodded as if she understood, giving each other a last kiss, first on the right side and then on the left.

"What did he say?" Jake asked.

"Tomorrow, the cemetery. We'll see where his mother, Elena, is buried."

"Beulah, how was it seeing him and talking to him?" Evelyn asked, when they returned to the hotel.

"He reminds me so much of Ephraim. And even Daddy. They even have some of the same mannerisms. How is that when he never knew either one of them?"

"It's a mystery," Evelyn said, and Annie saw her look at Tom and share an intimate moment of their own. Love and the results of love, a mystery indeed, she thought, as she looked at Jake.

Janice and Lindy sat around the fireplace, deep in discussion, when Annie slipped inside the room sometime later. She listened to their conversation while she dug pajamas out of the suitcase.

"Lindy, what kind of life could you have had together anyway? You're not a rock climber. You're nine-to-five. Let it go."

"I know, he's married now, I have to let it go. It's not him, it's the idea that I may never feel that way again. What if no one comes along that was like that?"

"Someone will come along better than that," Janice said. "Someone who will support you in your career, someone you can share similar interests with, not someone who goes off for months at a time to climb a mountain in Nepal. That's well and good if you're interested in the same lifestyle. Be patient, don't settle, and write your non-negotiables."

"My what?" Lindy said, as Annie settled herself in the vacant chair.

"Your non-negotiables. Write down five things you must have in the next relationship. Like his faith, or his sense of humor, or loyalty or integrity. Whatever the five things are for you. Then, measure everybody to that standard. You might not have gone out with this Rob guy if you'd done that."

"But we had so much chemistry."

"Look where chemistry got you. Seriously, it's one of the five things, but it can't be the only thing. Not enough for a marriage. Anybody got a cigarette?"

"Janice, not tonight," Annie said, laughing.

"If not tonight, when? I can't smoke in front of your grandmother."

"We raised tobacco, remember? You can smoke in front of my family."

Janice looked at Lindy. "I don't smoke, but these Italian cigarettes are so good."

"They're Marlboros," Annie said. "She thinks because they're bought here, they're better somehow."

"They are better, Lindy. I'll get us a pack and you can try one. You'll see."

"You two can smoke tonight if you want. I'm going to bed," Annie said.

"Delayed gratification is good," Janice said. "Bed tonight, smokes tomorrow."

Lindy giggled and Annie turned to look at her two best friends.

"I love you two."

Chapter Thirty

THE TRIP TO the cemetery had been poignant, as it was when she and Janice followed Benito there two months before. She learned that Benito's mother was the shopkeeper's daughter who her great uncle Ephraim had fallen in love with while he was stationed in Naples during the Italian campaign in World War II. He left Naples for the battle of Anzio, which is where he was killed in February 1944. Elena never saw him again. She bore his son without knowing Ephraim's fate, but finally believing the worst had happened. When Roberto Gianelli came along, Elena decided he would make a good father for her son and she made a life with him.

Although it could never be certain what Ephraim would have done had he lived, it was certain how Elena felt about him. Upon her death, with her second husband preceding her to the grave, she had placed *Maggio* or *May* in her name as if she had married Ephraim before his death. Annie wondered if maybe she did marry him in the best way they knew how.

Couldn't a couple still say vows to each other and before God, marrying each other until the legal aspects could be filed later when a war wasn't raging? The details of their love were lost to time now, with Benito as sole legacy of what had been.

They had made their way inside the U-shaped cemetery, lined on three sides with vaults from the ground to around twenty feet high. Each grave was marked by a white marble square in the wall with the name, birth date, and death date, along with a picture of the deceased and a vase holding real or artificial flowers.

Benito led Beulah by the hand to the vault, two stones up from the ground, where Elena's body rested.

"*Mamma*," he said, pointing to the inscription, *Elena Caivano Maggio Gianelli. N. 5 Settembre 1924—M. 17 Gennaio, 2000.*

A respectful silence had settled over the group as they watched Benito and Beulah stand in front of the vault. They left in silence, leaving Elena in her resting place.

After the cemetery, Paola, Janice, Lindy, and Annie went to the chapel to approve the planned placement of candles and chairs.

"I think we need some greenery around the candles," Janice said.

"Yes, I think so," Paola said. "The cypress trees will make nice cuttings and they have tiny cones we can use for decoration."

"It's a good thing we're on the move so much today," Lindy said. "I haven't stayed up that late talking in a long time."

Janice put her arm around Lindy. "You can sleep when you're dead. For now, we are in Italy."

Bundled against the cool weather and armed with scissors, the girls scrambled around the hillside below the medieval walls. They snipped cypress branches and gathered the tree's small cones in baskets provided by Angelina.

Paola proved to be an artist as she directed the placement of the greenery and cones around the simple, white candles that lined the aisles and provided a backdrop to the altar.

"Perfect," Annie declared, and stood back to admire the work.

"*Basta*, enough," Paola said. "*Andiamo a Montepulciano.*"

"I need to change clothes," Janice said. "Lindy, do you have the room key?"

"Here you go. Will you grab my purse? It's on the bed."

Lindy turned to Annie. "Have you heard from your dad?"

"When I call, it goes to voicemail. He could be in the air."

"Maybe he'll be here by the time we get back from

Montepulciano tonight."

"Rehearsal is not until tomorrow night; he still has time. How do you think Grandma's doing? I've hardly spent time with her since we arrived," Annie said.

"Beulah tried to plug in her hot rollers. Evelyn stopped her before she burned them out and gave her a converter. She was mystified that we all don't have the same electric voltage," Lindy said.

"I forgot to tell her that."

"She used her new bank card at the ATM machine in the square, although the euro conversion is a challenge," Lindy said.

"For a woman who stashes cash in a coffee can in the freezer, this is a big deal," Annie said. They laughed and then Lindy grew serious.

"Gosh, Annie, can you believe you're going to be married in a couple of days?"

"In some ways, I can't, but in other ways, it's like I've been heading toward this day all my life. I am nervous," she said. "It's a life-altering step, but one I can't imagine not taking."

***

"Want to ride with me and Vincenzo to Montepulciano?" Jake said. He held open the car door.

"Sure do," Annie said as Janice slid into the front with Vincenzo. Tom drove the van with Evelyn, Scott, Mary Beth, and Lindy; Beulah, snatching every minute possible with her nephew, rode with Benito, Luca, and Rosa.

"Vincenzo, tell us about Luca and Rosa. What are their personalities like?" Annie asked.

"Rosa, she takes after her *mamma*. She is good girl, very shy, likes music, and sings very nice. Anna is also musical. Luca, very smart and hard worker, but lately he make trouble."

"What kind of trouble?" Annie asked.

"Stay out too late, not do his lessons, and there are boys he is with we don't like very much. Not respectful. We are a bit worried about him. Fifteen is a hard age for children. How you say, crossroads?"

"I'm sorry to hear that," she said. "It must be hard to watch them go through the teenage years. I know I gave my grandparents their fair share of trouble. Jake, here, on the other hand, was the model son."

"Right." He squeezed her knee.

"Seriously, Vincenzo. Grandma was always saying, 'If you could be more like Jake.'"

"Of course, sons and the *mammas* or aunts, always easy. Sons and *papàs*. Different story."

***

In Montepulciano, they ate in a crowded restaurant known for large Florentine steaks served rare. Elbow to elbow on bench seats under a vaulted brick ceiling, they ate a sumptuous dinner of beef, bitter greens, and stewed white beans. The talk and laughter had kept Annie from thinking of her father, but as they approached Montefollonico in the darkness, she was eager to check with the front desk.

"No, Mr. Taylor has not arrived yet," the desk clerk said. "Should I still hold the room?"

"Yes, please," she said before turning away. Even if he arrived tomorrow, she had hoped he would come in time to enjoy being a part of the pre-wedding festivities. As it stood now, he would barely make it in time for the rehearsal and the wedding.

"Any word?" Jake met her in the lobby and clasped her hand.

"Nothing," she sighed. "Do you think something's happened to him? I suppose he could have had an accident."

"He never said for sure when he would get here. Let's not worry about it. I'll try calling tomorrow. If we don't get him, I'll see if I can call the bar."

Annie nodded. "We're supposed to go to Siena tomorrow. Should I stay back here in case he comes?"

"I don't think so. You have a group of people who have made every effort and sacrifice to be with us during the days leading up to the wedding. Let's not throw that away for the one who isn't here."

"You're right. How did I get so lucky?"

"I'm glad you feel that way. As a matter of fact, I'm thinking I should capitalize on that feeling you're feeling. How about a limoncello and a kiss—or two?" he grinned.

"How about we drop the limoncello?"

"Even better."

Chapter Thirty-One

THE NEXT MORNING, Beulah sat close to the fireplace in their hotel room after Evelyn had fetched her a *caffè americano* from the hotel restaurant. Evelyn had gone back out to have coffee with Tom, so she was alone with the big, steaming cup and her thoughts.

Why is it called an americano? It was far stronger than her Maxwell House, and that was about as American as it got. Then there were the espressos so stout they could stand a spoon on its end. Annie had explained that espressos were taken in tiny little cups and thrown back in a gulp. For people who seemed to appreciate lingering over long meals, the espresso habit was a mystery.

The Italians also liked their frothy cappuccinos in the morning, dolloped with a meringue-like topping, but it was actually foamy milk. Beulah liked her coffee black. She took a sip and stared into the fire, thankful it was a bit stronger since she wasn't sleeping as well. Her routine was upside down with the time change and an unfamiliar hotel. She had tried keeping her watch on home time, but it made her feel worse to look at it and realize it was three o'clock in the morning when she was waking up. It had been easier to change to Italian time and forget about home.

Flying at forty-thousand feet in a tin can, sleeping in her clothes, lurching through traffic with cars whizzing past at the speed of sound, and the rolling in her stomach that told her she was off her schedule had all been worth it when she laid eyes on Benito. She could not stop looking at him, just as she felt his eyes on her, even when she was looking away.

His wife, Angelina, was a lovely woman. Her nephew had found a good life partner, and the evidence of love in the family with their two children was obvious. Vincenzo looked less like her side of the family and took more after Angelina. Vincenzo's wife, Anna, was very quiet and shy. Paola, his single daughter who lived in London, had a good mix of both. The surprising resemblance to Benito, and of course Ephraim, was passed down to Luca, the teenage grandson. The one difference was that Luca had brown eyes instead of Ephraim's blue. Benito's granddaughter, Rosa, took more after Anna with her shy eyes and long, dark hair.

Beulah marveled at the similar mannerisms, such as the way Benito hung a finger through a belt loop, just as Ephraim used to do. There was also the half smile she remembered so well from Ephraim, an expression Benito had on his face almost all the time, as if he was about to tell a joke.

Lindy had already taken many pictures, treasures Beulah planned to frame, but not before taking them to church and parading them around to everyone she knew. She looked back now to the shame she felt when she realized Ephraim had a child in Italy, out of wedlock, disturbed that her brother was not the perfect hero. What had seemed bad at the time was now meant for good, and for that, she now rejoiced with prayers of gratitude.

She wiggled her toes and took another sip of the steamy liquid. Two things weighed heavy on her, even amidst this wonderful trip. One was the impending talk with Benito about his inheritance. She wanted to do it before she lost her courage. The temptation to simply enjoy the trip and their new relationship was strong. He was doing well, not rich by any means, but he had made a good life. Yet, she could not live with herself if she didn't put this thing right. Her family had not provided for him. Benito was Ephraim's son, and he deserved to be recognized as an heir.

She hadn't wanted to bring up such an awkward subject on their first meeting, but it was time. She would, sometime today during the visit to Siena. Her bank was prepared with the wire transfer, all arranged with Jake's assistance before she left. All that was now needed was Benito's bank information so the transaction could be complete.

Second, there was Eddie Taylor. Beulah feared he would not show up for the wedding, disappointing Annie once again in this most public of ways. He had always lacked courage to do the right thing. Still, she prayed with all her heart he would be a man and father and do this one, most important act for Annie.

***

Beulah rode to Siena with Benito, Luca, and Rosa, while the rest of the party followed in other cars. Luca and Rosa both spoke English and had peppered Beulah with questions about America. Luca switched back and forth into Italian so Benito could keep up with the conversation. Benito drove expertly down the hill into the Val D'Orcia, then toward the green signs indicating an *autostrada*, which Beulah took to be the Italian equivalent of the interstate.

"I go to school there," Luca said, and pointed to a building halfway up the mountain. "Rosa is in another school."

"Do you like school?" Beulah asked.

Luca shrugged his shoulders. "Eez okay. I prefer other things."

Benito gave his grandson a stern look through the rearview mirror and shook his finger.

Luca looked at Beulah sheepishly. "*Nonno* understands more English than you think," he said.

"He cares about you and wants you to do well," she said.

"*Si, lo so,*" Luca sat back in the car and stared out the window.

Once on the outskirts of Siena, Benito parked, and they waited for the others to gather so they could move as a group toward the medieval gate that welcomed them into the old town.

"*Siena e molto importante,*" Benito said, emphasizing the statement with his right hand, palm open. As Benito talked, Vincenzo translated.

"Siena influenced art and architecture in the Middle Ages and is a unique example of a medieval town this large. It was also the center of commerce and even banking until around the thirteenth or fourteenth century. There were many battles with Florence since they were great rivals. As we go inside, you will see the large square in the center called the *Piazza del Campo*. This is where the *Palio di Siena* takes place twice a year. Perhaps you have seen pictures before? There is much color and festivity during that time."

Beulah listened along with the others, fascinated by a place much older than even the oldest building in the States. *It's quite extraordinary,* she thought, as she realized how young America must seem to these ancient cultures.

"*Allora,*" Benito said, and stood. "*Andiamo.*"

"We go towards the piazza," Vincenzo said.

Beulah walked slow, not wanting to aggravate her knee, and Benito stayed with her, as they poked along behind the others. He noted points of interest while Vincenzo hung back with them to translate.

Ancient buildings hugged both sides of the street. Sometimes Benito took her hand and moved her to the side as a car or small truck edged along with the people. She could imagine the congestion in summer when the tourists turned out in droves. They turned a corner and spilled into the great piazza that sloped downward, a breathtaking site anchored by a great brick bell tower. Beulah stood for a moment and looked up, and then around, taking all of it in and pressing it into her memory for the years to come.

"*Bellissimo,*" Benito said.

"*Bellissimo,*" Beulah agreed.

"*Torre del Mangia,*" Benito said, and pointed to the tall tower.

The tower was made of red bricks, but the top seemed to be a gray stone, maybe marble, and was quite a feat of engineering so many years ago.

"*Torre del Mangia* means Tower of the Eater," Vincenzo said with a smile. "It refers to the first bell ringer, who must have liked eating."

"What do you think?" Annie came over from where the others stood and admired the piazza, and locked arms with Beulah.

"It is one of the most incredible things I've ever seen in my whole life," Beulah said.

Benito spoke to Vincenzo in rolling Italian.

"*Papà* says we see some churches and some art, and then we eat."

The churches in Italy looked so different from what Beulah knew back home in Kentucky. Magnificent structures with stone carvings, stained glass windows, and paintings called frescos painted in wet plaster on the walls and ceilings. She was proud of the fact her ancestor had laid the cornerstone of Somerville Baptist Church back in the 1800s. But by comparison, these churches were far older and grander.

The ceilings reached to the heavens, as if they were trying to capture God and hold him inside the building. It was so unlike the utilitarian metal churches that popped up everywhere in the countryside these days. While there could be too much focus on a building, there was also something beautiful about reflecting the creator through fine workmanship.

By lunch time, Beulah felt overwhelmed with all she had taken in with her eyes, and bodily tired with the extra caution over uneven brick and stone streets.

It was a great relief when they sat down to lunch. She ordered a salad, called *insalata mista*, but was a little disappointed to find out there was no blue cheese dressing to dollop on top of it when it finally came. Not only that, the salad was brought out after the meal instead of before. She contented herself with the red wine vinegar and oil that was placed on the table in place of real salad dressing.

There was always bread in baskets, Beulah discovered, no matter where they ate. Benito ordered a plate of cured meats and pasta dishes for them to share. There was comfort in having him make all the choices, even though the menu did have an explanation in English, due to all the tourists who visited Siena. After lunch, they ordered espressos and she wondered if now might be a good time to address the inheritance issue.

There may be a better time later, but the issue had weighed so heavy upon her, she hesitated to wait another day. With the wedding rehearsal tomorrow, any number of distractions might arise and keep her from it. While Paola was telling the rest of the group more about the history between Florence and Siena, she said a small prayer asking for the right words and for wisdom. Then she asked Vincenzo to move next to her and Benito in order to translate.

Beulah took another sip of her espresso, which tasted like liquid tobacco, and then decided to gulp the whole thing, feeling very Italian for the moment.

Vincenzo traded seats so he would be at the end of the table with his father and Beulah. She touched him lightly on the arm. "I'd like to speak to Benito about something very important. Should we stay here or go outside?"

"*Si*, of course, no I think here is fine. It will be more private than the street."

Beulah turned to Benito and addressed him directly.

"Benito, you are my brother's son. If Ephraim had lived, he would have inherited the farm where I now live along with me. Very little money came with it, but the land was paid for by the time my parents died." She paused and waited while Vincenzo translated.

"My husband and I worked the farm all our lives, but we had a great advantage by having land free and clear. I talked to an attorney, and we examined the inheritance and the value of the farm when it was deeded to us after my parents died. I don't think you have use for half a farm in America, but I plan to wire your half of the money, at its current rate as valued by our county."

There, she had said it. She waited while Vincenzo translated.

Benito listened, frowned, and then broke out into a landslide of Italian, waving his hands and shaking his head. All of this directed at Vincenzo. Beulah's heart sank. She had offended him in some way. Vincenzo started to translate, but Benito interrupted, his eyes hard, and now using both hands to emphasize a point.

Vincenzo responded in Italian and it seemed they argued for a moment. Then Vincenzo laughed and she recognized the word "*papa.*" Benito folded his arms, raised his eyebrows, and turned his head away as if he smelled something bad.

"You saw *papà's* reaction. He say 'absolutely not.' His stepfather was good to him, and provided for him as a son. His grandparents also took great care, so he was not without inheritance. What you have is yours. The farm should belong to you entirely." She felt Benito squeeze her hand. "Even more, he said you are his elder and a widow, and if anything, he should provide for you should you ever need it."

Beulah felt a tear slide down her cheek.

"He provide for me?" The thought had never even occurred to her. What generosity of spirit this man, her nephew, showed. All this time she had worried, even lost sleep, over her future. Yet, he was thinking he should take care of her. For the first time in the two years since the death of Fred, she felt the comfort of having a kinsman to lean on, knowing he was here if she ever needed it. Beulah squeezed Benito's hand, and she knew he saw and felt her gratitude.

"But is there anything I can give you? Anything at all to give you some kind of inheritance you should have from my parents?" She pressed, not wanting to hold anything back from this man.

Vincenzo translated and Benito was quiet a moment, then responded to Vincenzo. They went back and forth, growing more animated. Beulah recognized the word "*mamma*," although the language came out in rolling intonations that sounded like music.

Back and forth they went, hand gestures flying, and then Vincenzo nodded and turned to Beulah.

"There is one thing that might be considered."

Beulah pondered the request with equal part fear and excitement. There was nothing to do but to agree—it was very little to ask after she was prepared to give Benito half the value of the farm. Yet, it was a great deal of responsibility, and she did not want to fail them.

Before she got too far down the road of thinking about it—or worrying about it for that matter—Benito needed to discuss it with his family. Until then, she would not share their conversation; it was a matter that needed wisdom and prayer.

The day in Siena had been exhausting, both physically and emotionally, and she was rather glad there was nothing to do the next day other than rest and attend the rehearsal and the dinner afterward. The wedding was the following day, then Florence before they left Montefollonico. Beulah had pushed herself on this trip, doing things she never dreamed or even desired to do, yet how rich it made her feel now to have these experiences and memories.

She crawled into bed that night with thanksgiving for how the inheritance talk had turned out. To think Benito considered her family and wanted to make sure she was provided for had warmed her heart in an unexpected way. How she had missed her older brother all these years, and to now have Benito step up and take his emotional seat in her life was nothing short of a miracle.

When she did return home, she wanted to revise her will. The farm would go to Annie and Jake; but there would also be some money for Benito and his heirs, even if he would not allow it while she was living.

***

Beulah was sore in places she didn't even know she had muscles. She popped two Advil with her morning *caffè americano*. Despite the daily dose of pasta and bread, the exercise did seem to make her dresses loose. If she could push beyond the soreness and stiffness that came with it, she might walk more at home.

When it was time for the rehearsal, the group met the Gianellis at the great wooden door to the small church. When Paola opened it, there was a collective gasp.

Candles burned from stands and on windowsills to give the stone walls an effervescent glow. Greenery surrounded the white candles, and more candles and greenery decorated both sides of the altar. There was such a natural simplicity to the decorations, showing off the craftsmanship of the stone, and yet softening it at the same time.

"It's beautiful," Annie said.

"I want to get married here," Lindy said.

"Ask Paola to find you an Italian man," Jake teased.

"Uh, no way. I've heard too much about their reputation."

Vincenzo laughed. "There are exceptions," he said. "*Papà* and me. We hope Luca will be the same."

Lindy seemed embarrassed about her comment. "I'm sorry, that was a stereotype."

"It is quite well deserved, no need to apologize."

Paola went into action. "Okay, we get chairs tomorrow, Annie. Sorry not here now. There is also not much heat."

"We don't need many chairs, since half the guests are in the wedding," Annie said. "Since the ceremony is short, we shouldn't have to worry about the lack of heat."

"We take care. In the meantime, guests must stand."

Paola pointed to the altar. "Scott, here. Jake, there. Best man?"

"Tom," Jake said and motioned for Tom to join him.

"Okay, Nonna?" Paola motioned for Beulah, and she followed her great niece's hand signals to stand in the back. "I give you signal and Luca will take you to your seat. Then he walk Evelyn. After, he take *mamma*, and *papà* will follow. Lindy?"

"I'll stand here for pictures," Lindy said.

"Now, Janice come down first, slowly, then Annie. We pretend your *papà* is here. Stand here," she pointed to a spot for Janice.

With Paola directing things, Beulah took Luca's arm, and they went down the aisle to the imagined chair. Evelyn did the same, with Scott and Jake already standing at the altar.

"We need a *papà*," Paola exclaimed, as if the realization smacked her in the face. "*Papà*, you stand in." She motioned for Benito to go to the back of the chapel with Annie.

"Janice, you next."

Beulah watched Annie take Benito's arm, glad there was someone in the party who could complete this role, at least in rehearsal.

Annie smiled at Benito and they started down the aisle. "We imagine the accordion, okay?" Paola said, humming, and everyone laughed.

After the rehearsal, they loaded into cars and went down the mountain to a winery for dinner. Small candles illuminated the walkway to the antique wooden door. Down stone steps, the room opened into vaulted brick walls and ceiling, with a glowing chandelier hanging from the center. Wine bottles filled wooden racks from the floor to the ceiling on both sides of the room.

Annie clasped her hands. "It's magical."

Evelyn had outdone herself. It explained those morning trips with Tom down to the winery before everyone else had even had their breakfast.

Flickering votive candles lined the center of the white, linen-covered tables and reflected off the white china and many wine glasses placed at each setting.

"*Prosecco,*" Angelina leaned over and said to Beulah.

Prosecco. The sparkling white wine Rossella DeVechio had served when she stayed with Beulah while Janice and Annie were in Italy finding Benito.

Beulah thought back with shame over the way she acted that week. Especially now, when she saw how the Lord was working in that visit to lay the groundwork for better knowing her Italian family. Rossella had introduced her to the food and drink of Italians, paving the way for Beulah to understand the culture of her new family members.

Waiters in black suits brought course after course. Benito explained with pride the red wine was *vino nobile,* famous in Val D'Orcia. He also told them about the local *vin santo,* a sweet wine in which to dip a cookie, when it came time for the dessert course. Despite being a tee-totaler all her life, she realized there was a time and place for everything under the sun. This was a season for celebration.

Chapter Thirty-Two

ANNIE DREAMED HER father arrived in the night, and when she woke up on her wedding day, while Janice and Lindy lay sleeping in their beds, she dressed and went to the hotel reception, sure it was more than a dream.

"No, I'm sorry," the clerk said again, and Annie felt more than a little pity in the kind eyes of the middle-aged man.

She smiled and said, "Could you call my phone if he does arrive?"

"*Si*, but your fiancé has already requested the same. Should I call both?"

"Oh no, his phone is fine, thank you." *Put it out of your mind. He's not coming.*

Someone knocked at the door while she put on her makeup, lifting her hopes one last time.

"You're not supposed to see her," Lindy said.

"Only a minute." Jake's voice.

"Okay, but only because she's not in her dress yet."

"No hanky-panky while we're gone," Janice warned.

Lindy and Janice left them alone. Annie knew what he had come to say by the look on his face.

"He's not coming," she said.

Jake's eyes were full of sympathy. "No, he's not coming."

Annie tried to hold it back, but she burst into tears when Jake pulled her to his chest. She cried for a while and then silently listened to his heartbeat, drawing comfort from his body. She pulled back to look at Jake.

"You talked to him?"

"He called me," Jake admitted.

"After all my calls went unanswered."

"We talked for a long time," Jake said.

"He was drinking, I'm sure."

"Probably."

"What's his excuse?"

"He didn't offer anything."

"Well, that's new," Annie said and blew her nose with the tissue Jake handed her. "Usually there's some cock-and-bull story that he's made up."

"He said he's not worthy to walk you down the aisle. He hasn't earned the right."

"No, he hasn't earned the right. I wanted to give it to him anyway because he is my father. He hasn't earned anything. This was a gift I wanted to give him, to grant him the right to be my father for one day in the eyes of God and all our friends. Somehow, he manages to diminish the pain he inflicts on others, and make it about himself. It's always about him."

"You have every right to be angry."

Annie slumped into the chair by the fireplace. "I don't want to be angry. This is my wedding day and I want to be—no, I am—happy."

"That's right. Let's not allow him to take that happiness away from you today." He held her face in both his hands and kissed her gently on the lips.

***

"Good grief, you're a mess," Janice said after Jake left.

"We need to do your makeup all over," Lindy said.

"Is it that bad?"

Her two friends peered at her as if they were threading a needle. "It's bad," Janice said.

"I've got some of that yellow cream that takes away dark circles," Lindy offered.

"Grab it. I'll start on the hair," Janice ordered.

"Sorry about your dad," Lindy said as she began working the cream under Annie's eyes.

"Me too, but it's his loss. No offense, Annie, but what a jerk."

"None taken."

"Beulah's fit to be tied," Lindy said.

"I bet she is," Annie said. "This is not her first rodeo with him. It makes me realize the disappointment my mother and grandmother must have experienced, over and over again."

There was a knock and the door cracked open.

"Can we come in?" Beulah was standing on the threshold with Evelyn behind her.

"Sure," Lindy called over her shoulder.

"How are you?" Beulah asked.

Annie reached for her grandmother's hand. "I'm fine. Disappointed, but fine. It's not going to ruin this day. You all look beautiful." Evelyn was dressed in pale blue; Beulah wore light peach.

Beulah squeezed her hand and sat down in the chair beside her while Lindy and Janice continued to work.

"I can't believe Jo Anne's little girl is getting married," Beulah said, getting choked up. "She would have been so proud of the young woman you've become."

"No crying, people," Janice said, and put both hands up as if to stop traffic. They all burst into laughter.

***

Lindy left with Evelyn and Beulah after putting the finishing touches on Annie's makeup.

"Can you pin this on?" Annie said, handing the cameo to Janice. "Something old, something new, something borrowed and something blue," Annie said. "I've got everything but the something new."

"What about your shoes?"

"They're new. I showed Betty a few options and let her choose so she'd feel included."

"Then you're good to go," Janice concluded.

"Janice, thank you. If you hadn't been so honest with me, I doubt I'd be here today."

Janice shrugged. "You've been a good friend to me, Annie Taylor. That's what friends do, if they love each other." Janice pursed her lips as if to push back emotion. "Now, let's stop all this jabber and get to the chapel. You look great and it's time."

Vincenzo was waiting outside to drive them up the hill.

"*Ciao bella, cara la mia Annie,*" Vincenzo said and kissed her on both cheeks before helping her into the back seat with Janice.

"I must tell you something now," Vincenzo said, turning around to face her in the back seat. "Papà is well loved in Montefollonico. He help many people over the years. Many people want to show him respect. It became too much."

What was he saying? She looked to Janice for explanation, but her head was turned, as if she found something interesting outside the car window.

"What has happened to *papà* with finding his family, it has been a happy thing, not only for us, but for the whole village because *papà* is loved."

"I don't understand what you're getting at." Vincenzo started the engine and drove out of the hotel parking lot.

"You see soon," Vincenzo said.

Janice picked at her fingernails. When the car turned into the town square, people crowded along the sides of the street, as if watching a parade. They pointed, smiled, and waved at the car as it inched along.

"What's going on?" Annie asked, as she waved back.

No one answered and she kept waving as the street narrowed when they approached the chapel.

Vincenzo stopped the car and helped her out. The chapel doors opened wide with Lindy on one side and Paola on the other. The chapel was packed tight with people who sat and stood wherever space permitted.

Understanding washed over her and she turned to Vincenzo.

"You see, not intimate wedding you wanted. They wouldn't allow it," Vincenzo said.

Annie kissed her cousin on both cheeks. "I'm very happy."

"Did you know about this?" she whispered to Janice as they approached the doors to the chapel.

"I heard about it today when I heard one of the townspeople speak about it in Italian," Janice whispered back. "The Gianellis didn't have a choice."

Paola greeted them at the door. "I am sorry, Annie, did Vincenzo explain?"

After getting over the initial shock, Annie found it touching that so many people wanted to celebrate with her extended family. "It's beyond anything I could have imagined."

"Are you ready to begin?"

"I need a *papà* first. Please ask Benito if he would be my escort down the aisle?"

Chapter Thirty-Three

BEULAH SAW ANNIE on Benito's arm and all hope of keeping the mascara that Evelyn had so carefully applied that afternoon was lost. The accordion player pumped out "Here Comes the Bride" and the scene might have taken on a comical air had the participants not been so serious about their roles.

Benito stood straight as an arrow, his chest out, with Annie on his arm as they made their way down the central aisle with villagers crowding the tiny chapel. Body heat provided by all the attendees made the chapel downright cozy.

Jake's face broke into a gigantic smile when he spotted his bride, and Annie radiated joy. Both had eyes only for each other during her approach to the altar.

Evelyn's wedding dress had been transformed. The elegant, sleeveless gown accentuated Annie's pretty figure, the length providing a small train in the back with gently flowing folds.

Scott began the simple ceremony, and Beulah grabbed the Kleenex from her purse, while Janice did double-duty as matron of honor and translator for the villagers who packed the chapel.

Beulah imagined that the Protestant wedding seemed strange to the Italians, but was overwhelmingly pleased that so many of Benito's friends wanted to participate.

If it was at all like Somerville, curiosity about Benito's new American family fueled villager attendance. These people were so much like those from back home. They spoke a foreign language, had different cultural preferences, and ate different foods, but as a whole, this small, rural town had much in common with Somerville.

Scott performed the ceremony well, quoting First Corinthians 13. It was the same passage Beulah and Fred had chosen to have read at their own wedding so many years ago. Thinking of Fred brought fresh tears.

Beulah looked across the aisle at Evelyn, watching her only son give himself to another woman. While Evelyn was over the moon with happiness at Jake's choice, Beulah also knew that as a mother, she was likely to feel a twinge of loss. Tom held Evelyn's hand through the entire ceremony; Beulah reckoned those two would follow suit before too long.

That meant changes to her relationship with Evelyn and the way they went in and out of each other's houses, especially if Evelyn moved to town. *How can I be sad for something so exciting for Evelyn?* Jake's father, Charlie, had been a wonderful husband for Evelyn, but Tom would bring her a new life and new experiences. No, she could not grieve her friend's new happiness.

"Now that Jake and Annie have given themselves to each other by solemn vows, with the joining of hands, and the giving and receiving of rings, I announce to you that they are husband and wife," Scott intoned. "Those whom God has joined together, let no one put asunder."

Jake kissed Annie and grinned at her, and then, as if he couldn't stop himself, went in for a longer kiss. Cheers erupted. Scott announced them as Mr. and Mrs. Wilder and they led the way out of the church to a bouncy accordion tune. The wedding party circled around and went back into the chapel for pictures while everyone else made their way to the reception.

Lindy snapped pictures right and left, posing each family together. At the end, the accordion player offered to take a picture of the whole group so Lindy could be in it.

The reception party had been moved to the *Teatro di Montefollonico* with high-beamed ceilings, something Paola and Angelina had decided to do after their friends had made it clear that they wanted to attend. She had heard the villagers were providing all the food, everything fresh and homemade.

Benito led Beulah to a seat in the front of the room, then left her when someone called for him across the room.

"*Ciao bella*," a deep voice said. Beulah turned and saw a handsome older man, his white hair a stunning contrast to his olive skin. He sat next to her, a little close for Beulah's comfort. "You very beautiful," he said, looking at Beulah with such intensity, she shifted her eyes and blushed.

"You taste my wine?" he poured her a glass. "I make a *vino nobile* and eets the best." She had learned from Rossella DeVechio that it was difficult to turn down an Italian when it came to sharing food or wine, so she took the glass and sipped.

"Very good," she said. She preferred a big glass of iced sweet tea. Ice in anything, she found out, was unheard of around here.

"You taste my olive oil," he said. "Harvest only November." He poured out a vibrant green liquid on a plate and handed her a piece of bread. She took it and tasted the fresh, earthy oil.

"Very good," she repeated.

"You like?"

"*Giancarlo, cosa stai facendo? Questa è mia zia,*" Benito put his hands on the man's shoulders.

"*Non puoi darmi la colpa per averci provato,*" the man said, laughing. He got up and moved away.

Benito sat down next to her.

"This eez good day," he said in English.

"A *buongiorno,*" she agreed. "And a *bounanotte.*"

Vincenzo joined them. "They are preparing antipasto now, then there will be a pasta course, and then a meat course, followed by sweets, cheese, and fruit."

Beulah remembered the course order from the night Rossella DeVechio had made dinner for them at her house. Even though she made and dried pasta in her living room, Beulah couldn't for the life of her remember the name of the pasta now. Before she met Rossella, everything was either a macaroni, noodle, or spaghetti. She hadn't realized so many varieties of pasta existed.

"Do you have an answer yet?" Beulah asked Vincenzo.

Vincenzo translated for Benito.

"No, she is still thinking. I hope she will agree before you leave so we can make plans. It is the right thing. Papà and I are very sure."

"Would you like me to speak with her? If she wants, that is," Beulah said.

"*Si*, when the time comes, you must speak with her."

Paola waved to them from across the room and motioned Benito to come up to where she was standing next to Annie and Jake as they received guests wishing them well. Beulah jumped as several pops sounded all over the room.

Waiters carried trays of small glasses sparkling in the candlelight. Tonight, there was no question about it. She reached for one and waited for the toast.

"*Questo è un giorno molto felice per me. Sono nella mia città con la mia nuova famiglia americana e ho anche accompagnato mia cugina all'altare.*" Benito paused and nodded to Vincenzo to translate.

"This day is very happy for me. I welcome my American family to Montefollonico, and I walk my cousin down the aisle."

"*Per me questa è una cugina speciale . . . E' venuta qui a trovarmi, nonostante molti ostacoli, e mi ha voluto nella famiglia May.*"

"This cousin is special to me. She came here, despite many obstacles, to find me and invite me into the May family."

"*Questo brindisi è per la sposa e lo sposo, Annie e Jake e per mia zia Beulah, che hanno portato molta felicità ai Gianellis. Cin Cin!*"

"I raise this toast to the bride and groom, Annie and Jake, and to my aunt Beulah, all of whom have brought the Gianellis great happiness. Cheers!" Benito and Vincenzo lifted their glasses of prosecco and the whole room responded with "Chin-Chin," then drank. There was nothing to do but follow suit. It was a wedding, after all.

Chapter Thirty-Four

BEULAH COULDN'T REMEMBER the last time she had stayed up until midnight. However, quite a few things had changed for her in the last few months, and she reckoned a body wasn't too old to learn or experience new things.

At breakfast in the hotel restaurant, she found out Scott, Mary Beth, and Janice had already been picked up by a driver for the trip back to Rome. Janice was catching a flight while Scott and Mary Beth planned to get a brief tour of Rome before heading home. The party was down to Tom, Evelyn, Lindy, and her, along with the Gianellis.

Benito had recommended they spend the night in Florence so they could have a bit more time taking in the city, with him and Angelina traveling with them as tour guides. Paola was headed home to London and Vincenzo had farming responsibilities, so it was back to normal life for them.

Before they all parted ways, there was still the request to be resolved. Beulah had thought it over, and she had decided Benito's proposition had merit. She told them it was fine with her, but they wanted her to consider it while they spoke with Anna about it. Anna was the one who had the most to sacrifice should it come about, and Beulah knew her maternal tendencies might not allow it.

While the others packed up, Beulah waited for Benito in the gravel lot of the hotel reception area. His little gray Fiat pulled in and she slid into the front seat. They exchanged smiles and greetings, then drove down the hill to Vincenzo's farm house.

A plate of sweet breads and coffee awaited her, as Anna shyly motioned for her to sit down at the table.

"Rosa and Luca are not here," Vincenzo said, "so we can speak freely. Please eat."

Beulah took a croissant and tore off a piece of the flaky bread, enjoying it with the rich coffee provided her in a small cup. After a week in Italy, she wondered if she might try a richer coffee blend, one that was a little stronger than her Maxwell House.

"Beulah, we have had much discussion after *papà* and I spoke with you a couple of days ago and presented the idea. Anna was resistant at first, but now sees the benefits of getting Luca away. This became evident again last night as we caught him smoking with this group of older boys outside during the wedding reception. These boys are bad, they are known for stealing and drugs. He is a good kid, but if he stays long in this group, it will lead to trouble. We don't see another way other than to get him out of this situation for a while, so he can see there is a better way. We also don't want to presume upon your kindness. If you have any reservations, we can seek another option. Paola has offered to take him to London, although we are concerned that may not be best for him or her." He didn't bother to translate for his father, but she was sure Benito already knew what Vincenzo was going to say.

All six eyed her as if she held the fate of their son and grandson in her hands. She smiled. "Luca is more than welcome to come and stay with me for as long as you want. I am sure he can still get into trouble, but there are no gangs of boys roaming May Hollow Road, I can assure you of that."

Vincenzo and Anna broke out into relieved grins and Vincenzo quickly translated for Benito. Benito reached his hand across the table and grasped Beulah's hand.

"*Grazie mille*," her nephew said.

Now it was Anna's turn. "I have hard time with this," she said in broken English. "I want good for him but hard to let go." Anna wiped away a tear. Beulah felt how deeply this mother must love her son to give him up for the summer. "I thank you very much, to give time away."

"Is it possible for him to go back with us?" Beulah asked.

"No, he need visa and that will take some time," Vincenzo said, and then translated for Benito.

"But, we may send him as soon as possible. Then when we come in May, we can visit him. Maybe bring him home at the end of the summer, if all is going well," Vincenzo said. "But, if he cause you trouble, any at all, we put him on a plane home immediately."

Benito put his hand on her arm. "You his *nonna*," he said.

"Yes, *papà* say that while Luca is with you, he must obey. We tell him to treat you like grandmother."

"That sounds fine. I suppose I need to enroll him in the local school, and Jake can use his help on the farm."

"*Si*, yes, we want him to go to school and to work hard," Vincenzo said with gusto. "He works much on our farm. It will be great difficulty for me while he is gone, but it is for the best." Vincenzo translated and both Anna and Benito nodded.

"That all sounds good to me," Beulah said. "I'll wait for you to let me know when he can come."

"*Grazie mille*," Benito said again and stood up. "*Allora*, we go Firenze."

"Listen to *papà*," Vincenzo said. "He'll be speaking English before long."

"Much quicker than I'll be speaking Italian," she said. "Although, Luca might teach me a few more things."

***

It was their last night in Italy and Beulah worked at rearranging her suitcase before their final dinner with Benito. The hotel room was equipped with a little coffeemaker, so she made herself a cup while Evelyn was out squeezing in every moment of sightseeing around Rome with Tom and Lindy. She had begged off after seeing the famous Colosseum and the Forum, her sciatica flaring up and telling her it was time to take a rest.

What would Fred have thought about Italy? She couldn't help but wish he had been by her side marveling at the things she saw in Siena, Florence, and Rome. Truth was, she had never paid much attention to art, other than some nice print that might decorate a wall. Seeing the statue of David by Michelangelo in Florence and imagining the detail, time, and vision it took to create such a thing floored her, not to mention all the ancient monuments.

In Italy, everything seemed to be hacked out of stone, from the art to the houses, to the town squares Benito called *piazzas*. In Kentucky, wood was the natural resource. Limestone was also in abundance and used for the old fences and houses all around the central part of the state. Now that she thought about it, Benito might feel at home in the old stone house, should he stay there some day.

Benito's house had terracotta tile floors, and the same thing on the ceilings with dark wood beams holding it up. Lindy had taken pictures of everything, but Beulah pressed the images deep into her memory so she could pull it all out later after she got home.

She folded her clothes and placed them in the suitcase, leaving an outfit for the evening and her clothes for the trip home. Now she knew what it must be like for a barn-sour horse kicking up a run toward the structure that symbolized rest and all that was familiar. As delicious as the food had been, she was ready for soup beans and cornbread, with a nice Vidalia onion on the side and a tall glass of sweet tea.

There were the Gibsons, Stella, and Woody to check on when she got back. Evelyn had called a few times on her cellphone, but it wasn't the same as being in person and talking. There was the comfort of her bed and her room, where everything had a familiar place. The coldest part of winter was coming on soon and she wanted to be snugged up in her own home and cooking up a storm.

The trip had been satisfying, although quite exhausting. Oh, if her mama and daddy could have known their grandson. How they would have loved him. It gave a pang to her heart to think they never knew him. But to think she almost missed him as well, had it not been for the letters they saved.

Now she could look forward to Luca coming and living with her in the farmhouse. Annie's bedroom would be free, even if Stella wanted to stay a little longer. *And why not? The more the merrier.*

***

Dinner ended and the time for goodbyes had arrived. Beulah wiped a tear away as she hugged Benito and Angelina. Lindy took more pictures of them together, standing by the entrance of the restaurant in a section of Rome called Trastevere. The full moon hung low over the church in the center of the square. Angelina was on one of Benito's arms, while she was on the other. Behind them, Tom followed with Evelyn on his arm and his daughter by his side, a group promenade through the church square.

The next morning held a bustle of activity from the last-minute packing, taxi to the airport, security lines, and the long flight. She still feared the flight home, but she had decided her butterflies did not require a nerve pill this time, and that was no small victory.

For now, with the moon shining guidance over the Roman cobblestone streets, they enjoyed these last tranquil and precious moments as a family.

Chapter Thirty-Five

ANNIE WOKE UP the day after the wedding to the sound of Jake's rhythmic breathing. Her husband. How strange to be able to use that word with this boy she had grown up with. Yet at the same time, it seemed so natural. And last night? Just right, too.

Experiencing Jake's gentleness, strength, and desire for her manifested in the final, sacred act reserved for the time when they could celebrate it as man and wife, had been well worth the wait.

Annie smiled and snuggled closer to him. There was nothing she would change about her wedding. It was everything she had dreamed. Even her father's absence had been salved over by Benito acting as the man in her family and giving her away.

Now, the group would head home after travels to Florence and on to Rome while she and Jake went off on their own adventure.

They had a car and a guidebook, and some vague plans for traveling to one or two *agritourismi*, as working farms hosting guests were called in Italy. They had nothing firm, and the prospect of random traveling seemed delicious.

She slid softly onto the floor, put on her robe, and went to the kitchen. She added water to the base of the Italian coffee maker, spooned coffee in the small basket, screwed on the top, and turned on the gas burner. As it percolated so did her mind, brewing every detail and every conversation around the wedding.

There was a time in Tuscany two months before when Annie nearly chucked the whole thing, so strong were her fears about her family heritage and being too much like her father. She had worried she might leave Jake high and dry, maybe feeling that same smothering sense of responsibility her father felt after marrying her mother.

Annie felt the opposite. She wanted to be with Jake even more, to know more of what he was thinking and feeling in his heart and soul. To be joined with him physically in that most special bond. Her father's legacy had almost kept her from all this joy. Yesterday, he had threatened yet again to spoil her happiness by not showing up.

The coffee boiled and Annie turned off the gas as the realization of a truth came to her. *Dad will never be there for me and I need to accept it.*

Annie poured coffee into her cup and sat down in the sitting area, still hearing the comforting and steady breathing from the bedroom. She was no longer alone now. Jake was by her side, and would be for many years to come.

In the quiet early morning, Annie prayed her thanksgiving to God for leading them both back home at the same divine moment; for her grandmother, Evelyn, Tom, Lindy, Scott, and Mary Beth, all loving them enough to stand by them and witness their vows; for Benito and Angelina, Vincenzo and Anna, Luca, Rosa, and Paola, her new Italian family; and even for the villagers, who cared enough about Benito to extend their love and blessings to her marriage.

With this much gratefulness in her heart, how could she feel anything but pity for the lonely man her father had become? She took another sip of the coffee and stared at her phone. She would confront him.

There was no answer on the other end of the line, no voice warm with affection, nothing but a short voicemail message. When it beeped, she said what she had to say.

"Dad, the wedding was beautiful and I'm sorry you missed it," she hesitated. "I also want to say I love you and I forgive you."

***

A couple of days into the honeymoon, Annie and Jake sat by a roaring fire on a farm in Tuscany an hour from Montefollonico, sipping glasses of Brunello.

"Vincenzo asked me what I thought about Luca staying with Grandma," Annie said. "He'd love him to help you on the farm."

"I need the help," Jake said. "Being here has made me even more committed to making the farm produce as much as possible. Chickens, sheep, goats, pigs, maybe even a milk cow. An orchard for fruit. We'll need a lot of kids to help with everything." He grinned.

"I'm not quite ready for that yet, but give me a year or so. I'd like a little time with you before we bring kids into the mix," she said, resting her hand on his arm. "I do know what you mean, though. Getting away allows you to see more clearly what should be a priority. It's like stepping back and seeing the whole picture. When you're too close, you only see what's right in front of you."

"Has it made you rethink anything?" he said.

"This idea of providing hospitality on the farm, an American version of the *agritourismi* here in Italy, is growing. I can't figure out the lodging piece without an expense to build or renovate something. People would love the cottage, for example, but it belongs to Evelyn and it's right at her back door."

"Some things may be changing on that front. Tom asked my permission to marry Mom."

Annie sat up straight. "Jake Wilder! I can't believe you've known that this whole time and didn't tell me."

He deflected the couch pillow. "I found out the day of the wedding. I had other things on my mind after that," he said, and pulled her close.

She submitted and then pushed back. "Are you saying Evelyn might move into town?"

"I don't know for sure, but she asked me the other day if we wanted to live in the house if she did move. I said I would ask you, but I think you're set on the old stone house."

"Wow, I hadn't even thought about the farm house," Annie said. "What do you think?"

"It's up to you. On one hand, it's handy to the dairy barn

and the outbuildings, but if you were thinking of doing a bed and breakfast type of thing, living in the stone house gives us more privacy."

"The house has four bedrooms and baths attached, and then there's the guest cottage. If Evelyn is open to it, maybe we could pay her rent on the farmhouse and cottage, or even a fee based on the rentals so she gets more for it if it gets rented often. Someday, if we grow out of the stone house, we could always move there."

"It's a good thought," he said. "Now, I have another thought."

***

Beulah stretched out in her bed, appreciating the lumps and bumps of her old mattress. It was time to get up, but after tromping all over Italy and staying in one unfamiliar place after another, she savored the comfort of her own bedroom.

There was a chill in the air outside the cozy cocoon of her quilts. It was winter and her bones felt it. As comfy as her bed felt, the thought of her percolator and a nice cup of coffee motivated her to move.

In a few minutes, she dressed, cast a wistful eye toward Annie's empty bedroom, and went downstairs where she found Stella frying bacon and wearing an old apron.

"I hope you don't mind me trying to fix you breakfast this morning." Stella turned and smiled at Beulah, her eyes resting greedily on the sizzling meat, and the open pack of bacon and carton of eggs on the counter. Stella looked back at the counter. "I'll clean up my mess."

"I was thinking how good it looked," Beulah said. "You've learned your cooking lessons well."

"Can I get you a cup of coffee? I'll get it for you if you want to sit down there."

She sipped the coffee and waited while Stella dished up the bacon and eggs and put it in front of Beulah. Beulah rarely ate a big breakfast except on Saturdays, but since she had gotten back from Italy, she woke up in the mornings wanting lunch. By six o'clock, she was ready for bed. Annie said it would take a few days to get over the jet lag, but she hadn't expected her meal cycle to be turned upside down.

Stella filled her own coffee cup, adding cream and two teaspoons of sugar, then sat down across from Beulah.

"Beulah, I have some good news to tell you, but it might come as a little bit of a shock."

Beulah plopped her fork down on the plate and looked up at Stella, wide-eyed. *I don't know if I can take any more surprises.*

"I got on that dating site and was matched up with someone local, right off the bat," Stella said. "We've already been out a couple of times. It took me by surprise, since I knew this person, from a distance, and never thought he might be interested in someone like me."

Beulah took a gulp of coffee and waited.

"He's a man of faith, you'll be pleased to hear. And a widower." Stella seemed to be waiting for Beulah to put the riddle together.

"That's good, Stella. I can't fault you for that."

"He's a little older than me and he's got grown kids. He loves home cooking, so it's a good thing you've taught me so much. It's all so new, but it feels right. Anyway, I wanted you to know before it gets out to everyone else. We'll be sitting together at church this Sunday, and I'm sure the tongues will wag."

"A good way to start out a relationship," Beulah said. "Who is this lucky fellow?"

"It's Pastor Gillum."

***

The pictures from Italy spread out on Betty Gibson's coffee table.

"Law have mercy, he looks like your side of the family, except with the darker skin. I can't wait to see him when he comes over here. I'm still not over Annie getting married without me and Joe being a part of it. It's like she's robbed us of something," Betty said, and teared up.

Beulah ignored the tears, finding the best strategy with Betty's new emotional state was to simply move on. "We have the barbecue to look forward to in May. Annie's planning to get a few of the pictures from Italy blown up so everyone can see it and feel like they are a part of it. Honestly, even if she had married here, you weren't well enough to go anyway."

Betty blew her small, red nose, then sniffed. "How's Stella doing? I've missed her since she quit coming all the time."

"Oh, she seems to be doing fine," Beulah said.

"I think she has a man friend," Betty said. "I sat right here and kept an eye on her comings and goings while y'all were off traipsin' around. Twice last week, I saw a Lincoln drive in and out of there."

Betty eyed Beulah and waited for her to comment on this piece of juicy news.

"Is that right?"

"It reminded me of Pastor Gillum's car, but this car looked a bit more shined up than he keeps his. You know, he let himself go after Brenda died. Why, there's five women all eligible at church and he hasn't tried to date any of them. Don't think they didn't put themselves in his path. Every one of those women took him casseroles, signed up for the extra church committees, and volunteered to clean his house. He likes to eat too good to be single. In my opinion, he should find himself a good cook and settle down."

"Maybe Stella is a good pick?"

"Stella Hawkins? Have you lost your mind, Beulah? Why, she's not his type at all."

"You're probably right, Betty. What was I thinking?"

Chapter Thirty-Six

AFTER THE FIRST lazy winter afternoons and romantic evenings by the fire in the Tuscan farmhouse, Annie and Jake had stayed in three *agritourismi,* talked to the owners, viewed the dormant gardens, and toured the barns and operations. There had also been a trip to Florence and to Chianti where they walked hand-in-hand through the piazzas and museums. Annie cherished every minute of their alone time with each other. Soon enough, there would be other things to consume their time and attention. They had disconnected from home, knowing their family would call if there was an emergency. As the trip drew to a close, she felt refreshed and ready for their new chapter, excited to set up their own home together. As soon as they landed in Atlanta, Annie called Beulah.

"How is everyone?"

"Are you in Lexington?"

"Not yet, we're still in Atlanta, but we should be getting back in a couple of hours. Everything okay?"

"No. It's Vesta," Beulah said. "She's in the hospital. Vesta's nephew, Jerome, called this morning."

"Oh no," Annie said. "What's wrong?"

Beulah was silent on the other end of the line, as if she was deciding what to say. "Her heart's giving out."

Annie felt her throat close up. "I'll go straight there."

***

Outside Vesta's hospital room, family members gathered around a rolling cart with store-bought cookies and a thermos of coffee. Annie had seen the cart outside hospital rooms before and she knew what it meant—comfort the family as they waited for their loved one to pass on.

The room was quiet, other than the pumping of the oxygen machine and soft blips of the heart monitor. Annie recognized Jerome and Vivian from Vesta's description, and they recognized her. They embraced and brought her over to look down at Vesta's tiny frame lying on the bed. Her eyes were closed and her face looked peaceful, yet her breathing was labored.

"Aunt Vesta." Jerome leaned over close to her ear. "Annie's here to see you. Can you wake up?"

Vesta's eyes fluttered and she looked at Jerome, bringing him into focus. He pointed to Annie and Vesta turned her head slowly. Her almond eyes brightened a bit and she moved her right hand to reach for Annie, who clasped her hand and leaned down. "We just got back home," she said. Vesta grabbed her left hand and tried to lift it.

Annie raised it so she could see. "I'm married." Vesta's eyes then fell on the cameo Annie had pinned to her collar after digging through her luggage on the way to the hospital.

"I wore it for the ceremony. Everyone thought it made the dress, thanks to you." Annie's voice faltered and tears dripped off her cheeks.

Vesta shook her head as if to say, *Don't cry.* Then she pointed up to the ceiling and a smile brightened her face.

Annie nodded. "I know, but I'll miss you."

Vesta smiled, peace flooding her face, and then closed her eyes. It was the last time she was conscious. Annie gently passed Vesta's hand to Vivian; Jerome sat on the opposite side and held the other hand. Great-nieces, nephews, and cousins moved in and out of the room. Jake brought Beulah and they stayed for a while. After they left and the crowd was smaller, someone began a hymn.

It was a song Annie had known from her childhood at Somerville Baptist, but her throat was too constricted to sing. It was close to midnight when Vesta's spirit left her ninety-something-year-old shell, with all her family around her bed, singing her into eternity.

***

Annie, Jake, and Beulah sat together during the funeral and followed the procession to the cemetery where Vesta's body was laid to rest. After the funeral, Jerome invited them to his house for a meal.

With a spread of food that threatened to warp the folding tables, Annie, Jake, and Beulah ate and talked with Vesta's family and friends, hearing story after story of her life. Many former students came, along with teachers who had worked with Vesta. Along with the extended Givens clan and Vesta's church family, the house overflowed with loved ones. After the meal, they were about to take their leave when Jerome asked Annie to follow him back to a quiet bedroom.

"Come on, Jake. You too."

He closed the door on the loud talking outside and turned to Annie.

"Aunt Vesta was waiting on you to get home before she passed; that's the way I see it. You were awful special to her and she told me she wanted you to have all her books. She said you would know what they meant to her and you would put them to a good use. We'll load 'em up and deliver them to you sometime next week. You better know there's a bunch of them," he said, a glimmer of mischief in his eyes. "She took part of them to Richwood and we've been keeping the rest here."

"I'll take great care of them." Annie felt Jake's hand on her back.

"There was one book she wanted me to give you directly. There's a note in it for you."

Jerome handed her *Anna Karenina*. Annie laughed and it felt like a release after the day's heavy emotion. "This is the book she was reading when I first met her."

"I figured there was some reason," he said. "With Aunt Vesta, there was always a reason."

"Thank you for including me in your family," she said.

"From the way she tells it, we are family," he said and grinned.

"I believe we are. Oh, Vesta said she had a list in her Bible of everyone she wanted to invite to the historical marker dedication."

"It's right over here; let's look." He handed the worn and frayed Bible to Annie and she opened it, thumbing through the pages, much marked up and underlined. In the middle of the Psalms, she found the folded invitation list in Vesta's handwriting.

Later that evening, Annie settled by the fireplace after supper and opened Vesta's letter.

My dear Annie,

I feel the Lord calling me home soon. If that happens, I want to make sure you know how wonderful these last months have been and how special you are.

Our friendship brightened my days in such an unexpected way. I thank God for the day you came over to me and asked me about the old stone house. When you said you knew Anna Karenina, well, I knew you were going to be my friend.

Abide in Him and your marriage will be blessed. There's nothing on this earth so important.

Please don't be terribly sad since I am going to my real home and I am looking forward to it. I have had a good life and I have kept the faith.

All my love,
Vesta

Chapter Thirty-Seven

BEULAH PULLED ON a light sweater and went outside in the quiet dawn, breathing in the fresh country air of early May. It was going to be a bright, sunny day, the kind that shows Kentucky at its finest to the rest of the world on Derby Day.

She sat down on the old metal chair where she could admire the newly planted Roma and Oxheart tomatoes, the basil plants, and the straight rows where green beans soon would sprout.

Her Italian family had already been there for two days, and they had flown by, so she was up early, not wanting to miss a single moment.

Everyone had come except for Paola, who had work obligations, and Vincenzo, who stayed back at the farm to keep it running. He promised to come at the end of the summer when it was time for Luca to go home.

The morning after Benito arrived, she had taken them to see the old stone house and the May family cemetery. The stone house was finished now and decorated with Annie and Jake's antiques and furniture. Vesta's collection of books filled two bookcases, now proudly displayed in the living room.

Benito went through each room of the house, quiet and reflective, while he soaked up every detail. Angelina took pictures they could enjoy later. Beulah showed him Ephraim's room upstairs and the secret place where they found the letters. She told him where they stood when they hugged Ephraim goodbye, and how they received news that he had been killed in action. It was an emotional time, but they needed to experience it with each other.

Benito went around outside the house, looked at the creek, and when he was finished, they all climbed the hill to the cemetery where his father, grandparents, and great-grandparents were buried. At Ephraim's grave, Benito leaned over and laid his hand on the top of his father's white military tombstone. For a few minutes, no one could talk.

Later that day, they had helped plant the garden. At Benito and Angelina's recommendation, she had picked out some Marconi pepper plants and eggplant. While they watched, Luca had made the rows and dug the holes for the plants, with all three of them giving him instruction.

"MAMMA MIA," he had uttered at one point, throwing up his hands while they laughed at his feigned frustration. The sullen teen had already brightened after arriving in Kentucky, as if a load had been removed from his shoulders by leaving Italy. Who could understand the pressure teenagers faced these days? Beulah was grateful for her own youth in a simpler time and place.

With both Stella and Annie gone now, it was a pleasure to hear the chatter in the house at night. Anna and Rosa were still asleep upstairs in Annie's old room, and Luca was happy to take the couch since it gave him access to all five of her channels on the television. Benito and Angelina stayed in Stella's old room, which would become Luca's room after everyone went home.

Luca's help could not have come at a better time for Jake, and the hard farm work would help keep a fifteen-year-old boy out of trouble. Annie jumped in to help Jake wherever she could, but now she had a new project on her hands.

After Evelyn's April elopement with Tom, they had moved into his house downtown, freeing up the old brick Italianate and the guest cottage on the Wilder farm. Annie was decorating it and preparing it to lodge city folks who wanted a farm experience. Lindy moved out and rented a small house downtown, offering Stella a room within walking distance to the library. The young lawyer had plans to restore a loft over one of the businesses on Main Street, but as Beulah well knew, these renovations took a while.

"Beulah, what are you doin' sittin' there starin' at your tomato plants? Don't you know we have a potluck to manage? Good heavens, I hope you don't think you're going to leave me to do all the work." Betty Gibson surprised her and must have walked across the road and down the farm lane.

Beulah turned, about to answer Betty's interruption into her pleasant thoughts with irritation. Then she saw the amusement in her old friend's eyes.

"Land sakes Betty, it's not yet seven in the morning."

Betty pulled another metal chair up next to Beulah.

"That's my point. I'm already up taking my morning walk. You know I've lost twenty pounds already. I might fit in my old cheerleading costume if I keep a goin' like this."

"I surely hope you won't try to do the splits. You might split somethin' that can't be sewed up."

Betty chuckled. "I feel so much better with this weight off, I can't say it enough. I should have done it years ago. It's a crying shame it took a heart attack for me to do it. Of course, my bosom is still large, but it always was. Joe thinks I look like Marilyn Monroe, so I don't mind that too much."

Later, after Betty trotted off down the lane, her hips swinging and arms pumping, Beulah went inside and found Benito peering at the percolator.

"Cafe Americano or espresso?" she asked.

"*Si, espresso, per favore,*" Benito said.

Beulah nodded, feeling very cosmopolitan, and pulled out the Italian coffee maker Annie had delivered to her and the bag of Italian coffee.

Benito's face lit up. "*Fantastico, mille grazie.*"

"I hope you know what to do with it, because I sure don't."

"*Si,*" Benito said, getting the gist of her English. She had found it was easier to communicate with her nephew than she thought. It was as if they were anticipating each other's thoughts, a gift that transcended language.

***

As they gathered on the edge of Gibson's Creek at the entrance to the old stone house, Beulah looked around at the people milling about. Annie and Jake welcomed everyone, including Jerome and Vivian, along with several members of the Givens family and the pastor of Vesta's church. Tom, Evelyn, Lindy, Stella, and Pastor Gillum stood alongside Woody, Scott, and Mary Beth. Joe and Betty Gibson had brought their daughter Peggy and granddaughter Missy. There was Benito and his family, along with representatives from the Heritage Council, the state Historic Preservation office, and the Historical Society. Even members of the Stone Conservancy showed up after helping repair the stone house at no charge earlier in the year. The only person missing was Vesta.

Betty sidled over to her. "Look a there at Pastor Gillum holding hands with Stella. They'll be the next ones to marry, mark my word. Why, I saw it from the very beginning. I knew Stella was the perfect match for Pastor Gillum."

Beulah nodded. "You're always ahead of the rest of us."

Short speeches were given by state and local dignitaries. Once concluded, descendants were asked to come forward to assist unveiling the marker. May and Givens family members posed for pictures. Beulah stood next to Jerome, who reached for her hand. She grabbed Benito's until they were all holding hands together in front of the old stone house.

Hands in shades of white, olive, and brown clasped in unity. A glimpse of heaven.

Chapter Thirty-Eight

ALMOST TIME FOR the party to start. Annie looked around for Jake, and spotted him standing around the pit where Brett roasted the pig. Jake laughed at something Brett said, a sight that warmed Annie's heart.

When Brett had asked Annie to set him up with Lindy, Annie knew it would not go over well with Jake, especially with Lindy now becoming Jake's step-sister. But both parties were interested, so who was she to prevent romance? She gave Brett Lindy's phone number and he took it from there.

Now they were a couple, much to Jake's initial disapproval. Annie smiled, thinking back to the winter days when they had circled each other like two roosters. They had since become friends.

Jake left Brett and went over to the other fire pit where some of his farmer friends roasted whole chickens, flipping them between two stainless steel metal grids, and browning the hens to perfection on both sides.

"Are you enjoying the view?" Lindy said.

"I sure am. I never get tired of it," Annie said. "How's it going with Brett?"

"It's so good," Lindy sighed. "We're taking it slow, but I'm falling."

"You're over Rob?"

"Completely. I made my non-negotiables like Janice suggested and I realized Rob would not have made the cut. Brett fits every one of them, so we'll see, but I can't help thinking this could be it. How's it going with your first official overnight guests?"

"Since this stay is free, no one is complaining. I'm pressing them for feedback, so hopefully, we'll open at the end of this month."

"Who's staying where?"

"Suzanne and her family are in the cottage. All my New York friends are in the main house. That's Janice, Jimmy, and their kids; my old boss, Bob Vichy and his wife; and my flight attendant friends, Prema and Evie. We stayed up so late last night telling airline stories," Annie said. "You should have seen Bob when he got here. His face . . ." Annie giggled thinking about it. "He looked as if he had been dropped off on the moon. He kept saying, 'It's too quiet around here.'"

"Don't forget you were one of those New Yorkers a year ago," Lindy reminded her.

"I know, isn't that strange?"

***

The meal was beyond anything Annie could have imagined. Beulah, Betty, Evelyn, and Stella had been cooking up a storm over the last week. Dressed eggs, green salad, broccoli salad, seven-layer salad, green beans, mashed potatoes, baked beans, corn pudding, and collard greens went with the roasted meats. Pans of corn bread, gallons of sweet tea, and a table laden with Kentucky nut pies and bourbon bread pudding finished out the culinary selection.

Tom and Evelyn, the happy newlyweds, sat with Stella and Pastor Gillum and seemed in earnest conversation. Annie caught snippets of conversation about marriage after losing a spouse as she passed the table.

Beulah sat with Benito, Angelina, Luca, Rosa, and Anna with Janice helping to translate, next to her husband, Jimmy. Moving past, she heard Anna giving instructions to Luca on how he was to behave while living with Beulah. Benito was backing her up with the famous Italian hand gestures that needed no words.

In the barn lot, Janice and Jimmy's kids played with Scott and Mary Beth's children and Jake's niece and nephew, running and screaming from the hay loft to the corn crib to the old concrete water tank.

At another table, Bob Vichy and his wife sat next to Woody, along with Prema and Evie. Joe and Betty Gibson were also at the table. This she had to hear, so she lingered nearby a few moments and caught snatches of conversation.

"What's there to do at night around here?" Bob asked Woody.

"I take my pipe and sit on the front porch most summer nights. It's right peaceful."

"And you do that every night, all summer?"

"Well, now, sometimes I take an evening ride on my horse. They like it better when it's a little cooler."

Bob shook his head. His wife said, "Bob, we should book a stay down here at Annie's farmhouse. A little porch sitting might do us both good."

At the other end of the table, Betty Gibson held court with Prema and Evie.

"I was Tobacco Festival Queen for three years in a row. I broke a record that still holds," she said, her blonde curls bobbing.

"What is this Tobacco Festival Queen?" Prema asked. "I am not familiar with this concept."

Prema, you're in for it now, Annie thought, as she moved on to the next table.

Jerome and Vivian Givens and the other Givens family members sat with Jake's sister Suzanne, her husband, and Jake's grandmother. They compared school systems in Kentucky and Arizona. There was even a table of Richwood Manor friends. Annie's volunteer service at Richwood had taken the form of teaching an art class in charcoal pencil. She planned to tackle water color in the summer and move into acrylics for the fall.

Lonnie presented her with a bouquet of yellow roses upon his arrival, and Gin Taylor agreed to come after checking the *Farmer's Almanac*. Assured the moon was in the right phase for such an outing, she decked herself out in turquoise earrings and a long shift dress. Lonnie Caldwell caught her eye and winked. He was cozied up to Gin Taylor now, but Annie wasn't worried about Gin. That mountain girl could take care of herself.

Gin followed Lonnie's wink and motioned her over. Annie sat down on the seat next to Gin while Lonnie shifted his attentions to another of the Richwood Manor female residents.

"I hadn't seen ye lately to tell ye," she said, leaning in as if to tell a state secret. "Ye daddy dropped the claim. We all knowed ye was the reason. There's a widder woman that's mighty grateful for whatever ye did."

"I didn't know," Annie said, processing. "Thank you for telling me." The news surprised Annie. Her father had not responded to the message she had left on her honeymoon. In fact, she had no word from him at all since December, despite several phone messages and several invitations to the barbecue. Jake had called Pete's bar in Malaga to verify her father was still alive. Pete said he saw him every evening, as usual, but he also confessed to Jake that Eddie Taylor had grown sullen.

Annie suspected he was waiting for the barbecue to pass before responding so there would be no pressure for him to come. When he didn't show up at the wedding, a short flight away, she knew he would not be here on this day.

This news Gin shared with her made her think that he did care what she thought of him in some way. Otherwise, why had he dropped a claim? Certainly, it wasn't out of compassion. Still, she knew better than to expect anything more.

Annie left Gin with a squeeze on her shoulder and looked for Jake. She heard a few warm-up notes from the bluegrass band, and then the bearded musicians began the first tune of the night, strumming dulcimers, cellos, and violins. The upbeat tune would get guests on their feet dancing.

Benito tapped her on the shoulder. In halting English, he said, "Would you like dance?"

Annie smiled at him. "*Si, grazie.*"

He led her to the dance floor. Jake followed with Beulah, who laughed and shook her head, then to Annie's amazement, started dancing.

Soon, the dance floor was crowded with guests. As the next tune started up, Benito took Beulah by the hand, and Jake swung

Annie around in a twirl as the singer crooned, *"Blue moon of Kentucky, keep on shinin'."*

Annie looked up at the waning half-moon and whispered a prayer of gratitude. For Vesta, her mother, and her grandfather, all now in heaven. For her father, in all his brokenness, and for her family and friends here tonight. For her grandmother, who guided and raised her, and helped her find the way home.

Most of all, for Jake.

Acknowledgments

THANK YOU TO my dear husband Jess who so faithfully supports every project with a whole heart. I am grateful to my mother for her stories about the family farm and her old Kentucky sayings.

Thank you to the following professionals who helped construct aspects outside of my expertise: Bobbie Dille for her insight into assisted living homes; paramedic Mike Kavitch and Dr. Brian Ellis for details on heart attacks and doctor visits; Judge Bruce Petrie who did extraordinary work on researching the complicated case of Benito and his potential claim on the family farm; Kirk Correll for legal expertise; Elisabetta DeRossi for the Italian translation and cultural insights; and Roni Perry for helping me build an important character.

Thank you to Beth Dotson Brown, Rachel Correll, Emma Sleeth, and Adrienne Correll for reading the manuscript and giving me valuable feedback. Thanks to Preston Correll for his passion and wisdom on sustainable farming; and Leigh Correll for her olfactory details.

Thank you to Jordan Smith and Lea Ann Poynter for assisting in ways too numerous to mention; to my friend, agent and fellow

Italophile Jenni Burke; and to Koehler Books for believing in the May Hollow Trilogy.

I quoted four songs: "I'll Fly Away," by Albert E. Brumley; "If I Said You Had a Beautiful Body Would You Hold It Against Me," by David Bellamy; "The Yellow Rose of Texas," author unknown; and "Blue Moon of Kentucky" by Bill Monroe.

Finally, but most importantly, thanks be to God.

Author's Note

THE MAY HOLLOW TRILOGY highlights life in a small community, both in Kentucky and Italy. I find there are many similarities to the medieval village of Montefollonico, Italy and the small Kentucky towns I am most familiar with, including Stanford, Danville, Lancaster, and Perryville.

Somerville is a fictional Kentucky town inspired by Stanford, my county seat, both in size and geography. I created the name by combining my husband's home town of Somerset and my home town of Danville. It's a very agrarian place, surrounded by farmland and people who have worked the ground for generations.

Faith, family, food, and farm are common themes, which is why I felt so at home in Montefollonico when we chose it for Benito's community in Guarded.

It was natural to complete the trilogy with another visit to Montefollonico in Granted, bringing the story to resolution through the fulfillment of a community-wide celebration both in Italy, and back on May Hollow Road in Kentucky.

While I'm certainly an advocate of small-town life, I also realize this same type of community can be experienced in New

York, Los Angeles, and other major cities through the local neighborhoods, which seem like small towns within big cities.

Whether your community is a rural town or a neighborhood in a big city, President Lyndon B. Johnson once said it's nice to live in a place "where people know when you are sick, love you while you are alive, and miss you when you die."

I agree.

Discussion Questions

1. How does Annie's relationship with her father influence her decisions?

2. In Granted, you have two people who never ask for forgiveness, yet Beulah forgives Betty and Annie forgives her father. Do you agree with that? Should forgiveness be granted when someone doesn't ask for it?

3. There is tension between Beulah and Annie over Annie's father, Eddie Taylor. How are they viewing him with different lenses?

4. Stella thinks she loves Woody then realizes she loves more the idea of the community he brings rather than the person. Is it realistic to confuse those things?

5. Gin Taylor lives her life by the moon waxing and waning. Does that seem crazy to you or do you think there's something to the gravitational pull?

6. Betty Gibson is not an easy person to live with, yet Joe loves her and knows how to handle her better than anyone. Does this kind of commitment inspire you or not?

7. Annie runs into her old boyfriend, Brett Bradshaw, and mistakes his interest in her for a desire to rekindle their romance. Have you ever had an experience in your own life where you completely misunderstood someone else's intentions?

8. Jake continues to struggle with farming not quite being the ideal he envisioned. How have you seen him settle into a compromise with reality from the beginning of the trilogy to now?

9. How has Beulah changed when we met her in Grounded, through Guarded and now to Granted? How about Annie?

10. As we round out the story, do you feel satisfied with the way things have resolved or is there something you wish was different?

CPSIA information can be obtained
at www.ICGtesting.com
Printed in the USA
LVOW03s1422141117
556256LV00007B/879/P

9 781633 935501